Rescuing Rayne

Rescuing Rayne

Delta Force Heroes

Book 1

By Susan Stoker

Copyright © 2016 by Susan Stoker

ISBN: 978-1-68-230669-7

Edited by Kelli Collins and Missy Borucki

Cover Design by Chris Mackey, AURA Design Group
Cover Photograph: Darren Birks
Cover Model: Tyler Morgan

Manufactured in the United States

Table of Contents

Chapter One

CAPTAIN KEANE "GHOST" BRYSON leaned his head back on the seat and closed his eyes, ignoring the rain that was pouring down outside as if someone had turned a faucet on full blast. The gray day seemed determined to wreak havoc on the moods of every man, woman and child inside the crowded airport.

He used to hate flying commercial, but it didn't faze him anymore. As a Delta Force operative, and the team leader, his missions were always top secret and he and his fellow teammates typically flew commercially to get to where a mission would start or to get home.

Using a military plane would be more economical and probably safer in some respects, but the military liked them to have the anonymity of flying with everyday men and women heading to vacation or business trips. Ghost would never complain about it either...there were definite perks to flying under the radar, the occasional delays and cancelations notwithstanding.

Ghost had just completed one doozy of a mission.

The team had flown to Germany then headed to Turkey to assist in rescuing a kidnapped Army sergeant named Penelope Turner. Sergeant Turner had been snatched by the terrorist group ISIS while on a humanitarian mission in a refugee camp in Turkey. She and three of her Army Reservist comrades had been taken while patrolling the camp. The three men with Sergeant Turner had been killed, and their beheadings videotaped and publicized. Turner had been used as a propaganda tool to further ISIS's anti-American agenda.

The Navy SEAL team that had been sent in to get her out succeeded and extracted her from the camp with no issues, but when they'd been flying to the Special Forces base in Turkey to regroup and get out of the country, their helicopter had been shot down by insurgents in the mountains on the Turkish/Iraqi border.

Ghost and his team were sent in, after getting intelligence from a retired SEAL named Tex, to find the men and the Army sergeant. They'd gone in not knowing if anyone was dead or wounded, but in the end, the mission had been relatively simple.

The SEALs had done their job, and all that was left for Ghost and his fellow Delta Force operatives to do was rescue the Army Night Stalker team—some were wounded and some unfortunately killed in the initial chopper crash—provide some basic first aid to the SEALs, take out a few scattered terrorists, and call in a second rescue chopper for their entire group to get the hell out of Turkey.

In the short time Ghost had known the kidnapped Army Sergeant, he'd been impressed. Penelope had been feisty and definitely not broken by her time in captivity. His Delta Force team parted ways with Penelope and the SEALs at Incirlik Air Base in Turkey.

Ghost smiled, thinking back to Penelope's simple last words to him. "Thank you." He could tell the words were heartfelt and while Ghost knew she thought them inadequate, they meant the world to him. It wasn't often they heard a thank you due to the secrecy of their jobs, and Penelope had definitely meant it. He had no idea if he'd ever see her again, but because they were based out of the same Army post, he assumed they probably would at some point. She didn't know the Delta Force team was from Fort Hood, Texas, but hopefully, she had enough training to realize that if she saw any of them, she shouldn't acknowledge them as Delta. She'd most likely get debriefed and if she wasn't aware of how top secret their presence was at the Army base, she soon would be.

Ghost shifted in the uncomfortable seat in the waiting area at London's Heathrow Airport. He and his teammates had, as normal, flown out of Turkey into

Germany then split up. Fletch and Coach flew to France first and then were headed back to the States. Hollywood and Beatle were going home straight from Germany, Blade was going through Amsterdam, and Truck was taking a detour through Spain.

He could've taken a flight directly to Austin, but the Dallas/Fort Worth flight got in a bit earlier, and had an empty exit-row seat. It was a matter of convenience, but with the rain pouring down in sheets, Ghost thought that maybe he should've taken the later flight after all.

"Is this seat taken?"

Ghost turned toward the low, husky voice that immediately made him think of sex. He'd been aware that she'd been walking toward him, as he was of everyone who moved around him. He was always on alert, ready to take whatever action might be needed. It was engrained in the very marrow of his bones.

A brunette stood next to him. Her hair was pulled back into a bun at the nape of her neck. There were wisps of hair hanging around her face, which had obviously fallen out of their confinement. She was fairly tall, especially in the heels she was wearing. Ghost guessed her to be around five-eight or so. She was pleasantly rounded in all the right places. Her Marilyn Monroe physique was a turn on, as was the bright smile she was aiming his way.

Her accent gave away the fact she was American. She was wearing a navy blue skirt and shirt, and was pulling a blue suitcase and a small matching bag behind her. Obviously an employee of the airline, a flight attendant, she greeted him warmly.

Ghost shook his head and gestured toward the seat, inviting the woman to sit next to him.

"Thanks."

The woman sat down, opened the small blue bag, and fished out her cell phone. She turned to him and asked, "Going somewhere fun?"

Ghost wasn't sure he really wanted to get into a chat, but he was bored, and he might as well pass the time. He'd never been one to reject an opportunity to talk and flirt with a pretty woman. "Home."

His one-word answer didn't seem to daunt the flight attendant. "Ah, American. Where's home?"

"Texas."

"Really? Me too! How funny that we're going to the same place. Out of all the people I could've sat next to, I picked someone who was going to be on my flight." She laughed. "You *are* on flight eight twenty-three, right?"

Ghost nodded.

"Cool. But my place in Texas is really more of a place to store my stuff than a home, since I'm usually working. I currently have the European shift. I'm gone more than I'm home."

Ghost smiled inside. The woman was very pretty and her bubbly personality was pleasant. "Yeah, I travel a lot too, so I know what you mean."

She beamed. "Ah, I didn't really peg you as a businessman, but I guess looks can be deceiving, huh?"

"What did you peg me as?"

The woman tilted her head, contemplating his question. Her lips pursed and then she bit her bottom one. Amazingly, Ghost felt himself getting erect.

Jesus, was he that hard up for a woman? He tried to think about when he'd last had the pleasure of a woman's company in his bed, and was amazed to realize he wasn't sure. The team had been busy lately with ISIS ramping up their efforts to cause panic around the world, they hadn't had a lot of time to themselves back home. But it was more that he was tired of all the tag chasers in Texas…women who only wanted to sleep with military men to say they'd done it. Military men were accused of being sex-crazed, but the reality was, around military bases, there were plenty of women who saw marrying a military man as a way out of their destitute existences. Not only that, but some were obsessed with sleeping with as many soldiers as possible.

"Bounty hunter," she said resolutely.

Torn out of his internal thoughts of when he'd last

had sex, Ghost chuckled out loud in surprise at her deduction. "Bounty hunter? Really?"

"Uh-huh."

When she didn't elaborate, Ghost crossed his arms over his chest and smiled at her. "Why?"

"Let's see. Your eyes are constantly scanning the area, even as we talk. You're hyper-aware of everything around you. I bet you knew I was coming toward you before I even got here. You're sitting with your back to a wall, a typically defensible position. You ooze testosterone, you're more muscular than anyone else around here, and you're wearing combat boots."

"And you got bounty hunter out of all of that?"

She smiled at him, leaned back in her seat, and turned toward him. "Yup. Am I right?"

"No."

"So?"

Ghost knew what she wanted, but he was enjoying playing the game. "I'm a businessman."

She looked sideways at him for a beat. "So, you'd tell me but then you'd have to kill me...right?" She grinned, obviously also enjoying their flirting.

"Something like that."

She rolled her eyes. "Okay, spy was my second guess. I'm sticking with one of the two. Bounty hunter or spy. I'm Rayne Jackson, by the way. Spelled with a y and an e. Not like what's currently falling outside." She didn't hold out her hand but looked at him expectantly.

Rayne. Ghost liked that. It was an unusual name for an unusual woman. If she really did think he looked like a bounty hunter, she probably shouldn't have approached him. "Ghost."

"Ghost? Really?" She rolled her eyes again. "Okay then, Ghost. It's nice to meet you. And I'm amending my guess. I'm definitely going with spy."

"It's good to meet you too," he returned, ignoring her spy comment. It was a bit too close to the truth. "Think we'll get out of here today?"

She smiled at him. "So we're talking about the weather? Okay, I can do that. Are you in a hurry to get home?"

Not knowing why she was asking, but being cautious, Ghost answered, "Not particularly."

"Good, because in my expert opinion, we aren't going anywhere today."

"Hmm. Other than your profession as a flight attendant, what is this expert opinion based on?"

Rayne grinned. "Well, I'm not a meteorologist, but I've been flying through here for quite a while now, and every time it's rained this hard, the flights are either delayed or canceled."

"Shit," Ghost said under his breath. He didn't really need to get home, his team could handle the report back to the lieutenant colonel at the base, but he also didn't need the hassle of spending the night in London either. Damn the others, they were probably well on their way home by now. Stupid English weather.

"Yeah," Rayne commiserated. "Unfortunately, I'm pretty used to it by now."

Just then an announcement came over the loud-speakers in the busy airport.

Flight eight twenty-three to Dallas/Fort Worth is now delayed. Please check the boards for more information.

"Told ya," Rayne said with a smile.

"You really don't care that you could be stuck here?" Ghost asked. "Most women I know get extremely...ruffled...when their plans go awry."

Rayne snorted, and Ghost noted that even the small sound was attractive coming from her.

"No. I don't get...what was your word? Ruffled?" She shook her head. "I certainly didn't picture a man like you using a word like that. Does it usually come up in your super-spy conversations?" Her question was obviously rhetorical, because she continued before he could answer. "No, I don't get ruffled when flights are delayed or canceled. It's all a part of my day. Remember, I'm actually working, not on vacation. In fact, the delays and cancelations give me a chance to get out and see the city where I'm holed up. I've had dinner in the shadow of the Eiffel Tower, taken a gondola ride in Italy, and even smoked a joint in Amsterdam during one layover."

"Hmm, a woman of the world," Ghost joked.

Rayne laughed at him. "Not even close. Don't let my adventures fool you. I'm much happier sitting at home reading a book than going out, but I figure while I'm young enough, and I'm here, I might as well get out and see some of the cities most people only dream about visiting."

"Very mature of you," Ghost said honestly.

"Are you trying to tell me I'm old?" she joked.

"No, ma'am. I know better than to even hint at a woman's age."

"Good. Because at twenty-eight, I'm not old. Not even close."

Jesus, twenty-eight. It seemed so young to his thirty-six, He'd seen a lifetime of things she couldn't even imagine, but his body didn't seem to care. He was attracted to her, there was no denying it. "Twenty-eight...practically a baby."

"Whatever. What are you...thirty-two?"

"Six, but thanks."

"You are not."

"I'm not what?"

"Thirty-six. There's no way."

"So you're saying I'm lying?" Ghost sat up and put one arm on the back of the chair she was sitting in. She was hilarious.

"Not exactly lying, but you might be trying to make me think you're more worldly than you really are."

If only she knew how worldly he really was, she'd probably immediately get up and walk away. "I'm thirty-six. Want to see my ID?"

Rayne waved him off, laughing. "No. I'm just teasing you. So...what're you going to do if our flight is canceled?"

Ghost stared at the woman sitting next to him. He made a split-second decision. "Hopefully taking a pretty brunette to dinner and showing her some of the sights of London she might miss if she stayed in her hotel room and read a book."

He watched as Rayne blushed and stared at him for a beat. Then, surprising him, she said, "I'll take you up on checking out your ID now."

"My ID?" The change in subject threw Ghost for a moment.

"Uh-huh. I might go to dinner with you, but I've watched too many episodes on the crime channel. I'll text your name, address, and birthday to my friend back home. Then we can hang out here until we find out if our flight really is canceled. If you continue to be as interesting as you have been the last half an hour and you don't do anything completely creepy or stalkerish, like ask me to take off my panties so you can pocket them, I'd be happy to see the sights of London with you."

Again, Ghost was surprised, but pleasantly. He wasn't sure why, but the thought of Rayne being cautious and safe gave him a weird feeling inside. Knowing she was looking out for herself and trying to be careful was a total turn-on. Surprisingly so. He reached into his back pocket and took out his wallet. He pulled out his Texas driver's license and handed it to her without breaking eye contact. "I have a rule. I don't ask for anyone's panties on a first date."

She smiled, but didn't comment further. Rayne balanced his ID on her knee, took a picture of it with her cell phone, and then typed out a note to her friend on her phone.

Ghost knew the information she was transferring to her friend would never lead back to him. He was using one of his many aliases. Each team member had several they could use to make sure they could travel incognito to and from missions. Ghost felt a pang of regret for lying to Rayne, but he pushed it aside. She was obviously looking for a good time, just as he was.

She looked up at him. "John Benbrook? That's your name?"

"Yeah, what's wrong with it?"

"I don't know." Rayne wrinkled her nose adorably. "It just doesn't seem…like you, I guess."

"Call me Ghost," he demanded. "I don't use John that much anyway." It wasn't a lie.

"Okay…Ghost. Thanks for humoring me with your ID. And I still don't think you look thirty-six."

He smiled at her and put the plastic card back into his wallet. "So…how long have you been a stewardess?"

"Flight attendant."

"What?"

"We're not called stewardesses anymore. We're flight attendants."

Ghost smiled and apologized. "Sorry, my mistake. Flight attendant. How long have you been a flight attendant?"

"Around six years."

"Six years? You started young."

Hearing the question behind his words, Rayne explained, "Yeah, I majored in education in college. I did the whole student-teaching thing, aced the certification tests for the state and the whole nine yards."

"But…"

"But one, I couldn't find a job, at least not in the area I wanted, and two, turns out, I didn't care much for the kids."

Ghost burst out laughing and relaxed farther into

his chair. "Seems like that might have been something you figured out before you got your degree."

"Yeah, you'd think, right?" Rayne laughed. "I swear, I think the professors only have their students go to the well-behaved classes or something. I student-taught a few weeks and realized that teachers are really treated like crap. They aren't paid very much, and don't even get me started on the standardized tests and how the teacher is the one who gets punished if the kids don't score high enough. And another thing…when the kids act up, somehow it's always the teacher's fault and not the parents', or even the fault of the child."

She sighed, a deep frustrated sound that seemed to come from her belly. "I know. It's cliché, of course the teacher will blame the kids and parents, but seriously, I think if the US paid their teachers more, public schools would only get better and better."

"So you decided to what? See the world?" Ghost asked.

"Sorta. So there I was, with a degree I had no desire to use and no idea what I was going to do with my life. I had a friend whose mother worked for the airlines and I was bitching about finding a job I enjoyed and she suggested the flight-attendant thing." Rayne shrugged. "So yeah, I figured I could see the world while I decided what and where I wanted to work. And here I am, six years later, still seeing the world—or at least the airports of the world—and still trying to decide on what the perfect job is for me."

"It doesn't sound like a bad thing to do for a living," Ghost stated, thinking to himself her reason for signing up to be a flight attendant was eerily a lot like why he'd joined the Army when he was in his late teens. He hadn't been sure what he wanted to do with his life, and a friend in his graduating class was heading down to the recruiting station. He'd tagged along, and the rest was history. He'd climbed the ranks as an enlisted man, and then set his sights on being a Delta Force soldier...and an officer.

"It's not. Don't get me wrong. I enjoy what I'm doing, I wouldn't be doing it otherwise, but it's not what I want to do for the rest of my life. I really am a homebody. I might go out and try to see some of the cities that I have layovers in, but it's not much fun to explore by myself and sometimes the cities don't feel that safe."

"If they aren't safe, you shouldn't be wandering around," Ghost told her matter-of-factly.

"I understand that. But some of the places, I know I'll never get the chance to see again."

"That shouldn't matter. You could get killed, or raped, or kidnapped in some of those places...so you might see them, but it's not worth your life or your health."

Rayne nodded in agreement. "You're right. And just in case you're feeling smug that you can order me around, I'd already decided to be a bit more cautious when I'm overseas now that ISIS has gotten completely bat-shit crazy and has no moral compass whatsoever."

Ghost smiled at her cheekiness. "Good. How long before you think—"

His words were interrupted by the automated voice over the intercom.

We regret to inform you that flight eight twenty-three has now been canceled. Please see an airline representative to reschedule your flight. Heathrow Airport apologizes for any inconvenience.

Ghost stood up and held his hand out to Rayne. "So, since it's not safe to wander around by yourself…want to explore London with me?"

Chapter Two

RAYNE SAT IN the taxi next to John Benbrook, otherwise known as Ghost, and wondered what the hell she was doing. This wasn't like her. She didn't pick up random men in airports. She'd seen a lot of good-looking men throughout her travels, and had been hit on by many of them as well. But there was something different about this one.

He hadn't come on to her, not really. They'd been flirting, but he'd been polite and even a little bit distant. But the first time he'd smiled at her, Rayne's insides had twisted. He was good looking, rugged and scruffy, and somehow she knew underneath his tattered and slightly dirty T-shirt he was one hundred percent muscle. She wanted nothing more than to sit and talk to him…okay, she wanted more than that, but she'd take what she could get.

Now they were on their way downtown. It was still raining, and Ghost had made a phone call and gotten them a reservation at one of the restaurants in Park Plaza, a nice hotel near Westminster Abbey and the

London Eye. He said they could cancel it if they decided to go somewhere else, but he'd rather they had a back-up plan, just in case. It was still early in the afternoon, so Rayne assumed they'd have a late lunch or early dinner then do…

She wasn't sure *what* they were going to do. She supposed she'd play it by ear.

There were a ton of things she'd like to see in London, but having someone else with her made her feel like she should see what *he* wanted to do, rather than doing only what *she* wanted.

Rayne felt better after having sent John Benbrook's information to her friend, Mary, back home. Of course, if Ghost raped and killed her, who knew if her body would ever be found, but at least Mary would know who she'd been out with and could alert the local authorities.

Rayne hadn't lied to Ghost. She was a homebody. She enjoyed her job as a flight attendant, and she met a lot of very interesting people, but in her down time, she was content to stay at home and do things most people would consider dull. Reading, grocery shopping, watching movies with Mary, even knitting.

For now, she was living on the edge. Rayne had never had a one-night stand in her life. She'd always dated respectable, even boring men. She'd go out with them for a while, making sure it felt "right" before deciding to go to bed with them. But there was something about Ghost that made her want to strip off all her clothes and tackle him.

She shifted in her seat, embarrassed about not being able to take her mind off of what he might look like, naked and over her, as he propped himself up while he thrust—

"So…you do this often?" she asked nervously, cutting off her own thoughts to try to bring herself under control.

"Do what?"

"Pick up women in airports and take them out?"

Ghost chuckled. "Nope. You're my first."

Rayne raised her eyebrows and looked at him incredulously and with blatant disbelief.

He obviously was fluent in eyebrow language because his next words tried to reassure her. "Seriously. I don't pick women up."

Rayne looked at the handsome man sitting next to her. The combat boots and tight brown T-shirt he was wearing were rugged as anything she'd seen anyone wear before. *He* was rugged and manly. His hair was scruffy, and a bit too long to be considered fashionable. He was carrying only a small duffle bag. His cargo pants strained against the muscles in his thighs. He had a five o'clock shadow and his brown eyes were focused completely on her. She didn't want to be attracted to him, but she was. There was something about how he looked capable of looking after himself, and anyone around him, that drew her to him like a moth to a flame. It frustrated her though, because she knew she was probably one of an extremely long line of women who would bend over backward to make him happy, in bed and out.

"Yeah, I bet you don't. They throw themselves at you, don't they?" Rayne retorted gently, letting him know she wasn't buying his bullshit, but teasing him all the same.

He laughed under his breath and shook his head. "Doesn't matter how much they might throw themselves at me, Rayne, I only catch those I'm interested in."

Rayne thought about that for a beat. "I didn't throw myself at you."

"Nope," he agreed easily.

"What are we doing then?"

Ghost leaned forward. "You didn't throw yourself at me, and I knew you wouldn't. Maybe it's because you're so delightful." He shrugged. "Whatever the reason, I took our flight being canceled as a sign that I should do something about my attraction to you. It was nice to be the one asking instead of the one being asked or having to fend off unwanted attention. As to what we're doing? We're touring the city together...taking advantage of our canceled flight."

Rayne gulped but didn't say anything.

"But I have to warn you, Rayne. I don't do relationships. So today can go one of two ways. We can spend the day together, see some sights, laugh and have a good time, then go our separate ways."

"And the other way?"

"We can spend the day together, see some sights, laugh and have a good time, then see where this attraction between us goes. Then *tomorrow*, we'll go our separate ways."

She took a deep breath and tried to be brave. "So, you're saying if we sleep together, that's all it'll be."

"That's all it *can* be."

Rayne knew there was more that Ghost wasn't saying. She wasn't stupid. The man wouldn't have the nickname if he led a normal life. She wasn't the kind of woman to hop into bed with a man knowing there would be no relationship—but she wanted him. Mary would be proud as could be that she was doing something outside of the box.

Rayne could feel her nipples tighten just looking at Ghost. It was lust, but it was a lust she hadn't felt since she'd been in college and had seen a beautiful swimmer at a private party she'd attended one night. She couldn't remember the man's name now, but he was tall and slender, and had extremely broad shoulders.

She'd imagined him taking one look at her and falling madly in love, but apparently it wasn't to be. He'd gotten completely drunk and had to be helped home by some of his teammates after puking in the bushes.

Even all these years later, she still felt a bit of regret she never had a chance to explore her feelings toward that swimmer, so Rayne decided she'd have to be okay with one night with Ghost.

She couldn't help but let her mind wander. How would it feel to be skin to skin with him? Would his chest be covered in hair or smooth?

"I—" she began, not really knowing what she wanted to say, but feeling the press of the silence between them like a heavy blanket.

Ghost cut her off by putting a finger to her lips.

"Shhhh, don't decide right now. Let's play it by ear. No pressure. We'll spend the rest of the day together, see what we can see, and then we'll go from there. Okay?"

Suddenly feeling as if she'd just made a date to have sex like a whore on the streets, she blurted, "You won't be pissed if I don't want to—"

"Absolutely not." Ghost immediately reassured her. "Disappointed? Maybe, but upset with you? No. It's your choice. I've never forced a woman to do anything she didn't want to do in my life and I'm not about to start now."

"Okay."

"Good. You should also know, however, that I'm going to do what I can to convince you to spend the night with me. I'm attracted to you, Rayne with a 'y' and an 'e,' and I've already been imagining what you look like under that prim and proper skirt and shirt. That probably makes me a dog, but I'm just trying to be honest with you here. So whatever might go through your head today while we're out enjoying London, wondering if I've changed my mind or if I really want you, shouldn't be one of those thoughts."

Ghost didn't take his eyes off Rayne's lips. She'd taken her bottom lip between her teeth again as he'd been speaking.

He brought his hand up and palmed the side of her face, brushing his thumb across her lips. "Don't bite your lip, Rayne."

When her teeth let go of her lip, he leaned in, moving his hand to the back of her neck. Ignoring the taxi driver, Ghost got close enough that Rayne could feel the whisper of air from his words against her mouth.

"God, your lips were made for kissing. They're full and pink...and I can just imagine how soft they'll be against my own." He put a bit of pressure against her neck but didn't pull her all the way to himself. It was obvious he was waiting for her to make the decision on whether or not to kiss him.

Wanting this man's lips on her own more than she wanted to breathe, Rayne leaned forward the inch it took to close the gap between them, as if his lips were magnets and she couldn't resist the pull.

Their lips met and Rayne swore she felt something click between them the second they touched. She didn't have time to analyze the odd feeling because his tongue swiped across her lips and she immediately opened to him, letting him take whatever he wanted.

Ghost's other hand came up to the opposite side of her face and he tilted her head to a better angle. They made out in the back of the taxi, not paying attention to where the driver was taking them or if he was purposely taking the long route to get to the hotel to earn more money. Rayne knew it would be worth every pound if he was. Ghost's hands stayed at her face, never taking advantage, never moving farther down her body.

Rayne arched into Ghost and put her hands around him. She clutched at his back, trying to get closer. The lust she felt for him was crazy. It was insane. She didn't know anything about the man who was devouring her lips as if he'd never get enough, except that his name was John Benbrook and he lived in Fort Worth, Texas, but at the moment, she didn't care.

She had no idea how far their make-out session would've gone, probably not as far as *she* wanted it to, but the taxi driver cleared his throat and declared that they were at the Park Plaza Hotel.

Rayne pulled away from Ghost and refused to meet his eyes, knowing she was blushing. She realized she was more turned on by that one kiss than she'd been the last time she'd made love. She didn't want to seem desperate, but she was ready to say to hell with their tour and let him drag her upstairs to one of the rooms at the hotel and have his way with her.

Ghost brought one hand up and tenderly ran it over the top of her head, over her hair, and down her back. He wiped her swollen, wet lips with the pad of his thumb without a word.

Rayne finally worked up the nerve to look up at Ghost and the gleam in his eye made her feel better that her crazy attraction wasn't only one sided. He looked to be about a second away from throwing her down on the seat and making her lose her mind.

With one last smile, he pulled away and reached into his back pocket for his wallet. He pulled out a wad of pounds he'd exchanged at the airport and paid the driver.

Rayne took the time to gather her purse and open the door. She waited at the back of the taxi for Ghost and the driver. Finally they joined her and the driver opened the trunk and got out her overnight bag and Ghost's duffle.

"Come on, Rayne," Ghost said, reaching out and

grabbing the handle of her suitcase with one hand and pulling her into his side with the other. "We'll stash our bags with the concierge and see what trouble we can get into."

Relieved the sexual tension was broken, at least for the moment, Rayne fell into step beside Ghost and had a pretty good idea what her decision would be at the end of the evening. She wanted nothing more than to spend the night with the mysterious man at her side.

Consequences be damned.

Chapter Three

"**A**RE YOU SURE you don't want to change? It can't be comfortable wearing those shoes as we tromp around the city," Ghost asked for the third time.

"Did you see the last *Jurassic Park* movie?"

Ghost looked confused but answered affirmatively anyway.

"I'm like Claire. She went through that movie running from freaking dinosaurs in her heels and didn't bat an eye. I'm not saying I want one of those Indominuses to pop out from behind Big Ben or anything, but as long as you're not planning on entering us in a half marathon or something today, I'll manage just fine."

Ghost snorted. "A half marathon? Not exactly how I planned to exert my energy today. I just don't want you to regret your shoe choice halfway through the day. I'd prefer you to concentrate on other things."

Ignoring the subtle sexual innuendo—not sure if it even was one; she was feeling hornier than she'd ever been before and it was possible she was reading sex into his words when he didn't intend them that way—she reassured him, "Seriously, it's good. I'm on my feet all day almost every day, Ghost. It's fine. The airline has made sure our uniforms are comfortable...and that they can blend in away from work. I wouldn't choose this to wear every day, but for now, it's just easier and time is wasting. I'm starving!"

He chuckled and dropped the topic. "What do you want to eat?" Ghost asked as they were waiting for the concierge to come back with the luggage ticket.

"Fish and chips."

"You sound sure."

Rayne looked at Ghost incredulously. "I can't be in England and *not* eat fish and chips! It's got to be against the official tourist law or something!"

He smiled down at her and nodded. "Fish and chips it is."

The concierge came back with their claim ticket and overheard Ghost's comment.

"If you're looking for a good restaurant, I recommend Mickey's Fish and Chips. It's behind Hyde Park, but you can take the Tube there pretty easily."

Rayne loved listening to people speak with a British accent. She knew some people wouldn't understand a word the man had just said, but apparently, Ghost was not only fluent in eyebrow language, but British English as well. "Thanks. That would be great."

The concierge wrote down which subway trains

they'd need to take to get close to the restaurant, and then he went further and gave them directions as to which lines would bring them back to the hotel, Buckingham Palace and Westminster Abbey as well, and handed it to Ghost.

He thanked them and they made their way out of the hotel toward the train station around the corner.

Rayne smiled when Ghost positioned himself on the curb, keeping her away from the street, as they made their way through the pedestrian traffic and to the huge train station. He bought their tickets and Rayne loved the feel of his hand on the small of her back as they stood on the escalators, taking them down to the next level to wait for the correct train.

"You're pretty good at the whole subway thing, Ghost," Rayne teased. "You know that just makes me think you're a spy even more, right?"

Ghost smiled and looked at Rayne. Her cheeks were flushed with the heat of the day and the short walk to catch their subway car. Looking at her, he couldn't help but remember her enthusiastic participation in their kiss in the back of the taxi. He'd been pleasantly surprised at how she'd thrown herself into it as wholeheartedly as she had.

"I'm used to traveling, and London's public transportation is one of the best, and most easily navigable, in the world."

Rayne simply shook her head, as he wouldn't have heard her response anyway since a subway chose that minute to roar into view.

The doors opened and a large influx of people tried to push their way out at the same time the newcomers tried to push their way in. This was one of the reasons Rayne hated big cities and using the subway, she almost always came away with a few new bruises from fighting the masses.

Not today though. Ghost tucked her into his side and pushed through the crowd as if he was the King of England. He guided them to a bench and urged her to sit. Instead of settling next to her, he stood in front of her, once again protecting her from being jostled by riders getting on or off. He took hold of the bar above their heads and spread his legs enough for balance.

There were so many things Rayne wanted to say to him, but she felt self-conscious with all the people around them and the lack of privacy. She settled for smiling gratefully and watching him as he kept his eyes on the other people traveling in the car with them, as if they were terrorists and would blow them up. Rayne had no doubt that Ghost would leap into any situation and neutralize it. That was the kind of vibe she got from him, and it made her feel safe.

He stood with his profile to her and Rayne took the time to examine him. His biceps bulged as he held on to the strap above his head. His T-shirt molded to his body and Rayne swallowed hard. She was eye level with his crotch, and boy was it impressive. He was all man, and made her feel small and protected.

She tried to determine his height and finally decided since she came to about his chin that he had to be at least six-one or two. She was tall for a woman, and, even with her heels, was short compared to him. His body swayed with the movements of the train and Rayne closed her eyes, imagining his muscled arms around her, holding her body to his as he ever so slowly raised her shirt, never losing eye contact…

The train car lurched at the next stop and Rayne's eyes popped open. Ghost was looking down at her with an inscrutable look. She used to think she was good at reading people's faces, she had to be at her job, but she realized that she had absolutely no idea what Ghost was thinking. The car started moving, and he once again swung his gaze to the others around them, scrutinizing each person as if there would be a test when they got off about what everyone was wearing. Rayne had no doubt, if such a thing happened, he'd ace it.

After a few more stops, Ghost leaned down and told her, "Next stop is us."

Rayne nodded and stood up to make her way to the doors. She felt Ghost's arm go around her waist as the subway train began to slow. He was doing it to help her keep her balance, and to any casual observer it would've looked like a gentlemanly thing to do. But it felt like more to Rayne...it felt like a promise.

Ghost's arm brushed against her breast as he moved it down her body, and Rayne could feel every inch of *his* hard body against her back as he pulled her into him. His palm rested low on her hip and she could feel his fingers gripping her tightly. His thumb wasn't still, it was moving back and forth in a barely there caress. Even though only one arm was around her, Rayne felt surrounded by Ghost and as safe as if she were in her hometown back in the States.

The door opened and they shuffled out much as they had gotten into the car, with Ghost making sure no one bumped into or jostled her too harshly. After exiting the station and getting their bearings, they headed off toward Mickey's.

The small shop was typically British. A Union Jack flag hung outside and the restaurant was small and dark inside. The menu, written on a chalkboard behind the long counter, included all kinds of fried fish. The air was filled with the smell of fish, batter, and potatoes. It was heavenly and Rayne could feel her stomach growling.

"See what you want?" Ghost asked, stepping up to the counter.

"Fish and chips, of course," Rayne answered quickly. "Can't come to London and to a fish and chip shop and get calamari or something."

"Fish and chips it is then." Ghost turned to the young man behind the counter and quickly ordered.

Rayne offered to pay and got such a disgruntled look from Ghost that she backed away and smiled with both hands up in appeasement. "Okay, okay, calm down. I had to offer."

He shook his head, rolled his eyes at her, and pulled out some pounds to pay for their meal. They walked over to a small chipped table in the corner to wait.

She wasn't surprised when Ghost pulled her chair out, then took the seat with his back to the wall. She searched for something interesting to say.

"So…got any tattoos?"

Ghost grinned. "I'll show you mine if you show me yours."

"Deal." Rayne enjoyed the look of surprise on his face.

"Really? You've got a tattoo?"

"Don't look so surprised, stud. I'm not as dorky as I look."

"I would never call you dorky, Rayne. Polished, put-together and classy, but not dorky."

"Well, thanks, I guess."

"So…how many you got?"

Rayne sat back in her chair, crossed her arms in

front of her, and put one leg over the other. "Three. You?"

"Really? Three?"

"Really." Rayne watched as Ghost's eyes ran up and down her body as if he could somehow see through her clothes to the tattoos he now knew were under them. "And you can't see them with my clothes on."

As soon as the words left her mouth, Rayne blushed. They sounded a lot more suggestive out loud than they had in her head.

"Hmm, I can't wait to see these mysterious pieces of ink." Ghost's words were innocent, but the tone behind them was intense enough to make her bite her lip and look away from his focused gaze.

"Two fish and chips. Order up!"

The interruption was welcome and Ghost got up to retrieve their food. He carried the baskets overflowing with greasy pieces of batterd fish and thick fries back to the table and asked if Rayne wanted ketchup to go with her meal. Shaking her head, Rayne didn't wait for Ghost to start. She took a french fry, what the Brits called a chip, and bit into it with a groan. It was hot, almost hot enough to burn her mouth, but so greasy and so good.

They ate in silence for a while before Rayne asked, "How many do you have?"

Ghost knew exactly what she was talking about.

"One."

"Just one?"

"Yup."

"I guess a spy like you can't afford to have too many tattoos that could be recognized by the bad guys, huh?"

Ghost almost choked on the water he'd been drinking. He knew she was teasing, but her words were a bit closer to the truth than she knew. He played it off. "Oh yeah." He drew out the word and continued with a thick Russian accent, "Can't have the enemies recognizing my tattoos."

She giggled and pointed at him with a fry. "I knew it!"

Ghost leaned over and took a bite out of the errant fry, laughing when she shrieked at him, "Hey! That's mine! Eat your own fries!"

It'd been quite a while since he'd had such a good time with a female. Typically, either he or she was thinking too much about where the night would end, rather than enjoying the time at hand. And while he'd imagined what Rayne would look like, mussed and satisfied next to him in bed, he was actually enjoying the anticipation more than usual. It was as though a warm blanket wrapped around him, engulfing him in happy feelings, rather than the knife edge of lust he usually felt before taking a woman to bed.

They finished their meal and Ghost pushed his empty basket away, put his elbows on the table and leaned toward Rayne. "So, what do you want to do today?"

She immediately shrugged. "I don't know, what do *you* want to do?"

He tsked at her. "Come on, Rayne. I know you've thought about it. What would you do if it was just you and had a free day here in London?"

"If you really want to know…" Her voice trailed off.

"I really want to know. I asked, didn't I?"

"That doesn't mean you *really* wanted to know. People do that all the time, they—"

"Rayne…spit it out."

Instead of getting pissed at him for interrupting her, she laughed. "Okay, okay, Mr. Spy Man. Keep your shirt on. I definitely want to see Westminster Abbey and of course Big Ben. And if it's not too far away, Buckingham Palace."

Ghost nodded, assuming those would be on her list. "What about the Tower of London? Or the prime meridian?"

"The prime what?"

"Meridian. It's where the longitude starts over."

"Huh? Starts over?"

"Yeah. If you were looking at a GPS, it's the precise

location where the east numbers change to west. If you stand just right, holding the GPS, the Western coordinates would read, 000.00.000."

"Hmm, that sounds like something only a super-spy would be interested in seeing, to be honest."

Ghost threw his head back and laughed. Truly laughed for the first time in a really long time. He pushed away from the table and grabbed up their trash. "Come on, we'll start with Westminster Abbey and go from there then."

Chapter Four

GHOST WATCHED RAYNE'S face as they walked around Westminster Abbey. He'd taken hold of her hand when they'd left the fish and chip place, and hadn't let go. Luckily, she didn't seem inclined to let go of him either.

She was adorable. Rayne oohed and ahhed at everything. Ghost was a hard man. He'd seen too much in his thirty-six years to be surprised, or even impressed, by much anymore. But seeing London though Rayne's eyes was a completely different experience. He tended to rush through life, seeing things but not analyzing them past what threat they posed...unless of course it had to do with life or death. *His* life or death or the life or death of his teammates.

But Rayne's eyes were big as she listened to the tour guide discuss the various dead kings and queens who were entombed inside the huge church. Occasionally she'd squeeze his hand and lean over and whisper, "Wow" or "Can you believe that?" to him.

Of course, Ghost could only think about her curvy

body pressing against his side, the feel of her breast, her hipbone pressing against his...every movement made him hope she'd choose to spend the night in his bed rather than go her separate way.

The kiss they shared in the taxi was seared on his brain. She'd melted into his embrace as if she'd been doing it her entire life. The soft sighs and moans that had come from her throat as he'd devoured her mouth only made him long to hear them as he devoured the rest of her. She was a mix of innocent and jaded, and the dichotomy piqued his interest...big time.

"It's so hard to believe we're standing right where Prince William and Kate got married. This is such an amazing piece of history—and we're here!" Rayne whispered in a reverent voice.

They'd hung back from the small group of tourists following the volunteer guide. Ghost backed them into an alcove and pulled Rayne flush with the front of his body as he leaned against the ancient stones. He clasped his hands at the small of her back and smiled as she leaned into him, resting her forearms on his chest.

"I bet you've watched Princess Diana's wedding on the Internet, haven't you?" Ghost asked with a completely straight face, already knowing the answer.

"Oh yes," Rayne breathed. "She was so beautiful. She had that extremely long train that her little cousins helped carry. Did you know that Di and Charles decided to get married in St Paul's Cathedral instead of here because it had more seating? But she's been *here*. Right here. It's amazing."

Ghost felt the first stirrings of unease as Rayne continued on. "You're a romantic," Ghost said in a weird voice.

Rayne's head came back around and she looked up at him. She nodded. "Yeah. Always have been, always will be."

"The world isn't a fairy tale, Rayne," Ghost warned, again feeling a sense of foreboding creeping over him.

"I know it's not. I'm not an idiot. I might like to read romances and watch romantic comedies, but I'm a realist."

"I don't think—"

Rayne interrupted him. She leaned back and dug her nails into his chest. Ghost thought she was probably doing it unconsciously.

"Last week I was on a flight with a woman who was flying to New York to undergo an experimental surgery for colon cancer. She was traveling alone and I felt bad for her. So after I'd served the drinks, I sat and talked to her. Her husband couldn't go with her because he had to work. He didn't have any sick time left and she was on his health insurance. They couldn't afford for him to lose his job, so she had to fly up there by herself.

I can't imagine how scared she was, or how her husband felt about not being able to be by her side.

"The week before that, I noticed a woman with a black eye sitting next to a very big, very pissed-off man, who I can only assume was her husband. It was obvious she was being abused, but there was nothing I could do about it. Also the other week, I had the displeasure of having to try to please a man and woman and their two kids. The kids were out of control, and the parents didn't care. All they wanted to do was drink as many of the little bottles of alcohol as we'd serve them."

She leaned into Ghost as if it would help make her point. "I can tell you think being a romantic is a bad thing, and while I freely admit to wanting to find a man to spend the rest of my life with, I *do* know the world isn't always sunshine and roses. Most of the time it's overcast skies and poison ivy. That's why I read the books and watch the movies I do. If the only way I can experience romance is through my imagination and fairy-tale books and the weddings of English Royalty, I'm going to do it. Don't burst my bubble, Ghost. Please, let me have this."

Ghost wanted to argue, to tell her there were more assholes in the world than princes, and reading romance novels or watching sappy movies wouldn't ever change that fact. He wanted to make sure she knew that he wasn't a prince. He might not be quite as big of an asshole as the people he met in his job, but he didn't want her under any illusion that what he hoped they would be doing later would lead to a Lifetime movie or anything.

"Come on, come sit with me."

He towed her over to one of the many pews in the huge church and urged her down the bench until they reached the middle. He sat down and waited for Rayne to sit next to him. She sat uneasily and he could see the tight grip she had on the seat by the way her knuckles turned white.

Ghost hadn't meant to upset her, but he needed to make his point. He didn't want her falling for him. He knew he should get up and leave her to the rest of her day before she read more into what they were probably going to do that night than he could give, but he wasn't going to. He needed this woman. Her quirky personality had burrowed under his skin and he wanted her. More than he'd wanted a woman in a long, long time.

"I'm not a romantic guy, Rayne. I don't have it inside me to be in a relationship."

"Bull."

"Rayne—"

"No, seriously." She turned toward him on the bench. "I'll believe you when you say you don't want a relationship, but I will never believe you when you say you aren't romantic."

"I've never given a woman flowers in all my life. I've never proposed, hell, I don't usually stick around long enough to tell a woman I've had a good time."

His words hurt, but Rayne pushed it down. She'd known what she was in for when she'd first decided to bum around London with him. But she wanted to make sure he got where she was coming from, whether he liked it or not. "Fine, maybe you're a bit of a Neanderthal when it comes to relationships. You're not perfect. Great. I get it. But, Ghost, you *are* romantic."

When Ghost began to shake his head in denial, or disgust, Rayne wasn't sure which, she put her hand on his knee. "Let me finish."

Waiting until he finally nodded, she continued. "You've paid for every single thing we've done today, from the taxi, to lunch, to tipping the concierge at the hotel. When we were walking to the subway station, you put yourself between the traffic and me when we were on the sidewalk. You protected me from the crowds as we got in and out of the subway. You let me sit, while you stood near me, making sure no one got too close. You even carried my suitcase from the taxi to the hotel. Seriously, Ghost, you do these things and don't even realize you're doing them. That is a sign of a man who knows how to treat a woman. *That's* what women think is romantic. Screw flowers, they'll just die sooner rather than later. And even if you leave without saying goodbye to a woman, I'll bet everything I own you take very good care of her before you take off...don't you?"

She wouldn't have believed it if she hadn't seen it in person, but if she wasn't mistaken, a slight blush bloomed on Ghost's cheekbones at her words.

"So, call yourself a shitty boyfriend, but please, don't sell yourself short and say you aren't in at least some ways a romantic. Romance isn't about the outer trappings society has pushed down our throats from the time we were little. It's showing in all the little ways that you care about the person you're with. That you'll protect her if the shit hits the fan, that you'll provide for her, that you'll let her choose what she wants to do and where she wants to eat, even if it's not what you would pick for yourself."

Ghost didn't say anything for several moments, and Rayne had gotten to the point where she thought maybe he wasn't going to say anything, when finally he picked up her hand that was still resting on his knee and brought it up to his mouth and kissed the palm.

"Okay, you win. I know I should say goodbye here. I should leave you to enjoy London and carry on with your life as if you hadn't ever met me."

When she opened her mouth to protest, Ghost shook his head, and quickly continued on. "But I can't. I'm not sure I buy into your fantasy of what romance is, but I can't give you up yet. You're funny, interesting, and I'm attracted to you. I want to see those three tattoos of yours more than I want to walk away. But know…I *will* walk away."

"So it's a one-night stand then." Rayne's words weren't a question.

"Afraid so."

"Fine. I'm a romantic, you're bad relationship material, but I swear we're on the same page here, Ghost. Just relax. I'm not going to pull out an engagement ring at the end of the night. I'm also not going to chain you to the bed as Kathy Bates did in that *Misery* movie. It's fine."

Ghost nodded.

Rayne couldn't resist one last dig. "Damn, for a super-secret spy, you're acting a bit like a wuss."

She barely smothered a shriek, remembering where they were, when Ghost moved with deadly intent. She was lying flat on the pew with him pinning her arms above her head and resting his considerable weight on her upper body, keeping her immobile, before she could even try to evade him.

"Wuss?"

Rayne smiled, knowing he wasn't going to hurt her in the middle of the day in the busy church with all the tourists wandering around. "Well, in my defense, you *did* want to talk about your feelings a bit more than any man I've ever been attracted to before."

"One, I don't think I like you talking about other men when your nipples are hard and begging for my touch…"

Rayne glanced down and swallowed. He was right. The way he so easily manhandled her but was careful not to hurt her, and the feel of his hard body pressing into hers, was turning her on, and her body was showing it.

"…and two, now that we're on the same page, I can guarantee we won't be 'talking' much later tonight."

Rayne didn't say anything, merely lay under him, waiting for him to make the next move. When he didn't shift his hold for several moments, she arched her back the smallest amount and tested his grip on her wrists.

Finally, Ghost took a deep breath, ran his eyes down to her chest one more time, then brought them back up to her eyes. He leaned down and kissed her lightly and carefully on the lips, then sat up, pulling Rayne with him.

"You're gonna be the death of me. I can't make out with you in a pew in Westminster Abbey. I might be insane, but even I'm not willing to push my luck that far. Too many ghosts looking over my shoulder give me the willies. Come on, Buckingham Palace isn't too far from here. It's where Princess Diana, and Catherine and William, had their very public wedding day kisses. I figure you being the romantic you are, you would be interested in that, right?"

Ghost knew he'd made the right choice when Rayne's eyes lit up and she said breathlessly, "Really? You'll take me there?"

"Come on, Princess. Let's go look at a balcony."

Chapter Five

G HOST SMILED OVER at Rayne as the royal guards did their thing. The rain had stopped for the moment, but the clouds still hung low in the sky, a foreshadowing of the storm that was sure to return. It might not be raining, but the humidity in the air created a light mist, which he knew could turn into a downpour any second. But it was as if the weather knew Rayne really wanted to see the changing of the guards and the balcony where the British Royals paraded themselves when the world demanded and expected it of them.

"They do this every day?" Rayne asked breathlessly, not taking her eyes off the spectacle in front of them.

Ghost smiled. He'd been smiling like a fool all day, but didn't give a shit. Rayne made him happy. She saw the world through such a fresh lens. He would've thought no one could be that...clean, if he wasn't seeing it with his own two eyes. Fletch and the others on the team would give him no end of shit for the goofy-ass grin that had been on his face since he'd been in Rayne's presence. "Yeah, Princess. They do this every day."

She wrinkled her nose in the cute way she had. "But it's so...ostentatious."

Ghost busted out with a short laugh. "It might be ostentatious, but it's tradition. And the Brits are big on tradition." He loved how Rayne wasn't afraid to say what she was thinking. She hadn't held back with any of her thoughts throughout the day. She'd complained, loudly, that the tiles were wet in Westminster Abby and someone was going to fall and crack their head open, And while blood on the floor of the church was probably not a new thing for the centuries-old building, it probably wasn't a good idea in today's day and age of sue-happy tourists. Ghost had noticed that not long after Rayne's vocal observation, someone had brought out a carpet and unrolled it in front of the doors and placed a "wet floor" sign nearby.

"I get that it's something they've always done," Rayne continued, "but can't they do something else to keep up the tradition? I mean, the soldiers have to get sick of all the pomp and circumstance, and it's a traffic hazard. They have to stop the cars every time they change the guards. It's crazy."

Ghost held back his laugh and tried to change the subject. "So is the balcony everything you imagined it to be?" He expected an immediate affirmative answer, but as she was wont to do, Rayne surprised him.

She tilted her head and gazed up at the empty balcony on the other side of a large fountain in the middle of a roundabout. They were standing on the sidewalk on the opposite side of the huge wrought iron gates surrounding the palace. Ghost had tried to get her to get closer to the gates themselves, but she said she'd rather stand across the street so she could take it all in.

"Do you think they're in the palace now, looking out at us standing here and at the people walking by, wishing they had more normal lives? I mean, I'm here thinking how awesome it would be to be married to a prince, to live inside the palace and be waited on hand and foot, but as you so eloquently pointed out earlier today, the world isn't a picnic and it's probably not all that romantic to be a part of the Royal Family after all."

"Rayne—"

As usual, she talked over him. "I mean, Diana probably thought she'd hit the jackpot. She was young, much younger than I am now, and she grew up in England. Grew up thinking the Royal Family was all that and a bag of chips…American chips, not chips like french fries as they call them here. Then she married into it and we all know *now* that it wasn't a walk in the park for her. I just—" She broke off and looked over at Ghost and shrugged, almost embarrassed at how she'd been carrying on. She finished quickly, "Yeah, it's cool to be here to see the balcony."

"You want me to take your picture?"

"Really? Yes, please." Rayne posed on the sidewalk with a goofy grin on her face and pointed up toward the small balcony on the front of Buckingham Palace. Ghost handed back her phone, and Rayne pulled him over to her. "Come on, a selfie this time!"

Ghost knew he shouldn't. Knew he should tell her he had the type of job where he couldn't risk pictures of him showing up on the Internet. He could simply ask her not to post it anywhere, but even if she agreed now, she could forget, or get pissed, and it could somehow show up anyway. It just wasn't smart to be in pictures with hook-ups. Period. They'd been warned by the colonel, and everyone on the teams knew to avoid having their picture taken at all costs. But Rayne knew him as John Benbrook, not Keane Bryson, and after tonight, he'd never see her again. Besides that, he didn't think she was the type of woman to plaster her every movement on social media. She'd flat out said she'd never had a one-night stand before, so he thought it was pretty safe to pose for one picture with her.

Ghost put his arm around Rayne and pulled her close. She laughed and held out her hand with her phone.

"Smile!" she ordered. Rayne took the picture and turned the phone to check it out. She turned to him with a frown. "You didn't smile," she complained. "Come on, take another, and *smile* this time, dammit." Her words were stern, but the tone was teasing.

For reasons Ghost didn't understand—but he didn't stop to analyze his actions—he pulled out his own phone. "On mine this time."

Rayne smiled up at him, obviously pleased he also wanted a picture of them together.

"Okay. But be sure to get the balcony in it. Don't cut off our heads. Oh, and if you can get the—"

"Hush, woman, I got this," Ghost told her in a mock growl. "I'm a professional."

Rayne giggled and put both her arms around his waist and leaned in. "A professional? Professional what, is the question." She looked up at him again, smiling, joy leaking out of every pore in her body. "Okay, but don't blame *me* if you don't get the good stuff in frame."

Ghost looked down at the woman in his arms. He had one arm around her shoulders and the other was outstretched with his phone in his hand, ready to snap the picture. "I've got the good stuff in it, don't worry."

Rayne smiled and turned her head to look at his phone.

"Okay, on the count of three," she bossed. "One...two...three!"

Ghost snapped the picture and put the phone back

in his pocket before Rayne could snatch it out of his grasp to look at the photo he'd just taken.

"Ghost! I need to look at it and approve it!"

"Approve it?"

"Yeah, you know, make sure it's good enough to keep. I might look like a dork!"

"You don't look like a dork," Ghost told her with complete honesty.

"Whatever. You didn't even look at it and besides, guys' opinions can't be trusted."

"Really?"

"Yup. You don't care about things like hair and makeup or if the picture is blurry."

"Your hair looks fine, you aren't wearing much makeup, and the picture wasn't blurry."

"How do you know? You didn't even look at it! What if my eyes were closed? Then you'll see it later and be all sad because instead of being able to brag to your buddies about the chick you had in London, you'll have to—"

"I'm not going to brag about having you."

Rayne didn't understand the tone of Ghost's voice. She tilted her head and said seriously, "I thought all guys bragged about their conquests."

"First of all, *men* don't do that shit. It's a dick thing to do. Second of all, I have no desire to show your picture to my friends. This time is ours."

"But—"

"It's not that I don't want every one of my buds to be jealous as hell that I hooked up with a beautiful woman after a wonderful day in London...but what I do, and who I do it with, is my business. And yours. No one else's."

"Wow. Um, okay. But you should know," Rayne wrinkled her nose and shrugged apologetically, "I'll probably talk about it with my friend Mary. I mean, I won't go into details, but after that text I sent, she's going to want to know how it was. As of right this moment, I don't know *how* it will be, but if I had to guess, I'm thinking you're gonna knock my socks off. And since it's my first one-night stand, I'm going to have to spill to my bestie. Girl code and all that."

She felt Ghost chuckle against her. "You never say what I think you're going to say."

"Hopefully that's not a bad thing."

"It's not a bad thing."

"Okay. So...can I see the picture to make sure my eyes weren't closed?"

"No."

Rayne rolled her eyes at him. She finally let go of his waist and looked up at the sky as the rain started gently falling again. She sighed. "Okay, fine. You win. It's raining again," she stated unnecessarily.

"You had enough balcony?"

"Yeah." Rayne turned back to the big palace for a moment. "It really is beautiful though, isn't it?"

Ghost didn't answer.

Rayne turned to him. "Okay, I've tortured you long enough. What's next on the agenda?"

Ghost knew just what he wanted to do. "You ever been on a Ferris wheel?"

"Of course."

"Not like this one. Come on." Ghost took her hand in his as he hailed a cab.

Chapter Six

"I'M NOT SURE about this, Ghost," Rayne said nervously, holding tightly to his hand as they walked into one of the compartments on the famed London Eye. The day so far had been wonderful. Rayne had no idea how she'd gotten so lucky to have randomly chosen to sit next to Ghost in the airport, and then have their flight canceled, and now to be spending the day with him in the city. But she wasn't going to look a gift horse in the mouth. She'd simply go with it and hope everything worked out in the end.

"It's fine, Princess. You think I'd have us do anything where you might get hurt?"

"Uh…"

"I wouldn't. You're safe with me."

Rayne looked up at Ghost. *Safe with him.* If she could've, she would've melted into a puddle at his feet. He made fun of her for being a romantic at heart, but if he could only hear his own words. She'd tried to tell him how everything he'd done so far *was* romantic, but she was certain he didn't believe her.

The thing of it was, she *did* feel safe with him. There was no way anyone would bother them. They'd take one look at Ghost, and know instinctively he was a man not to be trifled with. It was what she thought the first time she saw him at the airport. "I know."

The taxi that had picked them up at Buckingham Palace had a very sketchy-looking driver. If she'd been by herself, she would've passed on it and either walked or hailed a different car. But not Ghost. He pulled her into the backseat, leaned forward with his phone, snapped a picture of the driver's identification, and then pushed a few more buttons on the phone. He'd then told the driver to take them to the London Eye and said in a deep, clear voice that meant business, "I've just sent your identification to a friend, an officer on the London Police force. If you value your job, you'll get us there in one piece. He's expecting a text from me in ten minutes, which is plenty of time for us to arrive. If he doesn't get it, the entire force will be looking for this taxi...and you."

The driver didn't say anything, but nodded, Rayne thought, nervously. She had no idea if Ghost really did know someone who worked on the police force here in London, but honestly, nothing would surprise her. She still didn't know what he really did for a living, but she was beginning to think her guess of spy or bounty hunter was closer than she'd thought. She'd been kidding at the time, but now she wasn't so sure.

The driver had pulled out into traffic and taken them to the famed tourist spot across from the Abbey without any general chitchat. All Ghost had said when they'd left the vehicle after arriving was, "Have a nice night."

"Come on, you'll love this," Ghost told her, bringing her back to the present and the huge sort-of Ferris wheel, leading her to the small bench in the middle of the compartment.

When the door shut behind them, Rayne asked in surprise, "We're the only ones in here? This thing can hold at least thirty people, what's going on?"

"It's raining and it's a random Wednesday night, Princess, there aren't a lot of people around. I slipped the guy fifty pounds and he agreed to let us have the compartment all to ourselves."

Rayne frowned. "You bribed him?"

"Yup."

"But..." Rayne couldn't think of a good protest.

Ghost laughed at her shocked reaction. "Just enjoy it, Rayne. It's fine."

"Okay. Whatever, but if you don't really have a friend on the police force and you get hauled off to jail when we get off, don't expect me to pay your bail."

They sat together holding hands as the huge wheel started to turn. It wasn't the same as the Ferris wheels back home in the States. This one moved extremely slowly, Rayne couldn't even tell they were moving, except for the landscape getting smaller and smaller as they rose into the air.

Rayne stood up and held on to the rail at the window. She felt Ghost come up behind her. He put his hands at either side of her hips and leaned into her, pointing out landmarks in the huge city as they slowly rose higher and higher above the River Thames.

"There's the Tower of London."

"Didn't people get tortured in the basement there?"

Ghost chuckled. "History's not your strong suit is it, Princess?"

Rayne tried to turn to protest, but Ghost put his hands on her hips and held her in place. He leaned down so his head was even with hers. "Relax. I was teasing. The Tower of London was where the royals originally lived. It's also been an armory, a treasury, and even the Crown Jewels of England are kept there and highly guarded. But, yes, to answer your question, it was also a prison at one time as well. However, you should know, despite what history likes to make people believe, there were actually only seven people executed there before the 1940s. Now it's simply a tourist attraction."

"Oh. That's kinda a letdown. I was liking that it was a big bad haunted prison where the worst of the worst were incarcerated. You know a lot about it," Rayne observed.

Ghost shrugged. "I like military history."

"Obviously."

Ghost smiled against Rayne's hair. He enjoyed it when she got a little snarky with him. She was a breath of fresh air compared to the people he usually dealt with in his life.

"What else am I looking at?"

Ghost pointed out other notable landmarks of the London skyline as they continued to gain altitude. When they got to the top of the wheel's projection, Ghost shifted them until they were looking once again at Westminster Abbey far below them.

"Look, Ghost! It's Big Ben!"

"Actually, its real name is the Elizabeth Tower."

"What?"

"The Elizabeth Tower. Big Ben is only a nickname. Before that, it was known simply as the Clock Tower."

Rayne turned in Ghost's embrace and looped her arms around his waist loosely. "Really? Good thing they changed it. The Clock Tower is a completely boring name for one of the most well-known clocks in the world. What else?"

"What else what?"

"What else do you know about Big Ben?"

Ghost grinned down at her. "Big Ben is the nickname for the clock and the tower it's in, but it's actually the name of the bell itself. Also, it's not the largest four-faced clock in the world...the largest is actually back home in the States...specifically, in Minneapolis. No overseas visitors are allowed to climb to the top of the tower, but United Kingdom residents are allowed, as long as they're sponsored by a Member of Parliament."

"Anything else?" Rayne asked with a smirk, amazed at how many random facts he knew.

"Yeah, there isn't an elevator. So anyone who wants to get to the top has to climb the three hundred and thirty-four stairs to get there...then come down all three hundred and thirty-four as well."

"Three hundred and thirty-four? Did you make that up? How do you know that? Have you been up there?"

Ghost smiled at Rayne, but didn't answer.

"You have! How in the hell did you manage that? Do you know someone in government as well as someone on the police force? You don't live here, right?"

"Right. I'm a US citizen, just like you."

Rayne stared at Ghost for a beat, trying to use her nonexistent mind-meld power to get him to tell her his secrets. Finally, she huffed out a breath. "I was right...you're totally a spy. Fine, don't tell me. You're probably best friends with the queen or something."

Or something was right, but Ghost wasn't going to let her know that. It was amazing the connections he had because of being a Delta Force soldier. He'd protected, and even saved, the lives of some powerful men and women in his career.

He turned Rayne back around so she was gazing out at the city again. The weak sun was setting and it was slowly getting dark.

Rayne sighed as Ghost gathered her into his arms. He put his hands on her hips and she shivered. God, he felt good.

Feeling her shiver, he ran his hands up and down her arms. "Cold, Princess?"

Jeez. Princess. Could he get any better? He'd called her that a few times already, but it was apparent he'd officially decided that was her new nickname. She should've been irritated, but she loved it. "No, not really."

"Come 'ere." Ghost pulled her into his embrace fully. His arms went all the way around her so his right hand rested on her left hip and his left hand rested on her right hip. She rested her hands on his forearms. Finally, she sighed.

"What's going on in that head of yours?"

"I've had a good time today."

"And?" Ghost prompted.

"And I don't want it to end. But," she warned as

she felt his hands tighten on her, "I'm scared."

His arms immediately loosened and Rayne missed them. He physically turned her so she was facing him. He put a finger under her chin and lifted it so she had no choice but to look at him. "Scared of me?"

Rayne shook her head. "Not exactly."

"Talk to me. Explain."

Rayne bit her lip unconsciously, trying to think how she wanted to voice her fears. "I heard what you said earlier today…and I agree with all of it. But, I've never done this." She gestured between them. "I was serious when I told you earlier that I'm a dork. I don't do one-night stands. I haven't had a boyfriend in two years. I like to read. You know I'm a romantic. Sleeping with you goes against everything I've ever thought about doing. It's not safe going to bed with someone you don't know. I don't know if you have the creeping crud, or if you're a sexual deviant, or what. For all I know, your ID was a fake and your name really isn't John Benbrook and you're not from Fort Worth. I'm just…scared.

"But you should know…I don't think I've ever wanted a man more than I want you. I've never had to forcibly think about something other than what your chest looks like, or how big your…well, how big you are, or even how your hands will feel on my skin. So, it's all freaking me out. All of it. John, I don't think I should—"

"Call me Ghost," he ordered immediately, and when she nodded, he continued, "You're absolutely right, it's not safe to sleep with someone you just met. But I'll tell you right now, I don't have the creeping crud, I'm not a sexual deviant, although if wanting to taste every inch of your skin, fuck you so hard you'll still feel me days later, then eat you out after you come apart on my cock is sexually deviant behavior, I'll have to amend that. And, Princess, you aren't alone in your attraction. I haven't stopped thinking about what's under this sexy outfit since you sat down next to me in the airport. We absolutely should do this. Every woman needs at least one one-night stand in her life. Please God, take what you want. Take me. I said it before, and I'll say it again, you're safe with me, Rayne Jackson."

"How much longer until this thing is back at the bottom?"

"I think we've got some time," Ghost murmured, tilting his head down to hers. "Plenty of time for me to taste these scrumptious lips again."

Rayne smiled up at the man in front of her and licked her lips in anticipation of his kiss.

"God," he groaned, "you're gonna be the death of me." And he lowered his lips to hers.

Chapter Seven

G HOST KNEW HE was making one of the biggest mistakes he'd ever made in his life, but he couldn't stop himself. If Hollywood was there he'd be smacking him on the back of his head telling him to *think*. But Hollywood and his other teammates *weren't* there. And Ghost couldn't resist the sweet, funny, slightly nerdy woman who was holding his hand and trying not to hyperventilate as if her life depended on it.

He'd felt bad when she was expressing her confusion and fear while they were on the London Eye, and she'd said she was scared his name wasn't really John, but not bad enough to stop what was about to happen. He *needed* Rayne. Needed her like a drug addict needed his next fix. A part of him knew he'd regret it if he didn't take her to bed...and not in a horndog way, but because he knew their time together would change him fundamentally.

He was being sentimental, but Rayne was the first woman in a long time who he was attracted to as much by her personality as he was by her body. She said what she was thinking, she wasn't afraid to show her emotions, and she was fun to be around. Yes, she was also hot, and he couldn't wait to get his hands on her body, but it went deeper than that. For the first time in his life he felt a connection to a woman.

It scared the shit out of him, but Ghost knew he couldn't walk away. Didn't *want* to walk away.

Hearing Rayne say she'd thought about what he might look like without his clothes on...that she wanted to know how big his dick was. Yeah, at that moment, he was putty in her hands and she had no idea. None. She said she was scared of him, but in actuality, it was the other way around. *She* terrified *him*. He'd never felt like he did right now, in all of his life. As though if he didn't get inside her, couldn't taste her, smell her, hear her come apart under his hands, that he'd feel like he'd never truly lived.

But it was more than that. Deep down he knew one night wasn't going to be enough. For the first time ever, he was contemplating trying to figure out how to meet back up with a woman...to see her again. He hadn't lied when he'd told her he was a one-night-only kind of man. First, his job demanded it, but second, he'd never found a woman who'd interested him enough to want to get to know her deeper than that.

That made him a dick, but so far, he hadn't had

any complaints. He always let the woman know straight up he couldn't give her more than one night in bed, and if she balked, he let her down easy and left. One or two had tried to change the rules to their agreement after they'd fucked, but Ghost still always left.

The fact was, he wanted to know more about Rayne, knew that one night with her body under him, over him, and in as many other positions as she could imagine and even some she couldn't...wasn't going to be enough. He knew it in the very marrow of his bones, but that didn't change the fact that he couldn't have what he wanted.

Ghost probably still could've resisted her and walked away, but when she'd said she'd never had a one-night stand before and hadn't had a boyfriend in two years, all he could think of was that she was clean. *Clean.* Keane Bryson didn't have "clean" in his life. His hands were covered in the metaphorical blood of all the men and women he'd killed for his country.

He'd seen too much hatred, jealousy, gluttony, selfishness, and straight-up stupidity in the world. Ghost hadn't even known someone as fresh and naïve as Rayne Jackson existed except in the fairy-tale movies she claimed to like to watch. And even if he had known, he knew *he* would never have a shot at her. But to have her stand in front of him and flat-out tell him she'd thought about how he'd feel against her skin was too much for him to resist.

Ghost wasn't a selfish man. His Delta Force team came first. His country came second. If someone needed food, he'd give his up. If they needed a weapon, he'd gladly give his over. He wasn't even afraid to give his life if it meant saving one of his teammates or someone he was supposed to look after on a mission.

But this? He couldn't give this up. Ghost thought he deserved to be selfish for once.

He needed Rayne. And he was going to have her. And not just once, but as many times as he could before it was time to go. He'd get her out of his system and then have the memory of the hot woman he'd seduced during a lucky layover in London.

They went into the lobby of the Park Plaza Hotel and after collecting their luggage from the concierge, almost ran into a woman in a wheelchair with her assistance dog next to her. Scooting around her with a murmured apology, Ghost kept his hand on Rayne, stepped up to the front desk, and secured them a room for the night.

Ghost could tell Rayne was embarrassed. She blushed as he asked for the largest-size bed they had with a view of the London Eye. She blushed as he gave the woman behind the desk his credit card. She even blushed when the lady in the wheelchair came back from outside and said hello as she went by them on the way back up to her room.

"You don't have to be embarrassed, Rayne," Ghost told her as the clerk went into a back room for a moment.

"I feel like I have *one-night stand* and *slut* tattooed on my forehead," she whispered.

Ghost leaned down and kissed her head. "I guarantee you don't. You are so far from a slut it isn't even funny. Relax."

He finished checking in, threw his duffle bag over his shoulder, grabbed the handle of her suitcase, and took hold of her hand with his free one. Neither spoke as they headed up the elevator and got off on their floor.

Ghost unlocked the door and held it open to let Rayne walk in ahead of him. He watched as she put her handbag on the dresser and went straight to the floor-to-ceiling windows. The room was nice, but it wasn't huge, as was typical with European hotels. Rayne pulled back the curtain and gasped.

The sun had completely fallen while they'd checked in and their room faced both the London Eye and Westminster Abbey.

"It's beautiful," Rayne breathed, looking at the lights of the city twinkling in the distance.

Ghost came up behind her and put his hands on

her shoulders. "*You're* beautiful," he told her honestly, brushing her hair off her shoulder, kissing her neck lightly.

"I think I can see Buckingham Palace from here too. Were we really this high up when we were on the Eye? Oh, what time does our plane leave tomorrow? You *did* get on the list for standby, right? Do we need to schedule a wake-up call?"

Ghost turned Rayne until she was facing him instead of the window, knowing she was skittish about the upcoming night. "Yes. I talked to the reservations woman and said to put me on standby and I'd confirm in the morning. Don't be nervous, Princess. We'll go at your speed, okay?"

He watched as she swallowed hard and nodded. "Okay."

"Why don't you get changed into something more comfortable? Then we'll sit and talk."

"Talk?"

"Yeah, talk. Then if you want more, we'll do more. If at any time you want to stop, we'll stop."

"Simple as that?"

"Yeah, Princess, simple as that. I told you once today that I'd never force you to do anything you didn't want to do, and that hasn't changed. Although I have to tell you…I'm hoping you won't *want* to stop and I'm going to do everything in my power to try to convince you to continue."

"I want you, Ghost. I'm just nervous. Thank you for being patient with me. I'll get there."

"Then I'll wait all night if I have to. Go on, get changed, I'll head downstairs and make sure our wake-up call is set up." He knew he didn't have to leave the room to set up the call, but he figured Rayne would be more comfortable if he wasn't there when she changed.

"Thanks, Ghost. I won't take too long."

Ghost pulled Rayne into his body and wrapped his arms around her in a hug. He waited, thrilled when he felt her hands tentatively snake around him and rest on his back. He pulled back, kissed her lightly on the lips, and squeezed her biceps. "I'll be back."

He took the elevator down to the lobby, went outside and leaned against the building after speaking briefly with the woman behind the desk. He didn't need to schedule a wake-up call for himself. He'd get up without any problem. He always woke early in the morning. The guys on the team could set a clock by him. He did ask for a call at six for Rayne though. She'd have to get back to the airport to get to work, and he didn't want her to miss the flight and get in trouble. Knowing what he was planning was a dickful thing to do, he still made the arrangements for Rayne to get to the airport in the morning without him. He'd warned her, so she knew she'd most likely wake up alone...or at least she wouldn't be surprised when she did.

Ghost waited as long as he thought Rayne might need to get changed and do whatever it was women did to get ready for bed, before heading back upstairs. He put the key in the lock and eased the door open. The lights had been dimmed and Ghost could just see Rayne's shape on the bed. He went over to his duffle bag, grabbed it, and headed into the bathroom.

He came out a few minutes later wearing a pair of gray sweatpants and no shirt. He padded to the bed and pulled back the sheet. He stretched out on his side and propped himself up on his elbow, facing Rayne.

She was sitting upright with her arms around her knees. Rayne was wearing a black tank top and a pair of bright purple loose pants. Ghost smiled.

"Purple, huh?"

He watched as Rayne smiled then turned her head toward him. "Yeah, I'm fond of bright colors."

"I can see that. Let's play a game."

"A game?" Rayne's brows furrowed in confusion.

"Yeah. Word association. I'll say something, and you tell me the first thing you think of when you hear it. Then you can tell me a word, and I'll do the same thing."

"What's the point?"

Ghost smiled again, loving how blunt she was.

"The point is to get you to relax a little bit...and to get to know each other a bit better."

"How is this game gonna help us get to know each other better? And doesn't that defeat the purpose of a one-night stand?"

"Soldier," Ghost said, without answering her question. The whole point of the game was to take her mind off what they were about to do and to get her to let down her guard.

"Fort Hood," she responded immediately.

"Why Fort Hood?"

"Because it's the biggest Army base in Texas, my brother is there, and it's what I thought of first."

Ghost silently swore. Figured with his luck her brother would be stationed at the same place he was. Even with that little piece of knowledge, he wasn't willing to turn his back on Rayne. He simply needed her too badly to walk away now. "Okay, your turn."

"London," she said with a gleam in her eye.

"Kissing you on the London Eye," Ghost answered immediately. He watched as Rayne smiled. "Sex."

"Awkward." As soon as she said it, she slapped a hand over her mouth and shut her eyes in mortification.

Ghost reached out and put his hand on her foot. "Sex has been awkward for you?"

"Unfortunately, yeah."

"In what way?"

"In every way. It's just weird. Getting naked with someone, figuring out where my hands are supposed to go, waiting for him to get done…it's just weird."

Ghost's pulse rate sped up, listening to her. It was obvious she wasn't a virgin, but damn he wanted to introduce her to passion. If she was lost in the moment, she wouldn't be worrying about where her hands were or if he got off or not. "Your turn," he said in a strangled voice.

Rayne leaned back against the pillows and dropped her legs, stretching them out in front of her. Ghost's hand moved from her foot to her thigh.

"Home."

The first word that sprang to his mind was "nowhere" but he knew he couldn't say that. "Fort Worth."

It was quiet in the room for a beat before she said softly, "Your turn."

"Tell me about your family."

"My family? I'm not sure that will put me in the mood, Ghost."

He chuckled. "Tell me anyway." He watched as Rayne relaxed even further. His plan was working just as he'd hoped.

"Well, I have a brother and a sister. I'm the middle kid. My sister is older than me by three years, and I'm two years older than my brother. Samantha is an actress and lives in California. She's been cast in a few films, but is still waiting for her big break."

"And your brother?"

"Chase lives down in Killeen and is a lieutenant in the Army. He's stationed at Fort Hood. He's always wanted to be in the military, he was accepted into West Point, and he's going to be a lifer. I've always kidded with him that there's no way I'll ever salute him…even if he climbs the rank to be a general." She laughed a little at herself.

"General Jackson?" he asked in what he hoped was a light tone.

"Yeah, ridiculous, huh? I guess it was just in his blood or something."

"You never thought about joining up? It would've been another way to see the world."

Rayne looked at him with such horror he had to smile.

"No freaking way. I'd make a terrible soldier. Heck, if there's ever an apocalypse, I'll totally be the first one killed by the zombies because I can't run to save my life."

"There's more to survival than running, Princess."

"Whatever. I suck at pushups, haven't done a sit-up since I was eight years old, and honestly? I don't follow directions very well."

When Ghost didn't say anything more, Rayne scooted down on the bed and mimicked his pose, turning on her side, propping her head up with her hand and leaning on her elbow. It looked as if he was thinking hard about something, so she let him think.

"I'll never look at the rain in the same way again," he said, seemingly out of the blue.

"What?"

"If it wasn't for the storm, the flight wouldn't have been canceled, and I wouldn't be here now, with you, so turned on I can't even think straight."

Rayne looked at him in surprise. "You are?"

"Yeah, Princess. I feel like I'm fifteen again, standing next to Whitney Pumperfield under the bleachers at the football game."

Rayne giggled, and Ghost continued with his made-up story. "She was a year younger than me, but she'd obviously been an early bloomer, because she had the finest set of tits I'd ever seen. And I wanted to get my hands on them…bad."

"Go on…did you?"

"Oh yeah…" Ghost paused for dramatic effect. "She let me kiss her for a while and I thought I was so suave. I moved one of my hands under her crop top and slowly eased it upward. I went straight for her bra and pulled it down. I squeezed her voluptuous tit and felt her nipple stab into my palm."

"And?" Rayne smiled and gestured for him to continue. "Don't leave me hanging here!"

Ghost scooted closer to her and put his hand on her

hip.

"And just as she moaned into my mouth, I blew in my pants and her best friend called her name from around the corner. She pulled away, and I lost my chance to do anything else with her."

"You came just from touching her breast?"

"Princess, I was fifteen. And you didn't see her tits."

Rayne laughed again and immediately tried to hide it from him.

"Yeah, I can laugh about it now, but back then I was mortified and pissed all at once. I wanted to touch her...all over, but later that night her friend convinced her that I only wanted in her pants and she refused to go anywhere with me ever again."

"*Did* you only want in her pants?"

"You heard me say I was fifteen, right?" Ghost joked.

"Yeah, right, sorry." She giggled at him.

Ghost thanked his lucky stars Rayne was finally relaxing. "As I said, right at this moment, I'm so turned on, I feel just like I did back then, standing with my hand on Whitney's chest." He moved his hand slowly up and down the side of Rayne's body.

"Are you going to lose it when you touch my breast?"

"Hell no. I've had some practice in control since then."

"Kiss me, Ghost."

"With pleasure." Ghost leaned forward and felt satisfaction pool in his gut when Rayne eased backward at his movement and lay on her back, opening herself up to him, looking into his eyes as if he was her first lover.

"I'm gonna kiss you, Princess. Then I'm gonna finally see what *your* gorgeous tits look like. I've been imagining it all afternoon. I know Whitney Pumperfield is gonna be a distant memory after seeing yours. Then I'm gonna strip off those god-awful purple pants and see if your legs are as long as they seemed today in that skirt."

"Hey! My pants aren't god-awful!"

Ghost ignored her protest and finished. "Then I'm gonna take you. I'm gonna take you soft and slow until you beg me to let you come. Then as you're coming, I'm gonna take you hard and fast, until you can't think of sex again without thinking about me. And Princess? I guarantee after tonight, you won't think sex is awkward ever again. You'll see what you've been missing all this time."

He paused, waiting for her to say something, to stop him. When she didn't move a muscle, not even to breathe, Ghost smiled down at her. "Oh yeah, Whitney has nothing on you."

As he leaned down to kiss her, he was thrilled when Rayne arched up to meet his mouth. Thank Christ.

Chapter Eight

RAYNE COULDN'T BELIEVE she was about to have a one-night stand with a man she basically picked up in an airport. He was honestly the sexiest man she'd ever laid eyes on. Muscular arms, six-pack abs, a tattoo of some words on his left side...he could've been a model if it wasn't for the variety of scars crisscrossing his torso. Scars notwithstanding, he was beautiful and she wanted her hands on him in the worst way. Why he seemed interested in plain ol' *her*, she had no idea, but she wasn't going to question it.

She wanted him. Bad. Rayne lifted her chin and licked her lips as Ghost's head descended toward hers. She kept her eyes open, not wanting to miss a second of the experience.

Ghost felt his heart beating in his chest as the anticipation of seeing Rayne naked, of getting inside her, pressed down on him. He couldn't remember being this excited to see a woman without her clothes on in a long, long time...probably since he was about fifteen years old.

His lips touched hers and Ghost put his right hand on her face while his left arm kept him propped up over Rayne. Their tongues tangled together as they relearned the taste of each other's mouths. He caressed her cheek with his thumb as their heads tilted one way, then the other as they devoured each other.

Ghost drew back and swallowed hard. He wanted to rush it. He wanted to be inside this amazing woman more than he wanted to breathe, but he didn't want to spook her, and perhaps more importantly, he wanted to give her romance. This might be a one-time thing, but the romantic part of him, usually buried deep, wanted to make this night one she'd remember for a long time.

"You taste like mint."

Ghost grinned down at Rayne. "So do you." After a beat, he asked, "You all right?"

Rayne nodded. "I'm good."

"Comfortable?"

"Uh-huh, why?"

"Because I have a feeling you're going to be on your back for a while."

Rayne laughed a little nervously and brought her hand up to grasp his biceps, noting absently that her fingertips didn't come close to touching as she wrapped her hand around him. "I am?"

"Yeah."

"I didn't really picture you as a missionary-style

man."

Ghost leaned down and kissed her jaw without an-swering. Then he moved to nip and lick at the skin right by her ear. He shifted and took her lobe between his teeth, sucking lightly and caressing her with his tongue. Finally he shifted his lips so he could whisper into Rayne's ear. "I'm a missionary man, a doggy-style man, a reverse-cowgirl man, and any other position I can get. I want you, any way I can get you, and I'm planning on using every minute of our night to keep you satisfied. But I want to start by feasting...and the best position for that is you, on your back. Under-stand?"

Her quick inhalation was answer enough. Ghost lifted his head and Rayne could see his eyes were dark with lust. His hand ran from her cheek down her chest, over her erect nipple to her waist. Without breaking eye contact, he lifted her tank top and eased his hand underneath it.

Neither of them said a word as Ghost's hand slowly slid up and covered her breast. She wasn't wearing a bra and his hand covered her completely and he squeezed.

Rayne shifted under him, feeling herself get wet at his confident touch.

"I can't wait to see these beauties," Ghost mur-mured reverently. "You're so soft and your nipple is begging for my touch."

"Ghost, please."

"Please what, Princess?"

He was smiling down at her, clearly enjoying her restless movements under him, knowing his touch was turning her on.

"Touch me."

"I am touching you."

"Ghost…" His name came out as a whine and Rayne was mortified as soon as the word left her mouth. She shouldn't have worried though.

"God, I love hearing you lose your mind. And I haven't even gotten started. Lift your arms. Let's get this tank off."

Rayne hesitated for a second. This was it. If she was going to back out, now was the time.

But the moment the thought entered her head, she dismissed it. She wanted Ghost. He'd been a gentleman all day. He'd protected her when they were out and about and he had a funny side hidden under his gruff exterior. He'd done nothing but reassure her he wasn't going to do anything she didn't want to do, and even if it made her similar to one of those stupid women in horror movies, she was going to trust him.

She lifted her arms.

Ghost took a deep breath and relaxed as Rayne finally raised her arms to give him the go-ahead to remove her tank. He'd wondered for a moment if she was about to call it quits, and it would've killed him, but he would've backed off. Thank Christ she was still with him.

Sitting up, Ghost straddled her hips and caressed her belly over the tank top, drawing out the moment. Looking down at his hands—and his prize—he slipped his hands under her shirt and ever so slowly pushed upward, taking the shirt with him as he moved. Her belly button was exposed, then the lower curves of her breasts and finally, as his hands moved over both nipples, her entire chest was bare to him.

She was beautiful. Not perfect, and he knew if asked, she'd probably point out all the areas on her body she thought were flawed. But her lushness only made him harder. His original thought that she reminded him of Marilyn Monroe was right on. Her hips were wide and her breasts were large. Her nipples stood up, as if begging for his touch. She had a bit of a belly, but all Ghost saw was heaven.

Not able to wait, and while pushing the tank top the rest of the way over her head and over her arms, Ghost leaned down and took one of her nipples into his mouth, and groaned. Her bud was hard, and he could feel it tighten more as he nipped at it with his teeth.

His hands now free, he brought them down and used one to plump up the breast of the nipple he was sucking, and the other he used to cover her other mound and squeeze.

He felt Rayne arch into his touch and smiled. Some men might be ass men, but he was most certainly a breast man. Without looking up, he moved to the other side of her chest. He nibbled around the curve of her ample mound and finally looked up to her face as his tongue came out and flicked the neglected tip.

Rayne was looking down at him with her mouth slightly open and he could hear her quick breaths. He looked back down at what he was doing. "There's nothing I enjoy more than playing with a pair of tits. And Princess, I have to say, yours are absolutely perfect."

"Better than Whitney Pumperfield's?"

It took Ghost a moment to figure out who she was talking about. Since Whitney was made up, he could answer her honestly with a smile. "A million times better than Whitney's."

He pulled back and sat up, hovering over Rayne once more. His hands didn't leave her chest as he continued to caress and squeeze her. "Yours are fleshy enough that if I do this," he squeezed her mounds together until they were touching, "I can imagine my cock sliding between them."

He ignored Rayne's gasp and went on, shifting so his fingertips were pinching her nipples. "Your nipples are large and stick out beautifully, giving me something to grab on to when I want to do this..."

Ghost twisted his fingers slightly, loving the flush of red that made its way up her neck. He knew he wasn't hurting her because her hips were undulating under his unconsciously. A little moan escaped her lips and he could feel her fingernails digging into his hips as she held on to him. Most importantly, she didn't tell him to stop, and she wasn't pulling away from him.

"You are beautiful, Princess." He soothed both hands over her breasts again, gently plumping them up and rubbing his palms over her nipples.

Something caught his eye and he leaned in closer to take a look. "Ah, tattoo number one."

Almost hidden, and it certainly would've gone unseen if she'd been standing, was a small pink ribbon tattooed on the underside of her left breast. There was a tiny purple heart next to it as well. The tattoo was tiny, probably only half an inch at most. Ghost leaned down and licked it. Then kissed it gently, before rising.

"Interesting place for a tattoo. That had to have hurt."

Rayne nodded at him. "It's for my friend Mary. She had breast cancer and I got it in solidarity for her. The pain it took for me to get it was nothing compared to what she went through."

"The woman you texted my info to?"

"Uh-huh...um, Ghost..."

"Yeah, Princess?" Ghost knew exactly what he was doing to her as he continued to stimulate her right nipple as he talked. He'd pushed up her left breast so he could see the small mark, and he could literally feel her heart beating as fast as a jackrabbit under his palm.

"Can we discuss it later?"

"Discuss what later?"

"Jesus, Ghost. My tattoo. My friend Mary. Breast cancer. All of it."

"Yeah, you're right, I was in the middle of something, wasn't I?"

Rayne nodded enthusiastically.

"Okay, Princess. That's one tattoo down. I can't wait to find the other two." He laughed when she moaned under him. He shifted his hips down her body until he was hovering over her knees. "Spread your legs for me."

Loving that she immediately did as he asked, Ghost moved so she could spread herself wider for him and settled himself on his knees between her legs. He scooted up, forcing her to widen her legs even more to accommodate him as he did. He put his hands on her hips and watched her face.

After a moment, she looked up at him. Her hands fluttered nervously next to her as if she wasn't sure what to do with them.

"I can smell how aroused you are for me, Princess.

Do you still want me? Want this?"

She nodded and swallowed hard.

"Thank God." He took the drawstring in his hand and slowly pulled, loosening the waist of her purple cotton pants. He pressed his thumbs into her hipbones and then methodically swept them back and forth over her pants, seemingly in no hurry.

Leaning down, he nuzzled the area right under her belly button and used his chin to push her pants farther down her hips. Looking up in surprise, he commented, "You aren't wearing panties."

"I know. I figured if I was coming to bed to be with you, I'd only be taking them off, so it seemed to me to be a time-saver to *leave* them off."

"Jesus, no wonder I can smell you so easily." His hands didn't move, but Ghost brought his nose down between her legs and inhaled deeply.

Shifting in embarrassment, and wanting him to get on with it, Rayne commented dryly, "You know, that'd be quicker if you used your hands."

Ghost swallowed a laugh. She was hilarious. "I know, but I'm enjoying taking my time."

"As much as I appreciate that, we do only have one night, Ghost. Can we get on with it?"

The gleam in his eyes as he looked up was electric. "You ready for me?"

"Yes."

Ghost backed away and stood up next to the bed. As his hands went to the waistband of his sweats, he gestured to her pants and ordered brusquely, "Take 'em off."

Rayne lifted her hips and pushed her favorite lounging pants down, using her feet to push them the rest of the way off and to the floor. She couldn't take her eyes off Ghost. He'd shoved his own pants off and was standing next to the bed taking her in as if she were a meal and he hadn't eaten in days.

But damn, he was fine. There was one additional gnarly scar on his left thigh, but otherwise he was flawless. She could see the tattooed writing on his side but couldn't read what it said. She was distracted by his cock, which was standing up long and thick, jutting from between his thighs. Before she'd gotten her fill of looking at him, Ghost threw one leg over hers and settled back between her knees.

He once again shoved his way up her body until her legs were gaping open around him. She bent her legs to accommodate him and gasped when he put both hands under her butt and lifted her hips.

Rayne grabbed on to his arms again and panted in anticipation. She'd had a few guys go down on her before, but none seemed this…intense about it. Ghost *had* said he wanted her to get lost in the passion between them, and it looked like she was about to be.

"Tattoo number two," Ghost said.

Rayne could see his attention on the small tattoo just outside her bikini line, almost on her inner thigh. He leaned down and licked over the Chinese symbol and she could feel the goose bumps shoot down her arms at his actions.

"What's it say?"

"You mean you can't read Chinese?" Rayne breathed as he licked over the ink again.

"Nope."

"Some spy you are. It stands for strength."

"Ummm, I like it."

"Th-thanks..." Rayne would've said more, but Ghost was obviously done talking about her tattoo because he'd begun slowly lapping at her clit. He hadn't wasted time working up to it, he'd just gone right for the gusto.

"Ghost...Jesus...oh my God...yeah...shit..."

Ghost gripped Rayne's hips tighter as she squirmed in his grasp. Once he had her where he wanted, he didn't want to waste any more time. She smelled divine, and he could see her lips glistening with her juices. He suddenly needed to see her come apart in his arms, to let go, to trust him to bring her there.

He felt her fingernails digging into him as she tried to hold on to something. Ghost loved hearing her incoherent mutterings as he feasted. His hands were busy, so he couldn't use them to help her get off, so he lowered his mouth and tasted her with one long lick between her folds. She was dripping wet, and Ghost pulled back for a second to take a good look at her pink slit.

She continued to squirm in his grip and he grinned. God. She was amazing. He lowered his head and once again set to work trying to get her to explode in his mouth. He flicked his tongue hard and fast against her clit and used his chin to rub against her lower lips.

"Yeah, right there. Harder…shit…yeah…Ghost…-I'm gonna…"

She didn't have to warn him, Ghost could read the signs. He continued his relentless pressure on the small bundle of nerves as she hunched up toward him and quivered and shook as her orgasm overtook her. He lowered her hips to the mattress but didn't stop his assault on her clit. Finally having a hand free, he brought it up to her entrance and slowly pushed in one finger as he continued his fast, hard licks against her.

He groaned as he felt her hot sheath clench around his finger. He pulled it out and added another. He kept a slow and steady rhythm as he pumped in and out of her. Ghost felt Rayne's hands move to his head as she tried to push him harder against her.

He pulled back a mere inch and blew on her clit. He glanced up and saw she was watching him. "You like what you see, Princess?"

"Uh-huh."

Without losing eye contact, Ghost said, "This is what passion is. It's getting lost in what's happening to your body. To want to watch your lover take his pleasure. You're beautiful, Rayne. Fucking beautiful."

Her head dropped back on the pillow at his words and she groaned. Her hips shifted under his hand, urging him to continue. Ghost bent his head down and re-concentrated on the task at hand, making sure Rayne was as lost to the passion blooming between them as he was. Ghost enjoyed giving head, but usually it was a means to an end. The wetter he could get a woman, the better the sex was for him.

But with Rayne, it wasn't like that. Seeing her orgasm under his tongue made him feel as if he was the king of the mountain. It wasn't about her taking a turn so he could get to his. He'd be happy making her come over and over again, even if he never got his shot.

It was that thought that made every muscle in his body tense, including the fingers deep inside her body. His teeth accidentally closed over her sensitive clit, and even though he immediately relaxed his grip, it was too late, she exploded once again in his arms. Ghost could actually feel her juices coat his fingers and she squeezed them until they ached. The thought of her doing that when his cock was inside her was almost too much.

He brought the hand that had been under her down his body and ruthlessly grabbed the base of his cock, preventing himself from exploding all over the sheets. Jesus fucking Christ.

Chapter Nine

G HOST WAS A man who always kept control of everything around him, including his body. The fact that he'd almost lost it while merely imagining how it would feel to be inside Rayne's body didn't sit well with him.

While she was still coming down from her second orgasm, Ghost reached over to the nightstand and grabbed the condom he'd put there before he'd joined Rayne in bed. Quickly sheathing himself, and grimacing at how sensitive he was, he crawled up Rayne's body until he was straddling her. He put his hands next to her shoulders and waited for her to open her eyes.

Rayne stretched lazily and slowly peeled her eyes open. Startled to see Ghost's face so close to hers, she smiled and brought her arms up to grab on to his biceps. "Hey."

"Hey back."

"That was…wow."

"You're beautiful when you come."

"Uh, thank you?"

"You're welcome. You ready for me?"

"Oh! Yeah, sorry. Your turn now." Rayne lifted her legs until they were bent at the knees again and tilted her pelvis up. "I'm ready." When Ghost didn't move, Rayne tilted her head back and wrinkled her eyebrows at him. "Ghost?"

"This isn't a *quid pro quo* thing, Rayne."

"I don't understand."

"You're acting like since I got you off, I can just shove myself inside you and once I orgasm we'll be even."

"Oh, well, you haven't...you know...yet, and I have."

"And you will again."

"Ghost, seriously, I know you're a super badass spy, but that's not how it works."

"Rayne, it *is* how it works. You want to know what I was thinking as I had my tongue inside you and you were coming around my fingers?"

"Uh, no, not really."

Ignoring her cute, flustered reply, Ghost barreled on, "I was thinking that I could watch you come all night and be completely satisfied, even if I never got my turn."

"What? That's just...I don't know what that is."

"It's honest. That's what it is."

"But, you're hard, you're ready." Rayne lifted her

hips until the tip of Ghost's cock brushed against her lower belly.

Ghost groaned, but forced himself to continue. "I *am* ready. But I want *you* to be ready. I want you to be sure. I can get off without entering you. We can do it that way if you want." He watched as Rayne's eyes dilated at his words. God, it made him feel so good that his words could turn her on.

"I want you inside me. Please, Ghost."

"Take me in your hand. Put me where you want me then."

Ghost knew he was skating on thin ice. Having Rayne's hands on him would test his control to the limit. When her hand reached between their bodies, brushing against his stomach, he clenched every muscle in his body and tried to think about anything but how good she felt.

He felt her grip his cock and tug as she tried to bring him closer to her. Ghost shifted until he felt her warm body against his and couldn't hold back a groan as he felt her nether lips part around his shaft.

Knowing she'd gotten him to where he needed to be, Rayne moved her hand away and to Ghost's side. She dug her nails in and pulled him to her. "Fuck me, Ghost. Please."

"Oh shit, Princess." It was as if her words let loose something inside him. He pushed slowly and relentlessly inside until he couldn't go any farther. Then he reached down and pulled Rayne's hips up and into him, and gained another few crucial millimeters. Ghost could feel his balls flush with the warm skin of her ass.

"Ghost, oh yeah. God, you feel good."

Ghost shut his eyes as Rayne's inner muscles squeezed against his shaft. Holy hell. He'd fucked his share of women. He wasn't ashamed of his sexual history, but this was something different. Rayne felt tighter, hotter, wetter...and more right than anything he'd ever felt before.

He opened his eyes and looked down. Rayne wasn't looking up at him, but had her head propped up on the pillow and was looking down their bodies to where they were joined.

Ghost pulled his hips back an inch, then pushed back in, loving the expression on Rayne's face as she continued to watch them. He did it again, pulling out even farther, before slowly pushing back in until she was full of him again. Ghost watched as Rayne began to pant and he felt her hips tilt up farther into him.

He did it again, and again, loving how Rayne kept her eyes on his cock as he pulled back, covered in her juices, then as he pushed back inside her. Normally he loved the sight of his cock being engulfed inside a woman's body, but he was getting more enjoyment out of watching Rayne this time instead. She sighed, she moaned, and she bit her lip as he continued his slow assault on her senses, but not once did she take her eyes off his cock.

Ghost knew he was getting close and pulled out until just his tip was surrounded by Rayne's hot body and paused...waiting. Finally her hips tilted up a miniscule amount and he slammed back inside her. She looked away from where they were joined and dropped her head back on the pillow and moaned.

Neither of them spoke, but with each thrust, Ghost knew they were communicating all the same. Desperate to feel her muscles contracting with her orgasm around his cock as they'd done around his fingers, he moved one hand between them and plucked at Rayne's clit as he hammered in and out of her. Finally, just as he thought he'd have to come without her, Ghost felt the telltale flutter of her inner muscles against him and felt her fingers grip him tighter.

"Harder, Ghost, God yeah, rub me a little harder...yeah, right there...Ghost!"

His name was a sigh and a warning that she was orgasming. She arched her back and her hips thrust up against his, helplessly lost in the release he'd forced on her.

Ghost held still for a moment as he felt the delicious contractions from deep inside her squeeze his dick, and finally let himself go. He thrust once, then twice, then held himself still as he felt the come boil up from his balls and spurt out the tip of his cock.

They both twitched and moaned through the small contractions of their muscles, and slowly Ghost lowered himself down onto Rayne. He gathered her close as they panted and tried to catch their breath.

Ghost loved feeling her inner walls continue to grip and release him as she slowly came back to herself. He ran a hand over her hair, feeling pride he'd put the sheen of sweat on her forehead.

"You okay?" he asked softly.

"No, I think you killed me." Her voice was low and gravelly and she cleared her throat as she opened her eyes. "But what a way to go."

They smiled at each other for a beat before Ghost commented, "I have to get rid of this condom. Don't move."

"I couldn't move if my life depended on it."

Ghost grinned, pleased with himself, and eased his hips back. They both groaned as he slipped out of her body. "Be right back."

"'Kay."

Ghost dealt with the condom in the bathroom and quickly rejoined Rayne. She hadn't moved a muscle and he easily slipped back into the bed beside her. He lay on his back and she cuddled into him, one arm thrown around his rib cage and her head on his shoulder. He wrapped his arm around her and marveled at how good she felt against him.

"I know I should be tired, but I'm not," Rayne murmured. "I feel mellow and relaxed, but not ready to sleep. Is that normal?"

Ghost chuckled. "I have no idea, but yeah, I feel the same way."

They were quiet for a beat, then Ghost asked, "So what's the most outlandish thing you've seen on a flight?"

"I thought the woman was the one who always wanted to talk after sex?" she asked teasingly.

Ghost shrugged. "Figured we might as well pass the time before we're ready to go again."

"Again?" Rayne propped herself up on an elbow and peered at him.

"Yeah. You didn't think once was going to be enough, did you? There're so many more things I want to do with you before our night is over, Princess."

She lay back down quickly, embarrassed for some reason. "Oh, okay, well good then. And I guess talking, while we're...recovering, is just as good as anything else we can do."

Ghost chuckled, loving how adorable she was in her embarrassment. He idly ran his hand up and down the part of her back he could reach. He grasped her other hand with his and played with her fingers as she answered.

"The weirdest thing I've seen on a flight, huh? Hmm, of course I've caught couples trying to get inducted into the mile-high club...but honestly, I can't imagine anything worse than having sex in a tiny airplane bathroom. That *cannot* be sanitary or comfortable!"

After Ghost chuckled, as she wanted him to, she continued.

"I guess I'd have to break your question into different categories. The most amazing thing I've even seen on a flight is when the pilot informed the passengers that we had two deceased American soldiers on our flight who were being taken back to the States, and one of the passengers started an impromptu collection for the Wounded Warrior Project. I swear almost every single person on the plane that day donated at least a dollar."

"That's amazing," Ghost said softly into the silence that followed.

Rayne sniffed once. "I know. I guess it meant more to me because of Chase being in the Army. He'd just been sent over to Iraq for his first tour and it hit me really hard that it could've been *him* in the coffin under us. I have the utmost respect for anyone in the military. It's a tough life, and they have to do things that us civilians would never understand. I admire them."

Feeling uncomfortable with the direction the conversation was going, Ghost tried to steer it back to safer territory. "So that's the most amazing, what's next?"

Rayne cleared her throat. "Okay, so the weirdest...it was on a flight from Gabon, Africa, to Paris. There was a whole family...and by a whole family, I mean at least twenty people. I don't know how they were all related, but in the middle of the flight, someone brought out a plucked chicken and started trying to cook it over a little Sterno flame thing."

"How did they get either of those onboard?" Ghost asked, appalled.

"I have no idea, obviously security is way different there than in the States, but anyway, here they were, trying to cook this bird, some of the other passengers were gagging and complaining, and the entire family started arguing about the chicken. Some wanted to be able to cook it, and others were against it. They were screaming and carrying on. It really was a weird thing."

"How did it get resolved?"

"One of the older women finally just smacked one of the younger men on the back of the head and said something stern. The chicken and the Sterno disappeared into someone's bag and that was that. As I said. Weird."

Ghost was enjoying the shit out of lying next to Rayne and listening to her stories. "Go on."

"Okay, so let's see…scariest moment? An almost-crash landing."

Ghost felt her tense next to him and he leaned up and kissed her on the forehead. "That would be scary, but obviously you're here, so it ended up okay."

"Yeah. Ghost…I don't know how to explain this to you. I thought I was going to die. We were in the middle of serving drinks and the plane went through some crazy turbulence. I mean, crazy like people who weren't wearing their seat belts were flying up out of their seats. I got thrown and my head hit the ceiling of the plane before I was dumped back down to the ground. We quickly pulled the drink carts back to the galleys and strapped into our jump seats. The pilot came on and said we'd been flying through a storm and had been hit by lightning and we were obviously going through some turbulence, and there had been damage to one of the engines so we were going to have to head to the nearest airport for an emergency landing."

Rayne paused and took a deep breath, then went on. "I was sitting next to the door with the little window so I could see outside. All I could see were these huge mountains. I thought we were going to crash into them. I was actually okay with that because I thought it wouldn't hurt. I didn't want to die, and coming face-to-face with the possibility wasn't fun, but I was okay with dying suddenly and without pain. We limped on for another twenty minutes before landing. It was bumpy and out of control, but finally we were safe on the ground and in one piece."

"And you're still a flight attendant?"

Rayne laughed grimly at the disbelief and awe in Ghost's question. "Yeah, crazy, isn't it? I figured, that had to have been my one brush with death. I got some counseling and really thought about it. We're all gonna die at some point or another. I enjoy what I do...at least for now, and I didn't want to be chased away from it. The pilot knew what he was doing, and while it was scary, it honestly happens all the time."

"That's an interesting way to look at it," Ghost commented.

"Yeah, well, it was that or go back to teaching," Rayne teased, laughing.

"I see your point."

"What about you?"

"What about me what?"

"What was a time when you were scared?"

Ghost frantically thought through his memories to see if there was anything he could tell her. Dismissing anything that had happened in his Army life, he tried to think of something that she'd believe. "I was held up at gunpoint once."

"Really?"

No. He hated lying to her, but he didn't really have

a choice. "Yes, really."

"What happened?"

"It was back home in Fort Worth. A woman I was dating and I were leaving a restaurant and a man came out of nowhere and stuck a gun in our faces and told us to give him all our money."

"Oh my God! What did you do?"

"Gave him all our money, of course."

"And what happened?"

"He left." Lying to Rayne didn't feel right anymore. Ghost wanted nothing more than to be able to tell her some of the real stories about when he'd felt scared...lying in the sand in Iraq, waiting to see if the man they were hunting would kill his own son in front of them or not...watching as his friend and teammate, Fletch, got the shit beaten out of him by some extremists who happened to get lucky and catch the two of them. It seemed like forever, but was only a couple of hours before the rest of the team showed up and got them out of there.

"That's it? He left?"

Ghost was brought out of his musings by her question. "Yup."

"And you were scared?"

Ghost couldn't help it, he laughed at her bafflement. "Princess, he had a gun aimed at the woman I was with...and I had a whole seduction planned for later that night. If he'd have shot either of us, it would've messed up my plans to get laid."

Rayne smacked him on the chest playfully. "Oh, you!"

Ghost smiled and grabbed hold of her hand, holding it flat on his chest. He idly rubbed his thumb on the back of it. "What are your dreams, Princess?"

He felt her settle in before she spoke. "I don't know. I used to think I wanted to have a huge family and live in a little house with a white picket fence, but after seeing as much of the world as I have, I'm just not sure that's what I want anymore."

"What *do* you want?"

"I'm not sure," Rayne whispered sleepily. "I enjoy seeing other countries. I like learning about other cultures, but I'm not comfortable either. Sometimes it scares me to be in countries that I know have constant terrorist attacks. I know I'm only twenty-eight, but I feel if I decide to do something else now that I've wasted all this time...with my degree, and in this job. I just don't know what else I should or could do."

Ghost wasn't pleased when he thought about Rayne being in dangerous cities and countries either, but he didn't have any answers for her. He kept his body relaxed under hers and stroked her back lightly.

"Mary works at a bank back home and she says she could get me a job there, but I don't think I'm a bank kinda person."

They lay there quiet for a bit, each lost in their own thoughts.

"I could always be a super-secret spy," Rayne teased drowsily. Her words were slurred and it was obvious she was on the verge of sleep.

"It's not all it's cracked up to be," Ghost replied almost inaudibly. "Sleep now, Princess. I've got you."

Not too much later, both were breathing deeply, sleeping the sleep of the sexually sated and feeling safe in the arms of the other.

Chapter Ten

RAYNE SHIFTED AND sighed. She felt *good*. More than good, great actually. She'd just had one heck of a dream… She went to stretch and felt herself held in place by a strong set of hands.

Her eyes flew open and she gasped as she looked down.

Ghost was laying on his stomach between her legs and he was lazily lapping at her sex. She groaned and threw her head back, her whole body suddenly alive and majorly turned on. "How long have you been down there?" she asked curiously.

"Long enough to watch you slowly get wetter and wetter and to learn that your body likes more direct stimulation on your clit rather than subtle manipulation."

"Oh good Lord, Ghost. Seriously?"

"Yeah. I'm serious. When I do this," he flattened his tongue and ran it roughly over her clit once and she jumped in reaction, "you cream more readily than if I do this," and he lightly licked around her bundle of nerves instead of directly on it. The latter felt good, but nothing like when he'd deliberately licked hard right over her bud.

"Yeah, okay...I believe you." Rayne felt one of his thick fingers push inside her folds and she held back the moan...barely.

"But I've been thinking—"

"Oh shit..."

Ghost continued as if Rayne hadn't interrupted him. "I've been thinking that I've seen two of your tattoos, but you said you had three. I haven't found the third yet. I checked out your ankles and arms while you were being lazy, and didn't see anything. So that only leaves one more place to check. Turn over, Princess."

"I want to check out yours, Ghost."

"And I'll let you...after. Turn over."

Feeling nervous because she had no idea what Ghost would think of her tattoo—it was very different from the others—she awkwardly turned over, buried her face in her arms, and held her breath.

"Up on your knees, Princess."

Ghost put pressure on her legs until she shifted and was on her knees, still bent over. She felt very exposed like this, with her butt in the air and her bits hanging out, but it was a perfect position for Ghost to get an up-close and personal look at her tattoo.

When he didn't say anything, Rayne commented

dryly, "It's a bit bigger than the other two."

When Ghost still didn't say anything, Rayne risked a look back at him. She wasn't sure what to expect. The tattoo *was* bigger than the others. In fact, it spanned her entire lower back. She hadn't gone into the tattoo parlor intending on getting the biggest tramp stamp she'd ever seen, but the artist had drawn up what she wanted and it'd been so beautiful, she'd gone with his suggestion to get it bigger than she'd planned.

"Ghost?"

"You have no idea how perfect this is." Ghost's voice was low and reverent.

Rayne finally felt him touch her. He ran his fingertips over her back, skimming the outline of the tattoo.

"Tell me what it means to you," he ordered softly and urgently.

She put her head back down and looked blindly at the clock on the table next to the bed. It was two-thirty in the morning. They'd only been asleep for about an hour and a half. "The eagle represents my job...a love of flying and of my country. The Army logo is in honor of Chase. I put a flower in one talon and a rifle in the other to represent both my siblings...Samantha loves carnations."

"And the lightning bolt?"

Rayne didn't understand Ghost's tone, but she continued anyway. "Remember when I told you about the scariest moment I had in the plane? With the lightning? It was kinda an important moment in my life...and I thought it went well with the tattoo."

"It goes well with the tattoo," Ghost breathed. He couldn't fucking believe what he was looking at. If he'd designed a tattoo for himself, it would've looked almost exactly like what was inked on her back. The eagle, the patriotic symbol of the United States, whose wings were spread and spanned her entire lower back. The tips of the wings barely wrapped around each side of her waist. The Army logo, the rifle...even the damn lightning bolt, which was incorporated into the Delta Force logo, was right on the mark. The only thing he wouldn't have included was the carnation...he'd change it to a fairy wand or something. He didn't think princesses carried wands, but somehow it still reminded him of Rayne.

Ghost felt himself harden painfully. His. She was fucking *his*.

He shook his head in denial. No, she wasn't his. She couldn't be. She thought his name was John Benbrook. She knew nothing about him. *Could* know nothing about him, for his safety and hers.

He leaned over, snatched a condom off the table and quickly smoothed it down his rock-hard shaft. He scooted up until he felt her heat against him. He lifted her hips until she was lined up perfectly. "Hold on," he murmured before sliding balls deep into her with one thrust.

He kept his eyes on the eagle as he pulled away and then pushed in again. Ghost ran his hands over her back, clenching his teeth against the emotion that pulled at him. She was perfect. Sweet as pie on the outside. Caring and loyal to her friends and family. But this huge tattoo on her back told him she had a rebellious side.

His.

Fuck. He had to stop thinking that.

"So I take it you approve of the tattoo?" Rayne moaned with a smile in her voice.

"Yeah, I approve, Princess. I fucking approve."

Rayne held her breath as Ghost fucked her with short, hard thrusts. She pushed back against him and came up on her hands and knees as he got more forceful.

"Touch yourself, Rayne. Make yourself come on my cock."

His words were gritty and raw, but they turned Rayne way the hell on. She balanced on one hand and reached down to where they were joined with the other. She stroked him once as he pulled out and she heard him swear.

"Touch *yourself*, Princess, not me."

"But I like touching you," she pouted.

"I like you touching me too, but any more of that and this will be over too soon."

"Party pooper," Rayne murmured as she turned her attention to her own body. As Ghost continued pumping in and out of her sensitive sheath, she flicked over her clit with easy strokes. She rubbed herself harder and harder until she could tell her orgasm was just a few flicks away.

"I'm about to come, Ghost."

"Yeah, do it. I wanna feel it."

Rayne rubbed against her clit once more and then caught herself with her hands as the orgasm moved through her. She shoved backwards as she trembled. She was thankful Ghost was behind her, holding on, because otherwise she would've face-planted right into the mattress.

"Oh God, Rayne, yes. You feel so fucking good. I gotta...shit..." Ghost pulled out of Rayne's still spasming body and tore off the condom. He pumped his shaft once, then again, and watched as his come spurted out of the end of his dick and landed on Rayne's back, right in the middle of her tattoo. He stroked himself a few more times, milking as much of his seed as he could. Then he took both hands and rubbed his essence into her back...and her tattoo.

He breathed great gulps of air as he watched her skin slowly absorb his come. It wasn't something he'd planned, or something he'd ever done before, but he wanted to mark her. Wanted to anoint that tattoo. That tattoo meant something to her, and everything on it represented his own life.

"Are you all right?"

Rayne voice was soft and worried. He'd obviously been rubbing her back for longer than he'd thought. Ghost's eyes dropped to hers. She was propped up on one elbow and looking back at him. He gave her tattoo one last caress, dropped his hands, and scooted away from her a bit, giving her room to turn over. He sighed in regret when her tattoo disappeared from view.

"I'm more than all right, Princess."

Rayne sat up and put her hand on his chest. "My turn to look at your ink now. Lay down."

Ghost smiled and lay down next to her, bending an arm and putting it behind his head. "Have at it." He gestured with his free hand to his side.

Rayne leaned down, ignoring her luscious nudity, and peered at the words inked on his left side. Ghost knew they wouldn't give away any of his secrets, he and his teammates had thought long and hard before deciding what they'd all get inked on their bodies. It was their code, their creed. The quote was a mix of why they fought and what their service meant to all of them.

I will defend my brothers & their women,
and remember that freedom isn't free.

Quiet professionalism rules the day.

Ghost knew it wasn't quite poetry, but he and his teammates liked it. The reference to brothers was because that was what they all felt like. The entire team knew they'd defend each other to the death, but they'd extended it on their ink to include the women they may or may not have in the future. It was important to all of them that they knew the team would have their women's backs…if it ever came to that.

And the last line was a reference to their job as Delta Force operatives. Not many people knew about them or what they did, and that's how it would stay.

Ghost waited as Rayne read the words on his skin. She ran her fingertips over each phrase, much as he'd done to her tattoo. He shivered; he swore he'd remember the way her hand felt on him, as she caressed what was the real him, for the rest of his days.

"It's beautiful."

"Yeah."

"It suits you."

Ghost tilted his head in question, and encouraged her to lie back down next to him.

As she snuggled into his side, her head resting on his shoulder and her arm thrown around his body, she nodded and said, "Yeah. I know I've teased you about being a spy, but if I had to really guess, I'd say you were military of some sort." When he tensed under her, she brought her hand up to his neck and laid it there reassuringly.

"I felt safe today. Completely. I didn't care that the taxi guy was creepy as all get out, because I was with you. I never would've ridden that crazy Ferris wheel thing if you weren't with me. And I never, I mean, *never* would've gone to bed with you if I didn't trust you. All I'm saying is that you're the kind of guy who I'd want by my side if I was fighting for my country."

Ghost didn't say anything, but shifted until one hand rested on the small of her back, covering her tattoo.

"I think you're pretty amazing too," he said in a low voice.

"Ummm. First time I've ever been thankful my plane was canceled."

"Me too, Princess. Me too."

Ghost held Rayne as she eased into sleep and throughout the next two hours. He wanted to do so many more things with her. So many positions he hadn't had time to try out, but she was obviously exhausted. She was sleeping deeply, even the feel of his fingertips on her breast didn't make her stir. Her nipples stiffened under his touch, but her breaths remained steady. Ghost wanted to take her hard-as-nails peaks in his mouth, then watch as they bounced and jiggled as she rode him, but he didn't have the heart to wake her.

He'd never felt like this before. Ever.

Typically, he'd be out of bed and on his way home about five minutes after his orgasm, but being with Rayne was relaxing...and exciting. Even if she was sleeping.

She was beautiful, her skin smooth and unblemished. Her tits big enough to hold, but not so big they overwhelmed her frame. She had a small belly, and thighs he could grab hold of and not be afraid he'd hurt her. There were so many ways he wanted to make love to her, to get to know her...but with each tick of the clock, Ghost knew his time with her was quickly running out.

Even knowing he was pushing his luck, he didn't leave her bed until an hour after he'd planned. After dressing, Ghost leaned over Rayne, who was now sleeping on her stomach clutching a pillow to her chest, and kissed her temple.

"Soar high, Princess," he whispered softly into her ear before standing up.

Ghost turned and walked to the door and stopped with one hand on the knob. Taking a resigned breath, he walked back over to the amazing woman in the bed and slowly tugged the sheet down, revealing the curve of her spine...and the tattoo that had made him lose his mind. He stared down at it, arguing with himself. It really was uncanny how she'd been able to capture the essence of who he was without even knowing him. Ghost knew he was being maudlin, but couldn't help it.

The side that wanted a memory of this night forever won, and Ghost quickly took out his cell phone and snapped a picture of the unique tattoo, being careful not to capture anything indecent in his photo. Her beautiful backside was for his eyes only.

He pulled the sheet back up carefully and leaned down one more time. He inhaled her scent, which by now was really a mixture of sex and whatever perfume she'd put on hours earlier, kissed his fingers and gently laid them on her lips, then turned abruptly and stalked to the door once more. He slipped out without a sound and disappeared into the large metropolis as if he didn't exist.

Chapter Eleven

A SHRILL RINGING woke Rayne from a deep sleep. She leaned over and answered the phone with a groggy, "Hello?" She heard the standard hotel recording for the wake-up call, hung up the phone, and sat up slowly. She looked next to her and saw she was alone in the bed.

"Ghost?"

Her voice echoed back through the empty room. Knowing in her heart she wasn't going to find him, Rayne twisted and put her feet on the floor anyway. She padded around the corner and looked in the bathroom. Empty.

She grabbed the tank top and pants she'd been wearing last night and pulled them on, then walked over to the window and peered out. The London Eye Ferris wheel was still and silent, waiting for another group of tourists, and Big Ben and Westminster Abbey looked as stately and majestic as they had the day before. In fact, everything looked the same, including the cloudy weather…but Rayne didn't *feel* the same.

Ghost had been upfront and honest with her from the beginning. He'd told her he was a one-night kind of guy, and that he didn't do relationships. She'd told him she was fine with that, and she was. But as he'd held her, and made her orgasm time and time again, her walls had crumbled. She'd begun to fantasize that they'd wake up in the morning and he'd tell her he couldn't live without her. They'd fly back to the States and date for a while before he'd finally propose to her.

It was ridiculous and she was too old to be living in a fantasy world.

Suddenly cold, Rayne went back to the bed and got under the covers. She pulled the sheet up to her chin and curled into a ball on her side. She turned her head and inhaled. God. The pillow smelled like Ghost.

Ghost. It was an appropriate name for the man. She knew next to nothing about him, except he made her feel safe. And wanted. And desirable. He had a tattoo and...what else? His name was John Benbrook and he lived in Fort Worth. She perked up a bit at that. She could look him up when she got home and then...

No. He left. They had one night together, that's all it was. He didn't want anything more to do with her. If he'd wanted more, he would've told her. Rayne knew it in her gut. She was a one-time fuck for him, that's all.

She threw off the sheet and climbed out of bed for the second time that morning. Fine then. She was a woman of the world. She could have a one-night affair and be sophisticated. Not that sleeping with someone the same day made you sophisticated in any way, but still. She could do this.

Rayne went through the motions of showering and getting ready for her shift at work. She'd be flying home to Dallas/Fort Worth, then she'd have two days off before she was set to fly again. She couldn't remember where she was scheduled to go next, but thought it was the Middle East rotation. It wasn't her favorite, but at the moment, she couldn't wait to get to work and try to forget the amazing man she'd met.

As she was leaving Park Plaza, the concierge handed her a note, saying, "Your gentleman asked me to give this to you with his apologizes that he had to leave early."

Rayne politely thanked the man, blushing because she was sure he knew Ghost had run out on her and they were practically strangers.

She'd stuffed the note in her pocket, not ready to read it yet, and arrived at Heathrow just in time to meet the other flight attendants she'd be working with and get ready for the flight. She'd held out hope that Ghost would be on her flight, as he'd planned the day before, but when it came time to close the door of the aircraft, he was nowhere in sight.

Four hours after the flight took off, and after the

first round of food and drinks had been served, Rayne took out the note Ghost had left for her. She'd been thinking about it for hours, and couldn't put off reading it any longer. She unfolded the small piece of paper and smoothed it out as she read.

Princess,

I told you I didn't do relationships...and I don't. But this morning, for the first time in my life, I wished I was a different kind of man. Stay safe.

~ Ghost

Dry-eyed, Rayne tucked the note into the book she'd been reading the day before her entire life was tilted on its axis. Knowing she'd think of things in her life as happening "Before Ghost" and "After Ghost" for quite a while, she sighed.

She rested her head on the seat behind her, and closed her eyes. She whispered to no one in particular, "If wishes were horses, beggars would ride."

KEANE "GHOST" BRYSON, occasionally known as John Benbrook, sat in first class, the only seat he could get on short notice that morning, and stared down at the picture on his phone. It was Rayne looking up at him and laughing as they stood in front of Buckingham

Palace. Even though it was misting, she looked like a ray of sunshine. She had both arms around his waist and he was gazing down at her as if she was the most important thing in his world. The balcony she'd so wanted to see was a blur behind them.

Ghost could almost feel her arms tighten around him and hear her laugh. He sighed and flicked his thumb to switch to the next picture. Ghost mentally reviewed how he'd alter the tattoo he was looking at for himself. He *needed* it. Putting her tattoo on his skin was the closest he could come to having her in his life.

As London disappeared behind him, Ghost knew he'd left the best thing that ever happened to him in the hotel. He'd almost walked back up to the room twice before dashing out the quick note and asking the concierge to give it to Rayne.

If he was a different man…but he wasn't. He was a Delta Force operative and he owed his life to his country for at least another five years. He wouldn't ask any woman to put herself through the worry that being married to someone like him would bring. He'd never be able to tell her where he was going or when he'd be back. They'd never be able to sit down and talk about their days together.

And God forbid they had children. The possibility of a child of his being left fatherless was way higher than average…even for a soldier. No, it had to be this way. Rayne would find another man, one who she could love and trust.

But that didn't mean Ghost wouldn't mourn what might have been. He wished he could've met Rayne years ago. He wished he had more time with her, or...

"Damn," he whispered to himself, cutting off his thoughts. "If wishes were horses, beggars would ride."

Chapter Twelve

6 Months Later

RAYNE SIGHED AS Mary berated her for what seemed like the thousandth time. "You've got to get your head out of your ass and get back in the game, Rayne."

"I know, Mary. I *know*."

"You say the words, but your actions don't match them. Look, we've talked about this. I know you had a wonderful time with Ghost, and I'm pleased beyond all that's holy that you finally took the plunge and had your first one-night stand…but he left London without saying goodbye, except for that cryptic note, and you haven't heard from him again. I don't understand what the problem is here."

Rayne sighed, put her chin in her hand, and absently stirred her Midori martini. She didn't know what her problem was either. Ghost *had* been upfront and honest with her.

He told her he didn't do relationships. He told her their time together could only be for one night. Shit, she'd even agreed with him. But somewhere between Ghost giving the creepy taxi driver a death stare that would've scared the bejeebus out of her, and running his hands reverently over the tattoo on her back, she'd fallen for him...hard.

They'd made love—no, had sex—several times during the night and she'd lost herself in him. He'd been tender and dominating at the same time. He'd teased her and even though he'd made it clear they were hooking up for only one night, she'd gone and done what he'd obviously been afraid she'd do—thought they might have something after the night was over.

Waking up in the hotel room, sore and satisfied but alone, hadn't been the best moment in her life. Even the note he'd left for her, saying that he wished he was a different kind of man, wasn't enough to allow her to forget him.

Mary sighed. "It's been six months, Rayne. He's not coming back. You can't do this to yourself. You have to get back into the dating world."

"You're right. I know you're right."

"Damn straight I'm right," Mary crowed, sucking up the last of her Diet Coke and rum through the small straw. "Come on, I'm not saying you have to take one of these yuppies home and screw him six ways to Sunday, but at least loosen up a bit and have some fun. Let's dance. Just dance."

Rayne nodded and leaned over to finish her drink. Mary might be right, but that didn't mean it didn't suck. It *was* time for her to move on. It was *past* time for her to move on. But no man she'd met since that amazing night in London all those months ago came close to making her feel one iota of what she'd felt when she was with Ghost.

When she'd first seen him in Heathrow airport, she'd sensed something about him. He was sitting with one arm resting on the back of the seat next to him. His back was against the wall and he was closely observing everyone around him. He oozed testosterone and even though many people gave him a wide berth, Rayne felt herself drawn to him like a moth to a flame.

She had no idea what gave her the gumption to stroll up to him as though he was a long-lost friend, but she had. They'd struck up a conversation and the next thing Rayne knew, they were touring London together.

Lunch, Westminster Abbey, Buckingham Palace, and the London Eye. It had been amazing, but it wasn't until they'd gotten into bed that her feelings had changed from lust to...more.

Oh, it was obvious Ghost had had some practice in the bedroom, but it was the way he'd been with her that had really made Rayne's heart flutter in her chest. It was stupid, he was probably that way with every woman he went to bed with, but even that thought didn't change the way Rayne felt.

He'd taken his time with her. He'd appreciated her body. He'd made her feel as though she wasn't a one-night fling, and that's what really hurt most of all. Even right up to the point when he'd been poised to take her, he'd still paused and asked if she was sure. He'd been a gentleman, and the dichotomy between the obviously alpha, take-charge badass, and the caring, sensitive-to-what-she-was-feeling, oh-my-God-did-he-know-how-to-make-her-scream man was as irresistible now in her memory as it had been while lying under him in that hotel room in London.

Rayne thought about her impulsive trip to the tattoo place. About three months ago, she'd gone back to the same artist who had done the ink on her lower back and asked him to add to it. She wasn't going to tell or show Mary, but since she'd never kept a secret from her best friend, she'd ended up keeping it quiet only until it healed. Then she'd shown it to her, and Mary had simply said, "Oh Raynie. It's beautiful. I don't think you should've done it, but it's beautiful."

Rayne hadn't thought her tattoo was anything special, but remembering how Ghost had reverently run his hands over it, and marked it with his release, still had the power to make her break out in chills. She wanted to somehow immortalize the night...make it seem more permanent than it was.

She'd never thought she'd be a tattoo type of person, but it had started with the small Chinese symbol for "strength" on her bikini line. Mary had been diagnosed with breast cancer and they went together to get the ink, vowing no matter what happened to be strong. Then when Mary had beaten the cancer, Rayne had gotten the small pink ribbon added to her skin. She'd had it done on the underside of her left breast. It had hurt like nothing she'd ever felt before, but she got through it thinking about how what Mary had to experience was so much worse.

After a long talk with her brother one night, she'd made the decision to get her third tattoo. She'd wanted something small and ladylike, but had somehow walked out of the tattoo parlor with a design that spanned her entire lower back. She wanted to regret it, but couldn't. It represented her family, and that meant the world to her. The eagle was standing upright with its wings spread, almost curling around each of her sides, it was that big.

When Ghost had taken her the last time, and she'd been bent over in front of him, he'd had an almost visceral reaction to seeing her tattoo. She had no idea why, only that he'd taken her harder and more intensely than he had any other time that night.

Rayne had asked the artist to add Big Ben so it was sort of behind the eagle, still on her back, but near her left side. He'd drawn a perfect rendering of the stately English landmark beside the eagle, somehow incorporating the bolt of lightning into the design of the clock. She'd had him make the time read two-thirty…the last time Rayne had remembered looking at the clock when she'd been with Ghost.

She'd then had the artist add the words "Quiet Professionalism" in fancy script writing around the top of the clock. Those words had been inked on Ghost's side and they fit him to a tee. He'd never be the kind of man to stand up and bring attention to himself, but he'd do what needed to be done without bringing any undue notice to himself.

The last addition to her already way-bigger-than-she-ever-meant-it-to-be tattoo was a small ghost floating around the peak of the clock. It looked out of place with the rest of the ink, and even the artist had protested, but she'd insisted and now had a permanent reminder of the most amazing day and night of her life.

Rayne had thought she'd regret it, but did it anyway. Now, even three months after the fact, and no closer to speaking with the one man who'd touched her heart in a way even she didn't understand, she didn't regret that tattoo. It settled her, made her feel good inside.

"Are you coming?" Mary's voice was impatient and Rayne could tell she was at the end of her I'mindulging-my-best-friend-in-her-doldrums mood.

"I'm coming, keep your pants on, woman," Rayne teased, pushing back from the small table they'd been sitting at in the large country and western bar.

Rayne joined Mary on the large wooden dance floor and they smiled and laughed as the song changed into one they could actually dance to. Neither of them knew how to dance very well, but they *did* know how to two-step.

They probably looked silly together. Mary was tall and slender. Her brown hair fell around her shoulders and as she moved, the layers of pink and purple she'd added peeked through. Rayne was about the same height as Mary, but she wasn't slender. She would never again shop at the trendy stores that only carried sizes zero to ten, but she didn't care. She liked food, hated to diet, and knew she was a normal size. She ignored the media that tried to tell women size six was average.

Rayne didn't care about size anyway. She'd never been made fun of, didn't have any deep dark secrets about people picking on her or abuse in her past. She loved Mary, who was naturally a size six, no matter what she ate, darn her, but she had lost weight from the cancer. She was probably more like a size two or four right now. People were people, it didn't matter if they were a size two or a size thirty-two.

Rayne laughed with Mary as they danced. A few men tried to hit on them, but for once, it seemed that Mary wasn't keen on getting her friend laid.

Later that night, as Rayne lay in her bed, tipsy from the alcohol, she thought once again about Ghost. Mary was right; it was time to put him out of her mind once and for all. It'd been six months. If he was going to track her down and declare his everlasting love, he would've done it already. But he hadn't.

Without asking permission, Mary had tried to track him down using the information on the ID that Rayne had texted to her from the airport all those months ago. Rayne had wanted to be safe, and she'd figured sending a picture of Ghost's driver's license to her best friend would at least make sure that someone knew who she was about to set out into London with.

It'd been a good idea—except Mary hadn't had any luck finding out where John Benbrook was. She'd actually driven to the address in Fort Worth that had been on the ID and found a huge apartment complex. When she'd inquired at the leasing office, they didn't have any current tenants with that name, and they wouldn't give her any information about past tenants either, saying something about privacy laws.

Mary wasn't ready to give up, but Rayne had finally put a stop to it, saying that probably half the people in Texas had an old address on their licenses. Who really went to the DMV the second they moved anyway?

If she was honest with herself, Rayne knew she'd much prefer it if John, a.k.a. Ghost, tracked *her* down, rather than the other way around. But lying in her big bed, remembering the look of regret and sorrow on his face after he'd taken her from behind, his eyes on her tattoo, would stay with her for a long time.

It killed her to think he regretted the time they spent together. But even with the cryptic yet sweet note he'd left for her, it was obvious their short time together was just as he'd claimed it would be...a one-night thing. One beautiful, never-to-be-forgotten night, but one night all the same.

Rayne turned over to her side and ignored the slight spinning of the room around her in her drunken state. The words came out soft and heartfelt as she closed her eyes and made the final decision to get on with her life once and for all.

"Wherever you are, John Benbrook, I hope you're safe and happy. I'll never forget you."

Chapter Thirteen

G HOST GESTURED TO his Delta Force teammates silently. Blade and Hollywood came up behind him and covered him as they made their way through the streets of Cairo.

Egypt had become more and more unstable as the months went by. The militants wanted control of the government, and didn't care who they killed in the process of getting that power. So far, the United States was officially staying out of the small skirmishes that were breaking out across the country—especially in the capital city—but unofficially, Delta Force and other special operations forces were being sent in to gather intel and to see if they could ferret out the ringleaders of the Muslim Brotherhood.

The group had been designated a terrorist organization by many Middle Eastern countries after a revolution a few years ago. The Muslim Brotherhood was generally a movement and not a political party, but after one of their supporters had been voted in as President of Egypt, and the *coup d'état* that followed, the Brotherhood had been shunned. They were now gathering back their power, and the United States and other countries were worried another bloody protest or takeover was in the works.

The trio moved silently through the empty pred-awn streets, acting on a tip they'd received late the night before. The group was supposed to be holding a meeting at a mosque east of the city, and Ghost and his team were checking it out to try to see how many people they'd managed to sway to their way of think-ing.

If there were fifty to a hundred people, the govern-ment wouldn't be very worried. It was unlikely so few men could mobilize to overthrow the government. But if it was more, then additional actions would need to be taken to try to mitigate the risk.

Ghost signaled to Blade and Hollywood and they disappeared into the gray morning light. If Ghost hadn't been looking right at where they went, he wouldn't have seen them. They blended in with the shadows surrounding the massive building until Ghost lost sight of them. He knew the rest of the team— Fletch, Coach, Beatle, and Truck—were around as well. They'd moved in from two other directions, but they were now also somewhere in the shadows, lurking and watching.

Ghost's job was to watch the front, and observe the

vehicles that may or may not arrive and who got out of them. For now, all was quiet…too quiet, which meant they were in the right place. In a city such as Cairo, overflowing with people, the streets should have some movement, even at this hour of the morning. The eerie quiet and unusual lack of people was a sign of something nefarious going on.

As it sometimes did, an image of Rayne popped into Ghost's head as he stood in the shadow of a nearby building, staring at the old mosque. She'd gazed around Westminster Abbey as if she'd never seen anything more beautiful in her life. Ghost ran a hand over his chest, rubbing over his heart, without knowing he was doing it.

He missed her. Rayne had a light outlook to life that Ghost had rarely seen. Jeez, he'd only known her for a day, but she was fun and upbeat and he'd genuinely enjoyed spending time with her. He knew she was probably a great flight attendant. During their time together, she'd put him at ease and made him feel as though he was the only thing she was concentrating on. He could totally see her chatting with passengers and easing the fears of the skittish fliers, and generally being friendly and open and making the not-so-great experience of flying a better one for the passengers.

That thought led to the next…if she could put *him* at ease, she could do it to any other guy on her flights.

The thought of her smiling at, or laughing with, or even dodging the advances of the horny businessmen who were bound to be on her flights made his hands clench into fists at his side.

Ghost took a deep breath, hoping to calm himself. It didn't do a lot of good.

He had no right to be jealous of any other guy. He'd been the one to leave her. It'd been for both their sakes, but it still rankled. A vision of Rayne lying under him, her head thrown back in the midst of an orgasm, popped into his brain and he literally stopped breathing for a moment. He'd relived every single second of their time together in his brain again and again since he'd left her side six months ago, but that one picture…of him making her explode the last time he'd taken her, played in his mind as if on rewind.

She'd been absolutely perfect. She'd trusted him to do whatever he wanted—no, needed—to do to her. She'd lain in his arms afterwards as trustingly as if they were longtime lovers instead of just having met that day. Ghost could remember the way she tasted, the way she laughed, her fingers brushing rhythmically over his chest hair as they rested between bouts of sex, the twinkle in her eyes as she teasingly called him a super-spy.

Every single thing about her was ingrained on his brain, and the images seemed to be getting more vivid as time went by, instead of less. It was the weirdest thing he'd ever experienced, and the flashbacks to their time together would come at the most inopportune moments...such as this one.

Ghost flinched as a truck eased up to the entrance of the large building. Fuck, he had to pay attention to what he was doing. The last thing he needed was his memories getting him, or his team, killed.

More humans than should logically fit inside streamed out of the vehicle and into the mosque. It was like one of those clown cars in the circus...he counted at least twenty people exiting the truck and making their way silently into the building. He didn't miss the rifles and other weapons the men carried either.

After about thirty minutes of more and more people arriving, Ghost eased away from the side of the building he'd been leaning against and down a dark alley. He crossed over another few streets until he got to the pre-arranged rally point. The other guys were already there. Without a word, they got into the truck they'd left there and headed back to their meeting location. Their job this time was not to interrupt the meeting or to detain any of the militants. Their job was to watch and report.

It looked as if this wasn't a small-time operation. There were way more than a hundred men involved. It was obvious the Muslim Brotherhood had gained a lot of support and the people of Egypt were going to have a battle on their hands...probably sooner rather than later.

As Beatle drove them silently back to their rendezvous point, Ghost's thoughts turned once again to Rayne. How was she? Was she safe? Where was she now? Was she on a job? Was she dating anyone?

He shook his head. He didn't have the right to even wonder that. But as he licked his lips, Ghost could almost taste her on them. She'd been so wet and slick under his mouth. He remembered waking her up the second time by going down on her. He'd been enjoying himself for quite a while before she'd stirred in his arms.

He'd taken his time, nuzzling and learning her preferences. Even while asleep, her body had reacted to his. He'd kept his touch light, so she wouldn't wake up until he was ready, but he couldn't help taking her bundle of nerves into his mouth. As soon as he'd sucked, she'd stirred under him and cream had blossomed between her folds as if readying just for him. He'd taken one finger and eased it—

"Ghost, we're here."

Ghost's thoughts were abruptly broken off by Fletch's announcement. He nodded, once again the leader of their team. "Debrief in ten. We'll report back to headquarters and get the hell out of dodge."

"Sounds good. See you in ten," Fletch answered for the group.

Ghost watched his men head into the small building and took a deep breath. He had to get Rayne out of his head. He'd considered finding a nice horny single or divorced ex-pat and losing himself in her for a night, but the thought hadn't even made his dick twitch. Dammit. Something had to be done, but Ghost had no idea what.

It was as if Rayne had crawled inside his heart and wouldn't leave…even though he'd told her he was a one-night-only kind of man. It was as though even his brain was conspiring against him. It wouldn't stop replaying their time together. As if that would somehow make a relationship between them possible.

Ghost almost snorted as he gathered his gear and headed toward the building. A relationship between them would never work. First, he'd lied to her…about almost everything, from the second he'd met her to the moment he left that hotel room. Second, he was Delta Force, a member of the most secretive group the US Military had. He couldn't tell Rayne anything about what he was doing, where he was going, or even when he'd be back. There was no way that could work in a relationship.

And third, he was always in danger. Always. From the second he left, and even when he returned home, someone was looking to kill him. Kill him for what he'd done in the past, and what they were afraid he'd do in the future. Delta Force soldiers were on the top of Al Qaeda, ISIS, and every other terrorist organization's hit list. They'd do anything to get their hands on one of them...if only to make them an example for every other soldier.

Ghost shook his head as he dumped his gear and got ready for the meeting with the team. It couldn't work. One way or another he had to get the beautiful Rayne out of his head. Once and for all.

"Wherever you are, Rayne Jackson, I hope you're safe and happy. I'll never forget you."

Chapter Fourteen

"WHEN ARE YOU coming down to visit?" Chase asked his sister impatiently.

Rayne sighed. "I wish I had time, but I leave in the morning for an international run."

"Where are you off to this time?"

"France, then Italy, then Egypt, then back up to France, then home."

"How long?"

"I think this one is about two weeks."

"I haven't seen you in forever, sis," Chase whined.

Rayne smiled, hearing the little boy he used to be in his voice. "I know, but I'll be back at the end of the month and we can get together."

"I'm going to hold you to that," Chase scolded. His voice turned serious. "I don't like that you'll be in Egypt. Promise you won't do anything crazy, like get a wild hair to explore by yourself or anything."

"Of course not. Egypt is perfectly safe, Chase. Cairo isn't exactly terrorist central these days," she said evenly.

"But you've seen the news. Bad stuff still happens over there. I heard just the other day that most of the cruise ships have taken the Egyptian ports off their itineraries. And trust *me* when I tell you, it's not safe." Chase's words held more than the usual amount of worry a brother had for a sister.

"It's *not* safe?"

"No."

When he didn't elaborate, Rayne tried to reassure him. "Chase, seriously, I'll be fine. It's just like most other trips I take there. I have the Athens-to-Cairo route. We fly in one day and out the next. I'll end up doing that three times, then we have an extra day off in Cairo, then it's back to Paris and back home. I've done it before. It's not a big deal."

"Well, again, don't walk around by yourself. Actually, it'd be safer if you hung out in the hotel on your day off, but I don't suppose you will."

Rayne smiled and secured her cell phone against her shoulder as she got a cup down from her cabinet and set about pouring a glass of orange juice. "You know me. I enjoy exploring different cities. I don't know if I'll ever have the chance again. I promise I won't go by myself. If I can't convince anyone to go with me, I'll stay in the hotel, bored out of my mind and sad that I'll be in Egypt and won't see one camel, but safe. Happy?" She didn't tell Chase that touring by herself held no appeal after spending time with Ghost in London.

"No, but it'll have to do. Call me the second you land at DFW. You get a week off after this run, right?"

"Right."

"Good, you can come down and visit me here at Fort Hood."

It wasn't so much a question as an order, but since it was what Rayne wanted to do anyway, she didn't complain. "Sounds like a plan. You heard much from Sam?"

"You know our sister...hanging out with the rich and famous out there in Los Angeles."

Rayne laughed. She *did* know her sister. "Who is she dating now?"

"I have no clue, but she did tell me she got a bit part in the newest *Jurassic Park* movie that's being filmed now."

Rayne groaned. "Don't tell me...she gets eaten by a giant made-up dinosaur?"

Chase laughed. "Probably. You saw the last one, there were a ton of extras running around getting snatched up by those flying meat-eaters. But you didn't hear it from me. I'm sure she wants to call and tell you herself."

"My lips are sealed. I'm so proud of her, and you too."

Chase's voice got soft. "I know. But seriously, sis. Stay safe. Trouble's brewing over there in Egypt and I hate that you'll be in the middle of it."

"I'm not going to be in the middle of anything...well, except the city. Relax, Chase. I'm almost twenty-nine. Old enough to take care of myself."

"You might be older than me by two years, but I'll always worry about you."

She swore sometimes Chase was an old soul. There was no way he acted twenty-six. She had no doubt he'd rise in the ranks of the Officer Corp at a record speed. But not wanting to get maudlin, Rayne changed the subject as she sat on the couch and idly flipped the channels. "How're things going for you?"

"Good. I'm up for promotion next month."

She knew it. "You're so going to make captain. It's more than about time."

"I hope so. I'm ready."

"You'll be great. Do you have any idea what your first assignment might be?"

"No clue. But it doesn't matter. I'll love whatever it is."

"Will you have a PCS?" It had taken Rayne a while to learn all the Army acronyms, but she'd done it. PCS stood for Permanent Change of Station...meaning when the Army moved a person from one base to another.

"I'm sure I will."

"That sucks."

Chase laughed. "You've just been spoiled with me here in Texas."

"True."

"I'll let you know as soon as I know."

"You better."

They both laughed, enjoying the banter. Finally, Rayne said regretfully, "I gotta get going."

"Hot date?"

"Ha. No. I have to finish packing and make sure Mary's all set with watching my condo and getting my mail and whatnot."

"A hot date sounds more interesting. Didn't you and Mary go out the other night?"

"Yeah...and?"

"You didn't hook up with anyone?"

"Good Lord, Chase. First, as if I'd tell *you*, second, I don't do one-night stands." That was a little lie that he'd never know about.

"Gross, Rayne, I wasn't talking about taking a guy home for the night. I was talking about whether you met anyone you might think you'd want to *date*. You know...dinners, movies, walks on the beach."

Rayne laughed. "We don't have any beaches up here in Fort Worth, and no, it was a country and western bar. I wasn't going to meet the future Mr.

Rayne Jackson at a bar. Seriously!"

"Hey, don't knock it, Mr. Right could be any-where. Have you tried any of those online dating sites?"

"Okay, we are officially done with this conversa-tion," Rayne stated firmly. "My little brother is *not* giving me dating advice. And I don't see you out there in the dating pool, Mr. You-Should-Get-Out-There Jackson."

Her brother laughed. "Okay, okay, truce. You're right. I'll butt out of your dating life if you stay out of mine."

"Deal. Now, I really have to go. Stay safe, and I'll call when I land in a couple of weeks and we'll work out when it's best for me to come down and visit for a few days."

"Sounds like a plan. Love you. I'll talk to you later."

"Bye, Chase. Love you too."

"Bye."

Rayne clicked off the phone and rested back against the cushions of her couch, trying to work up the energy to get up and finish her packing like she told her brother she had to do. It seemed as though it was getting harder and harder to work up the enthusiasm that she used to have for her job. She didn't mind the flying part, but every time she had a layover in a foreign city, it reminded her of Ghost...and that part hurt.

She had no problem telling Chase that she would

not wander around Cairo by herself. She had no desire to explore any of the cities she had layovers in any-more…not without Ghost. He'd made it fun, and she'd never felt safer than when she was with him. A hand on her back, putting himself between her and people walking too close to them…it didn't matter, it was those little things that she always missed when she was out and about on her own now.

It was the thought of Ghost laughing with her as they discussed…whatever it was they'd talked about in Westminster Abbey, that made her push up off the couch and head to her room. He'd been so patient with her, even if he wasn't outwardly a romantic. She only remembered him smiling at her, laughing; even when he disagreed with what she was saying, he'd been patient and not condescending. It was literally as if she made a list of the things she wanted in a man and he'd met every single one. And he'd come into and out of her life so quickly she didn't even have a chance to realize what she had before it was gone.

Rayne flipped open the top of her suitcase and set about filling it with only the clothes necessary for her trip. She didn't have time to be sad over what would never be. There was no doubt the man had faults, she just hadn't been around him long enough to figure out what they were. She was going to move on…slowly but surely. Maybe this would be the trip she could put Ghost behind her once and for all.

Chapter Fifteen

RAYNE SMILED AT the group chitchatting behind her in the bus. They'd landed in Cairo and the flight crew was sharing a bus from the airport to one of the nicer touristy hotels nearby. She enjoyed flying with the same group of flight attendants for several shifts. It made the work easier, and time went by faster.

There were four couples on the bus with them, discussing their plans for the next day. Apparently, they were going to spend a few days in the capital city before heading off to see the "famous" Egyptian pyramids.

"Hey, any of you guys want to come with us?"

The question was asked by a heavyset Hispanic woman. She was with her husband and they'd held hands for what seemed like the entire flight, and even after they'd deplaned, Rayne noticed that the large man seemed extra protective of his wife and kept her hand in his as much as possible. It reminded her of how Ghost had been with her, although she tried to push the memory aside.

Rayne turned around in her seat and asked, "Pardon?"

"I asked if you wanted to come with us tomorrow. We set up a private tour thingie and the max number of people is ten, but we only have eight. The price is really reasonable and we'll get to see a lot of great stuff...Giza pyramids, Sphinx, the Egyptian Museum, and we'll end up in Tahrir Square and will get a tour of The Mogamma government building."

"What's the deal with the square? Isn't it just a big downtown area?" Rayne asked.

The woman, obviously excited about the topic, exclaimed, "Oh no! There's so much more than a traffic circle and random buildings. It's where the country gathered to protest Hosni Mubarak's rule. There were probably a quarter of a million people in the square demanding his resignation. And it worked! Then a few years after that, it's where there was a revolt about the new president, once again demanding his resignation. It's all just fascinating and it'll be so cool to be standing where history was made!"

The pilot, copilot, and three of the other flight attendants all declined politely, but Rayne thought this might be just the thing she needed to get out of the doldrums. Going with a group to see the city was perfect. Safety in numbers and all that.

She turned to Sarah, one of the newer flight attendants who she'd flown with over the last week and a half or so. "Wanna go? We have tomorrow off."

Sarah shrugged and agreed. "Sure, why not?"

"Very cool!" the Hispanic woman cried excitedly. "My name is Diana. This is my husband Eduardo. We're from Houston. Sitting in the back is Paula and her boyfriend, Leon, then there's Becky and Michael, and finally Tracy and Steve. We all know each other from Houston, we go to the same church. We've always wanted to see the Great Pyramids, and finally we just bit the bullet and decided to go for it."

Rayne smiled politely at each of the couples and turned back to Diana. "So what are the details?"

"Tomorrow we're meeting in the lobby around nine. We'll be picked up and should get back to the hotel around three. It's only six hours, but we'll see as much of the city as we can in that time. It's so cool you're coming with us!"

They discussed price for a bit and as the bus was pulling up to the hotel, Diana exclaimed, "This is gonna be epic! See you in the morning!"

"She's a bit enthusiastic, huh?" Sarah mentioned dryly as they collected their bags and headed into the hotel lobby.

"Yeah, but that's better than not caring. Did you see that other couple? All they did was scowl at each other," Rayne commented with a laugh.

"True. As much as I want to see the city, I'm beginning to wonder if we'd be better off on our own."

"Nah, it'll be fine. How bad can it be?"

"OH MY GOD, could this get any worse?" Sarah asked under her breath as they watched Michael berate the tour driver.

The morning had started off well enough. They'd all met in the lobby at precisely nine in the morning and had met their driver, Hamadi. He had a minivan that they somehow all managed to squeeze into. It was a tight fit, but it *was* Egypt, after all. It's how everyone traveled.

They spent the morning looking at the pyramids of Giza…they weren't *the* pyramids, but they were still very cool. Rayne hadn't ever thought she'd see a real-life Sphinx either. They took a ton of pictures and then spent a couple of hours at the Egyptian Museum. Then they wandered around the square Diana had been so excited to tour.

Now they were at The Mogamma government building. It didn't look like much to Rayne, but she was going with it. After the walk through the large square surrounding the building, they were now waiting in line with hundreds of other tourists for their chance to tour the inside of the massive government building.

They were all tired, and a bit hungry, but Michael and Becky weren't dealing well at all with the circumstances.

"I hope you don't expect us to tip you after all this. I thought we had an exclusive tour? How long are we going to have to wait in this line? It doesn't look exclusive to me!" Michael raged. "Standing out here in the sun—baking. Ridiculous!"

Rayne looked at the driver. He'd been very patient, and Rayne even thought he'd done a wonderful job in maneuvering the van around the crazy traffic in the city, but she hadn't heard one positive word out of either of the couple all day.

"Don't mind him," Rayne said softly to Hamadi, turning her back to Michael. "You've done an amazing job today. I don't think I would've ever seen so many cool things if we were on a regular tour. Thank you."

The man smiled briefly at her, a smile that didn't reach his eyes. "Karma will take care of him," he said to Rayne seriously, if a bit dramatically, then turned to the group in general. "I have the tickets, but we have to wait in the line for security to get inside. Once we're in, we will break off and have our exclusive tour of the beautiful building."

"That sounds lovely," Paula said. She'd been the peacemaker the entire trip, trying to keep Michael's bad mood from spreading to the rest of the group. "I can't wait to see inside."

"I still say this is bullshit," Michael huffed. "What could they possibly be looking for anyway?"

Sarah leaned over and whispered to Rayne, "How about guns, knives and bombs? What an idiot."

Rayne smothered the laugh that wanted to come out and looked at the ground, trying to regain her composure. There was always one in every group. One person or couple that was stuck up and spoiled and just didn't understand cultures different from their own. She had no idea how they were even friends of Diana's and the other couples. They were all laid-back and sweet, and Michael and Becky just didn't seem to mesh with anyone.

Rayne thought of Ghost for the thousandth time that day. She tried not to, she really did, but she couldn't help it. When Michael had berated Hamadi in earshot of everyone around them, she *knew* Ghost wouldn't have stood for it. He would've ripped the guy a new asshole and made it look easy in the process.

Ghost would've made her feel safer. Cairo wasn't horribly unsafe, as she'd argued with her brother, but Rayne felt uneasy nevertheless. His words, that it wasn't the best place to be walking around, kept rattling around in her head. She felt better being in the group with the guide, but there were times she'd looked around after being dropped off to see a certain site when she'd observed their guide talking with other men in out-of-the way corners.

He didn't do anything really to make her feel uneasy, but she felt uneasy all the same. He was allowed to talk to his friends when they were touring the various landmarks, but every now and then she'd catch a look on his face that wasn't that of the easygoing guide he'd tried to show to them all day. Somehow Rayne knew Ghost would've made her feel better, told her she was imagining her unease. Or even told her she wasn't making it up, and he'd take her by the hand and take them back to the hotel so they could—

She cut her thought off before she could finish it. Dammit, she was supposed to be getting over Ghost. Going on this tour today was supposed to be the first step in doing so...unfortunately all it was doing was making her miss him more. It had been a mistake, and Rayne could only hope they'd get through the tour of the government building quickly. Her bed back at the hotel was calling her name. She had a book to read and a person to forget.

They finally made it to the front of the line and all of them went through security with no issues, except for Steve. He had a small knife in his pocket that had been confiscated. He wasn't happy it had been taken from him, but he'd acted with maturity and hadn't pitched a fit as they all knew Michael would've if it had been *his* knife that had been taken away.

Rayne thought about the hair clip she was wearing. Chase had given it to her last Christmas and at the time, she'd just laughed at him, but she'd been wearing it every day nonetheless. It was a simple design, but it was touted on the package as the Swiss Army Knife of barrettes.

There were three screwdrivers hidden on it, including a Phillips head, and a larger and smaller flat head as well. There was a hole that could work as a small 8mm wrench, one side was marked to use as a ruler, but the last two features were the most important to Chase. One side of the barrette actually had a serrated edge. It wouldn't cut through anything terribly thick, but if someone was determined enough, it probably could do some damage. And the last feature—which, as Chase had pointed out, the manufacturers probably hadn't even thought of, or at least wouldn't advertise—was that the point of the barrette could be used as either a pick or some sort of weapon in a pinch. Chase had told Rayne to go for an attacker's eyes if she ever had to use it to defend herself. That should give her enough time to run like hell. He'd told her to never stay and fight if she could run.

Not once had the hair clip been looked at twice at any of the security checkpoints she'd ever been through. That probably should've made Rayne nervous, but she was happy to have the added protection and peace of mind that it gave her. Not that she was some kind of James Bond by any stretch, but if push came to shove, she just might be able to use it to help herself get out of a situation.

Just as Hamadi said, after they got through security they were met by another man who led them off in a different direction than the rest of the tourists standing around them. Hamadi said he'd meet them at the end of the tour and disappeared into the throngs of tourists waiting for their tours. Their new guide spoke heavily accented English, which Rayne could barely understand. She was more than ready to be done for the day. She was tired and hot, and honestly, touring a government building wasn't high on her list of things she wanted to do.

The new guide led them through one room after another, explaining the purposes of the rooms and talking about some of the art on the walls. Finally, after about fifteen minutes, the Egyptian man guided them into a room that had no windows and not a lot of furniture. It had high ceilings and ornate carvings on the walls.

"Wait here," he ordered, his voice echoing in the cavernous room. "I be back."

Before anyone could say anything—rather, before

Michael could complain about it the same way he'd been bitching about everything else—the man was gone. He'd exited through one of the three doors and the sound of it shutting behind him echoed through the sparsely decorated room. There was an uncomfortable-looking short sofa covered in fake fur and two wooden chairs that looked, if they were actually used, as if they'd collapse under the person sitting on them. A large brown rectangular-shaped rug with tassels all the way around it was on the floor. It was the type of furniture one would expect to see in a museum, not a functioning governmental building.

"Michael, I'm tired. This is boring. I thought we were going to get to see thrones and jewels and stuff. This sucks."

Rayne sighed inaudibly. She'd thought the tour was going to be more exciting than it was as well, but she wasn't going to bitch about it as Becky was.

"Don't worry, I'll find Hamadi and tell him to take us back to the van. It's almost two-thirty anyway, we can cut the tour short I'm sure," Michael told Becky, not even asking the rest of the group if that was okay with them.

He walked to the door the guide had gone through and tugged on the knob. It didn't turn in his grasp. Michael turned with confusion to the group. "That's weird. It seems to be locked."

"Are you sure?" Sarah asked. "Maybe it's just stuck or something."

Michael tugged harder at the door. It still didn't budge.

Leon, a tall gentleman in his sixties, with hair as white as the clouds that had been wisping in the sky outside, went to one of the other doors in the room. He tried the knob, and it was obvious that it was also locked.

Clearly more than a little alarmed, Steve hurried to the door they'd used to enter the room, and found that it too was locked. Everyone stood for a moment looking at each other in confusion.

"I'm sure Hamadi will be here soon. I mean, we're on an official tour. They can't leave us locked in this room forever," Tracy said with complete confidence.

"This is total bullshit!" Michael seethed, kicking the door their guide had disappeared through. "I can't *wait* to hear his explanation for this goatscrew."

As much as Rayne disliked Michael, she had to agree with him on this one. It didn't make any sense, but there wasn't anything they could do other than wait.

Thirty minutes went by, then an hour. Rayne had wandered over to one of the walls and sat down against it, curling her arms around her up-drawn legs while they waited. Sarah had sat down next to her.

Leon and Paula were sitting on the sofa. Since they were the oldest of the group, everyone agreed they should have what little comfort it allowed. Paula was crying softly as Leon tried to comfort her. Tracy and Steve were sitting with their backs against the opposite wall, as they too waited for Hamadi to arrive.

Michael had paced the room for a while, ranting and raving about asshole Egyptians, which didn't make sense as almost all of the men and women they'd met on their tour had been very polite and accommodating. He'd even banged on each of the doors and yelled at the top of his lungs, trying to get someone to come and let them out...with no luck. Becky had been pissed at first as well, but as time went on, it was obvious she was getting scared...as scared as the rest of them.

Eduardo and Diana were sitting on the two chairs in the room, and once again, Eduardo hadn't let go of his wife's hand. He would lean in and whisper in her ear in Spanish and she'd nod, then a few minutes later, he'd do it again. They were the cutest couple Rayne had ever seen. It just sucked that they were all in this kind of situation...whatever this situation *was*.

Sarah leaned over and whispered to Rayne, "What the heck is going on?"

Rayne could only shake her head. "I have no idea. None of this makes any sense really."

"Do you think the guide meant to lock us in here?

Or was it an accident?"

Rayne had been thinking about the exact same thing. "I think he had to have known. I mean, we didn't really see many people in the last couple of rooms we went through, and it certainly seemed as though he knew where he was going...didn't it?"

When Sarah nodded, Rayne said louder, so the others could hear her, "Diana, how did you guys arrange for this tour?"

She lifted her head and Rayne could see the worry on her brow. "It was at the airport. We had come through customs and were waiting on the bus when Hamadi came up to us and asked if we wanted a tour. He was very nice and spoke excellent English. We haggled a price and he said he would pick us up at the hotel this morning."

"Did you tell him there would be eight of you?"

"Oh yes. He urged us to find two others to join us as he said he had room for ten in his van. That's why we asked you and Sarah to come with us."

It was a method many locals in not-so-prosperous countries used to try to rob the rich tourists coming into the city. Rayne's thoughts were running rampant. She thought back to the things her brother had tried to teach her about security. Dammit, one of the first things he'd taught her was never to talk to or go with anyone who wasn't with a legitimate tourist company.

She'd thought everyone knew that, but apparently not. She hadn't even thought to ask Diana and the others more questions about how they'd booked the tour. She'd just assumed they'd taken precautions. Diana had told her she'd met Hamadi at the airport, but Rayne hadn't realized until now that he didn't work for a reputable tour company. She mentally kicked herself. Chase would be disappointed in her.

"They'd planned for ten, although eight would've worked," Rayne said to no one in particular. "I saw Hamadi talking to several groups of men as we went through the different tourist spots today. Maybe they were in on it?"

"In on what? What the fuck are you babbling on about, woman?" Michael asked caustically.

"On whatever this is. On why we're sitting locked inside a windowless room in the middle of a government building on Tahrir Square," Rayne retorted, not bothering to try to be nice anymore.

"I'm sure they just forgot about us. As soon as they find us, we'll go back to the hotel and laugh about this," Paula said in a watery voice.

Just then a large boom sounded from somewhere in the building. Then another, and another that made the floor beneath their feet shake.

"Oh my freaking God, what was that?" Sarah asked, standing up quickly, as did Rayne.

"Come on, everyone over here," Rayne ordered, falling back on her flight attendant training. The room shook again and plaster actually flaked off the ceiling and rained down on the small group.

The four couples and Sarah and Rayne huddled against one of the walls, away from where they heard the loud thuds. Sarah and Rayne tried to reassure the group, using their experience to try to keep everyone calm, even though none of them knew just what they were being reassured about.

When another boom sounded, much closer than any of the others, Rayne looked around the room. "Sarah! Help me with the couch." The two women dragged the small couch over in front of the group. "Everyone kneel down behind this. It's not a lot of cover, but it's better than nothing."

Michael was silent. He apparently had no comebacks or rude remarks when in the middle of a dangerous situation. The group huddled behind the minuscule cover of the couch, wondering what in the world was going on.

Chapter Sixteen

G HOST AND HIS team sat silent on the C-17 transport plane as they flew across the Atlantic Ocean. They'd come back from their fact-finding mission in Egypt two weeks ago and now were returning—but this time it wasn't a fact-finding mission, it was a rescue.

All hell had broken loose in Egypt and the US government was frantically trying to get all Americans out of the country. The militants had made their move, in the middle of the day, in the middle of the week. It was bold; no one had expected it, which had helped to make their aggression successful.

The coup had begun in the middle of the city, in the same place everything had gone down a few years earlier, although now the streets around the government building and in the square were deserted. In the past, they'd been teeming with news crews and other media, but this time the threat of violence was keeping everyone away. They'd set off a series of bombs in the square and with that distraction, they'd taken over the government building.

Their plan was simple and effective. The group had hundreds of men posing as tour guides. They'd slowly but surely infiltrated and learned the layout of the building. They'd laid in wait, even bribed the security officers. They'd planned well, each of the men bringing in as many tourists as they could round up, and now there were countless Americans and others being held hostage inside the large governmental complex, and it'd become a political nightmare.

The militants were parading the captured men and women in front of some of the windows in the huge building and they'd begun executing them when the Egyptian government didn't react fast enough to their demands.

The US Army had already sent several units to the area and they were working with the Egyptian Army to secure the streets around the besieged building, but it wasn't until the bodies of two men and two women were thrown out the third floor window of one of the buildings that Delta Force and the SEALs were called in.

The bodies of the killed tourists lay where they'd landed; any attempts to recover them had been thwarted by the militants. They obviously liked having them on display for the hundreds of news crews that had taken up residence in the buildings around the square.

Filming from the windows suited them just fine.

Ghost had been surprised to see the SEAL team at the airport that they'd assisted six months ago in Turkey. The SEALs had been escorting Sergeant Penelope Turner home after successfully snatching her from right under the noses of ISIS when either their plan had been discovered, or the terrorists had gotten lucky, and they'd been shot down en route to safety. Ghost's team had swooped in, cleaned up, and escorted the SEALs and Sergeant Turner to a safe base, where they'd parted ways.

They hadn't spent very much time with the other men, but Ghost and his team had a lot of respect for how the SEALs had acted and how their team had operated on the mission. It was no hardship to work with them again. Ghost suspected his longtime friend and brother-in-arms, Tex, had something to do with them meeting up again today. It wasn't as if he could make the actual decision on what missions they were assigned to, but the man had an uncanny ability to do things others would think impossible. A suggestion here, a coded message there…and voila! Ghost honestly wasn't surprised to learn that each of the men on the SEAL team not only knew Tex, but were close friends with him as well.

Tex was a man who knew everyone and he was a former SEAL himself, so it was only natural that Wolf and his team relied on him for intelligence and information. Tex had been wounded on a mission and had medically retired from the Navy, but it seemed he was just as active today, if not more so, as when he'd been on the teams.

Ghost had greeted Wolf warmly. "Good to see you, Wolf."

"You too, Ghost. Let's get a move on, we can debrief onboard."

Ghost and his team usually flew commercial to try to stay under the radar, but for this mission, time was of the essence, and it was more important to get over to Cairo and help rescue the remaining hostages than it was to try to be stealthy. As far as anyone knew, they were a part of the SEAL team, not Delta Force.

After the thirteen men got settled on the plane and they were in the air, as the highest-ranking soldier, Ghost started the debriefing and didn't beat around the bush.

"Okay, here's what we know...which isn't a lot. Reports are sketchy coming out of Cairo, more so because no one seems to know exactly what's going on inside the building. There's no definite number of militants and no real count of how many hostages there might be."

"So we've got a whole lot of who-the-hell-knows-what," Wolf bit out, obviously pissed off.

"That about covers it," Ghost agreed.

"As much as it sucks, we're gonna need to take a day or two for reconnaissance," Fletch stated. "We can't make a move until we know where those hostages are being held."

"Agreed," Abe, one of the SEALs, stated. "The last thing we want is to go in balls to the wall and get innocents killed."

All the men hated the delay, but it was a necessary one.

"All right. Let's discuss Plan A. Then we'll figure out a Plan B, C, and D. If all else fails, get the fuck out of there and to safety with as many hostages as you can find," Ghost ordered, smoothing the map out on the table in front of them.

Mozart, another of the SEALs, groaned. "Easier said than done."

"No shit," Beatle agreed.

"Okay, here's the plan…"

The men strategized, argued, and discussed various plans of action all the way across the ocean. Finally, hours after they'd taken off, the military plane landed. All thirteen men on board were locked and loaded— ready to take out as many bad guys as possible, and bring home as many hostages as they could get their hands on.

RAYNE BIT BACK the moan of fright that threatened to come out of her throat. They'd been stuck inside the locked room for what seemed like hours, but when they were finally freed, the situation wasn't anything they had imagined it would be.

A gruff-looking Egyptian man had opened the door and been followed in by three others. All four men were holding automatic rifles and they'd immediately started ordering them to do something in Egyptian.

It was Michael—of course it was Michael—who was stupid enough to complain to the men that he didn't understand what they wanted. He was rifle-butted in the face for his insolence. Afterwards, Michael hadn't complained again.

They were herded into another room, which held about twenty other tourists, and another five or so men and boys with loaded weapons. Rayne and Sarah huddled close together, not wanting to get separated. The other couples had done the same thing, and Rayne couldn't help but get a lump in her throat at watching how Leon, Eduardo, and Steve put themselves between the men with rifles and their wives. Finally, after another hour or so, their entire group was moved into another room, this one again with no windows. The doors were shut once more and they were all locked in.

The thirty or so of them spent the next day confused, hungry, and terrified out of their minds. Rayne felt disgusting in her T-shirt and jeans and, as inappropriate as it was, wished she could wash the sweat and fear off with a scalding-hot shower.

A couple of times some of the men banged and kicked at the doors, with no luck. Finally, after they were all frightened beyond belief and beyond the need to rebel, the group was led once again to another room. This one looked as if it had been a ballroom at one time.

There were ornate carvings and paintings on the walls, and red tapestries hung as curtains from the windows. The incongruence between the opulence of their surroundings and the way they felt—beaten down, smelly, hungry, and scared—was jarring. Overall, there were probably around sixty or so hostages in the large room. Rayne couldn't tell what country everyone was from, except not everyone was speaking English. There was what sounded like French, German, Spanish, and some Slavic language thrown in as well. But at the moment they were allies, thrown into this awful situation by fate, and nationality didn't matter.

Sarah and Rayne immediately went to the back of the room, away from the windows and doors, and sat down against the wall. Rayne whispered urgently to Sarah, wiping sweat from her brow from the warm room and the stress. "Don't do anything to call attention to yourself. Nothing, you hear me? Don't get hysterical, if no one else is. Try not to throw up. Don't yell at anyone, don't get in any arguments. If you call attention to yourself, you're making yourself a target, and that's the *last* thing you want to do in a situation like this. Blend in or die, Sarah. I'm not kidding."

"How in the world do you know these things? I don't remember them teaching that to us in flight attendant school," Sarah questioned in wonder.

"My brother is in the Army. Counterterrorism. He taught me."

The women were quiet for a while as they watched what was happening around them. Rayne wasn't surprised when Michael tried to make himself the leader of the large group. Rayne could've told him it was the wrong thing to do, but he wouldn't have listened to her anyway.

For the first day or two in the ballroom, their captors ignored them for the most part. They brought in slabs of some kind of meat and cheese, and buckets of water for them all to share, but that was about it. After they'd emptied one of the buckets, it was put in a far corner for use as a bathroom.

When Michael started getting mouthy with the guards and demanding to be let go, Rayne could tell they were losing their temper.

On the third day of their captivity—Rayne didn't know why they were being held captive or by who, but supposed it was a moot point anyway—the guards apparently had had enough of Michael and some of the other more demanding hostages.

The entire group was ordered to line up. Women in one line and men in another. Rayne watched sadly as Diana and Eduardo, Leon and Paula, and Tracy and Steve said tearful goodbyes. No one had any idea what in the world was going on, and being separated from each other suddenly seemed like a death sentence.

Becky and Michael flatly refused to do as their captors said. Michael stood next to his wife with his arm around her shoulders and declared, "No. You can't separate us. This is my wife and she is very delicate. We aren't going anywhere; you need to let us go. You're all gonna die anyway, so you might as well give up now!"

Rayne couldn't believe how stupid Michael was. She had no idea what he thought his little speech was going to accomplish, but it was evident that it irritated the man who was trying to get everyone in order.

He pulled out his rifle and shot Michael in the head, and when Becky started screeching, put two bullets into her without a word of warning.

The room was silent as their bodies fell to the ground with a thud. No one dared scream. No one wanted to piss off the unstable man who'd just murdered two people in front of them without seeming to think twice about it.

"Anyone else want to complain about your treatment? Anyone else want to be set free?"

No one said a word.

The man, apparently still pissed off, turned and shot the man in line closest to him, then killed the closest woman as well. He gave no explanation, simply turned and walked out of the room, saying something to the other captors in Egyptian before he left.

"You men, yes, you four in line. Pick up bodies and throw out window, there," another captor ordered. His English was broken, but more than understandable.

Rayne watched, trembling and weak from fear and hunger, as the men did as they were told. Michael and Becky's bodies were dragged to the window and tipped out. Next came the other man and woman, who'd done nothing except stand too close to Michael.

Everyone was silent as the women were herded out one door and the men were led away through a door on the opposite side of the big room. Everyone had thought, or was deluding themselves into thinking that the situation would end nonviolently up until that point. Now they all knew they were expendable. There was no telling when their captors would get sick of them and decide it was easier to throw their dead bodies out a window than feed them, give them water, or deal with them in any way.

For the first time since they'd been locked in that first room, Rayne thought there was a higher-than-average chance she wouldn't live through whatever was going on. She'd never see her brother and sister again. Would never go dancing with Mary. And would never, ever have the opportunity to see Ghost again.

Why that last thought was the one that made her the saddest was beyond her, but a lone tear made its way down her cheek as Rayne meekly followed behind Sarah to wherever and whatever the militants had planned for them.

Chapter Seventeen

FLETCH KEPT HIS binoculars trained on the building in front of him as he spoke to Ghost. "The curtains are pulled back in this room. Looks like three in the top-right room. Armed with AK-47s, probably around thirteen, mid-twenties and mid-forties."

"Any hostages?" Ghost asked in a quiet voice.

"Not that I can see, but I'm guessing they're there. The men are holding their weapons as if they're guarding someone, or some people. In the rooms where there haven't been any hostages or curtains, the weapons are slung across their backs. They're probably sitting."

"Any chance we can move to do a head count?"

"Doubtful. We'd have to get up pretty high to see down into that room, and there aren't any buildings around here that'll work for that."

"Dammit," Ghost swore. "It's not good that they separated the men from the women."

Fletch lowered the binoculars and looked over at his friend and teammate. "It's not. But this isn't anything new. What's up with you, Ghost?"

Ghost sighed but remained silent.

"Does it have anything to do with that new tattoo on your leg?" Fletch pushed.

"I told you before, I'm not talking about it," Ghost ground out between clenched teeth. Even though he was close friends with Fletch, it didn't feel right sharing what had happened between him and Rayne all those months ago. And his tattoo was special. Sacred. Not something to be gossiped about as if they were giggling pre-teens.

Fletch sighed. "Look, I'm not an idiot. None of us are. We know that something happened on your layover in London earlier this year. Not talking about it isn't helping you. You know better than to let shit stay bottled up inside. It festers. You've got a hair trigger and you seem to be letting things like this situation bother you more than you used to. I'm not saying that's a bad thing, but you can't let this get to you. And you are, much more than you ever did before."

"It's not festering, and I'm not fucking talking about it."

Fletch went on as if his friend hadn't just shut him down. "If I had to guess, I'd say this was over a woman. You met someone and had a great time…and now you regret sleeping with her, which isn't like you, but whatever. Was she fat? Ugly? Will she not leave you alone? Is that the problem?" Fletch knew it wasn't any of those things, but he kept pushing to see if he could get a rise out of his friend. Any reaction was better than the blank look on Ghost's face when he refused to talk about whatever it was that went down.

"Let me guess, she was a shitty lay. No, I have it—did she give you VD? Is that the issue? Because if it is, you can go to the doctor and—"

"For fuck's sake, Fletch, she didn't give me VD. Christ."

"So there *was* a woman."

Ghost ran his hand over his face wearily. Fletch had been on him for weeks, trying to goad him into letting something slip, and it looked as though he'd finally gotten his way. But Fletch was a good friend, someone Ghost trusted. And Lord knew he needed to talk to someone about this shit. Guess they were going to gossip as if they were pre-teens after all.

"Yeah. She was…awesome."

"So what's the problem?"

Ghost turned to his friend. "We're Delta."

"And?"

"Isn't that enough?"

Fletch shook his head. "Look, I'm not saying any relationship would be easy, but you know it can work."

"I lied to her, Fletch. Every fucking thing out of my mouth was a lie."

"You tell her you wanted to be her boyfriend?"

"No."

"You tell her you loved her?"

"Fuck no."

"That you'd call her? Write? Send her gushy love letters?"

"Dammit, Fletch. No."

"Then I don't see the issue."

"I liked her. She was…feisty. Sweet. Down-to-earth. Loyal."

"Wow," Fletch breathed. "I never thought I'd see the day that horndog Ghost fell head-over-heels for a woman."

"I'm not head-over-fucking-heels, asshole."

"I'd say you are. Look at you, man. You went and got a tattoo that not only blows your cover as Army—the huge fucking Army logo did that, if nothing else—but you got a fairy wand tattooed on your body as well. And not once in your description of this woman did you say anything about what she looks like."

"So?"

"So?" Fletch shook his head. "Buddy, every time you've ever described one of the women you've slept with, you started with her tits. Or her ass, how beautiful she was, how short, how tall, how curvy…something about her body. This woman? Not one damn thing."

Ghost stared long and hard at his friend. He was right. Oh, Rayne was beautiful, but he wasn't about to discuss her with his friends. She was his. "Fuck, man, I didn't even give her my real name."

"So what?" Fletch returned immediately.

"She thinks I'm John Benbrook."

"You didn't give her your nick?"

"I did."

"So she knows the real you."

"Ghost isn't the real me."

"Bullshit. Ghost *is* you, and you know it. The name fits you better than any nickname I've ever heard of before. You're light on your feet and can get in and out of places undetected in a way none of the rest of us can. You're spooky how you know when we're in deep shit and have to get the hell out. If this woman was calling you Ghost, then she knows the real you."

"I lied about everything else too. I made up a girlfriend for my fifteen-year-old self. I made up where I was from. I lied about being held up once. Jesus, Fletch, I fucking lied to her about everything."

"What about the sex? Were you faking it then too?"

Ghost had no idea the lines in his face smoothed out and a look of contentment stole over him as he spoke. "No. Not one thing was faked when we were in bed together."

"When we get back, you have to find her, Ghost."

Fletch held up a hand to stop the argument he knew his friend was going to make. "If I ever meet a woman who makes me look like you do right now, you can bet I'd never let her go."

When Ghost didn't respond, Fletch continued. "You lied. I get it; that sucks. She's gonna be pissed. But you're Delta, man. Top secret. You were on the way home from a mission. There are a thousand reasons why you lied, but you didn't lie about the most important thing, Ghost. The way you felt when you were with her. That speaks a thousand times louder than any of that other shit."

"Jesus, I feel as if I'm on Dr. Phil or something," Ghost griped.

Fletch smiled. "I might not be the smartest man on the block, but if I had a sweet, feisty woman waiting for me at home, who could take my cock night after night and leave me with the memories you obviously have until the next time I could get home, I'd do anything in my power to hold on to her."

Ghost nodded. Fletch had always been the more introspective one of their group. He was closed off and secretive, and didn't trust easily, but once you got past all that, he was steadfast in his loyalty.

A large blast sounded in the building across the square and both men immediately turned their attention back to their job. The binoculars were back in front of Fletch's eyes and Ghost tried to ascertain where the blast came from.

"Northwest corner of the complex. Smoke," Ghost told Fletch.

"Oh shit," was his response.

"What? Shit what?" Ghost asked urgently, looking down at his friend and seeing he hadn't swung his gaze to the northwest corner, but was still looking at the room they'd last discussed.

"There are definitely hostages in that room. No tangos in there with them anymore, but there's a group of women pounding on the door with all they've got. Oh shit, it's—"

His words were cut off when the entire corner of the building, right where the room full of hostages had been, disappeared from their view under a fiery blast and a column of smoke.

Chapter Eighteen

"**W**E CAN'T JUST sit here and do nothing," Sarah exclaimed, obviously at the end of her rope.

"What do you want to do? Demand to be released like that guy who got shot?" one of the other women being held with them jeered caustically.

Rayne didn't blame Sarah for being antsy. They'd been moved around several times since they'd been separated from the men. Diana, Paula, and Tracy weren't dealing very well with wondering if their men were all right. Rayne would've felt the same way if she'd been with Ghost and he'd been separated from her. Fighting amongst themselves wasn't going to help anything.

She glanced over at the three men, actually two men and one boy, who were guarding them at the moment. The guards had been switching out, but it was obvious they were a ragtag bunch who didn't really know what was going on day to day, they were just following orders.

At one point, the boy had come over to their group.

He hadn't said anything, and hoping to try to make him see them as humans and not as animals that should be shot, Rayne had broken the rule Chase had demanded she learn about blending in and never standing out, and smiled at him. The boy had stopped and looked her in the eye. He'd nodded at her and went back over to the two men on the other side of the room. Rayne hoped that his nod meant that he saw her as a friend and not an enemy. That she'd humanized all of them to him. Maybe he had a sister he loved. He had to have a mother...right?

Rayne tried to keep her voice clear and calm, just like she'd been taught to do in emergencies on the plane. "You're both right, we should be thinking about what we might be able to do if we get the chance, but we also can't demand things; that will just irritate them more."

"What should we do?" That was Paula. Always looking to others for direction.

The thing was, Rayne had no idea. There were about fifteen of them in this room at the moment. There had been seventeen, but their captors had taken two of the women away, and they'd never returned. Rayne didn't want to think about what might be happening with them. She glanced over at the gunmen. They were talking with each other, and only occasionally glancing over at them. Rayne supposed their group didn't look all that threatening at the moment...they were sitting in a small circle, huddled together for comfort.

"Okay, this is a new group of gunmen, right? We haven't seen the same men since we've been in here. So they're rotating the guards out."

"And?" It was an Australian woman named Pat who spoke up. "What good is that knowledge to us?"

"I'm not sure, but at this point, any information is better than none," Rayne returned easily, keeping her voice carefully modulated. Even though she was irritated, she couldn't let it show.

"Here's what I think," another woman, probably in her early twenties, piped up. "I think we ought to charge them. There's fifteen of us, and only three of them."

"But they have guns," Paula said nervously, wringing her hands.

"True, but I'm thinking a couple of us can distract them, while the rest tackle them."

Rayne barely resisted rolling her eyes. It was the worst plan in the history of plans. It was as if she was in the middle of a bad B-movie. At any moment, the chick would tear off her clothes and parade herself around and the good guys would burst in and save the day. It just wasn't going to happen.

The door to their room was suddenly flung open

hard enough that it banged against the wall and made every single one of the women jump in fright.

There were two men who entered, armed of course. One held a box as well as a rifle and the other one immediately started talking to the captors in the room in a language they couldn't understand.

The women all stood up and huddled together against the wall, sensing something was about to happen, but not knowing what.

The boy, who Rayne had smiled at not long before, pointed over at her when the newcomer barked a question at him. Rayne held her breath, wondering what the men were doing.

Rayne really didn't like being singled out. Shit. Chase had warned her. When this had happened to the other two women, they'd been taken out of the room and hadn't returned.

The man with the box placed it on the ground near the other two captors and came toward her. Rayne backed away as much as she could, which wasn't far considering there was a wall behind her.

The man grabbed hold of her arm and wrenched her toward him roughly. Rayne heard Sarah whimper, but not one of the women said anything. They'd learned from the last time to keep quiet, otherwise they'd get hit.

Rayne gasped as her other arm was grabbed in a

rough grip by another captor. She was dragged out of the room between the two men, with the boy following close behind. She glanced back one more time and caught the agonized look of grief on Sarah's face before the door shut firmly behind them.

"Where are we going?" Rayne asked, not really expecting an answer.

"Boys become men," the tall, bearded man next to her said in a rumbly guttural voice.

"What?" Rayne hadn't expected an answer, so she hadn't been concentrating on understanding his thick accent.

"Boys become men," he repeated, not at all seeming to be put out at having to say it again.

"I don't understand."

"Typical. Americans stupid. Never understand."

Rayne wanted to protest, but kept her mouth shut. She changed tactics and tried to memorize where they were walking. If there was any chance she could get away, she had to know which way to go. The last thing she wanted to do was run right into a nest of terrorists when she was running for her life.

They walked, half-dragging her along several corridors. The building was huge. Rayne was afraid she'd be lost in the maze of hallways for the rest of her life.

A large explosion sounded somewhere behind her, and the men stopped and waited for something. The ground shook under their feet and Rayne shuddered.

"That was your friends," one of the men holding her said, a bit too happily for Rayne's peace of mind.

"What?"

"We just blew up the room they were in. Teach lesson to the world."

"Oh God," Rayne moaned, as she was once again hauled roughly down the hall. They'd blown up the room with Paula, Sarah, Tracy, and sweet Diana? Could they have survived? Why was she spared? She had so many questions, and absolutely no answers.

The boy behind them said something in a whiny voice that grated on Rayne's nerves. The man to her left barked at him in a pissed-off tone that would've had Rayne cowering if she wasn't already. The boy mumbled something and they were on their way again.

They came to a door at the end of a long hallway and the boy hurried around to open it. Rayne was propelled inside by the two men. The room was dark and smelled horrendous...like sweat and body odor, and a coppery stench that could only be blood. It was taking a while for her eyes to adjust to the dim light so she didn't fight the hold of the two men as they dragged her to the corner of the room. It wasn't until she felt a cold band wrap around her ankle, so tightly it pinched her skin, that she realized she was in big trouble—and she began to try to wiggle out of the tight hold of her captors.

There was laughter around her, and Rayne glanced down at a man kneeling at her feet. The one who'd just wrapped an iron cuff around her ankle. It was attached to a long chain, which was bolted to the wall. Behind her was a rusty bed frame with a thin mattress on it, which had several dark spots.

The man at her feet said something and again, everyone around them laughed.

"He said you have fat ankles," a modulated, accented voice said from across the room.

Rayne would've been offended—she did *not* have fat ankles—if she wasn't so scared. They were perfectly normal, thank you very much, but she was too frightened to open her mouth to rebuff the claim. She'd always thought if she was ever in a situation where her life was threatened that she'd be brave and could smart-mouth her way out of anything, but that had been a pipe dream. She was absolutely terrified at what was going to happen to her in this horrible room and couldn't say a thing to try to defend herself.

There had been six men waiting for them as they'd entered, all wearing gray robes that covered them from their shoulders down to their feet. None were wearing any sort of head covering or mask. They were sitting on a platform of sorts...three men on the bottom row and three on the top row. They all had long beards and were watching her with lecherous intent. It looked like some kind of pagan ritual or something.

The man who had fastened the cuff around her ankle picked up a huge knife from the floor. It was rusty and had serrations on the blade. Before Rayne could move, her biceps were pulled behind her back, wrenching her arms at an awkward angle and holding her immobile. She frantically wriggled and squirmed, futilely trying to get out of the hold.

"If you struggle, there's a greater chance of being cut," the accented voice said.

"Why are you doing this? What's going on?" Rayne desperately needed answers.

The man at her feet took his time. He brought the knife up to her pant leg and oh so slowly began to slice upwards. Rayne could feel the tip of the blade against her leg, but couldn't tell if it was actually cutting her or not. Her legs felt numb—hell, everything felt numb.

"In our culture, a boy becomes a man when he first takes a woman."

"Oh shit." Rayne was beginning to understand.

"I see you understand. You should feel honored. Moshe chose you to be his first."

Rayne finally found her spunk and her tongue. "That's not your culture. Egypt is a beautiful country filled with wonderful people, and that's not the way of its culture. It might be *your* way, assholes, trying to pretend it's normal and right, but it's not. You're brainwashing your children to be killers and rapists."

Her head was flung backwards with the force of the smack one of the other men delivered.

"It's also the way of our culture to make sure women know their place. And their place is to be quiet and to speak only when spoken to."

"Fuck that," Rayne muttered, only to cry out in pain when she was hit again, this time not with an open palm, but a closed fist. It hurt, but she knew that whatever these psychos had in store for her would hurt a whole lot more. Her breaths came out faster and faster as her destroyed jeans fell to the floor. There was more laughing from the men as she stood before them in her black lace underwear. She'd felt sexy when she'd put it on, however many days ago it had been. Now she felt defiled and dirty.

There was a conversation between the men and the boy that Rayne didn't understand, but the man gleefully translated for her. "Moshe's father praises his son and tells him he chose well. You have spunk, and your thighs are thick and full and will cushion him as they should. Your hips are wide and can bear many sons."

"Oh God, please, don't do this. Let me go."

The man with the accented English continued as if she hadn't spoken. "The ritual is to take you seven times. Seven is a lucky number in our country. Once he fills you seven times, he will be a man."

Rayne couldn't get enough air in her lungs. Seven times? She was going to be raped by this man-boy seven times?

"It is our job to critique him, to tell him the best ways to master a woman, to make her compliant under him. He knows you will fight him at first, it is expected, but by the time his ritual is done, you will be broken and will do whatever he tells you and will take whatever he wants to give to you. You might as well accept your fate now, American whore. The two before you fought valiantly, but in the end took our new men with no struggle, as proper women should."

Rayne closed her eyes and prayed. Not for rescue, but for a quick death. If she could get ahold of the knife the man was using to cut off her shirt now, she would plunge it into her own heart.

The words in the room sounded as if they were coming from a long way off and Rayne felt disconnected from her body. It was as if someone else was being held, having their shirt cut off, being laughed at...not her.

She thought about her brother, Chase, about how he'd feel learning what had happened to her...if he ever learned. And her sister, Sam. Sam was happy as a clam in Los Angeles chasing her dream of becoming an actress. And Ghost...

Oh God, Ghost. What she wouldn't give to be able to see him one more time. If she lived through this, she swore right then and there to not let these animals take away the beautiful memories she had of Ghost making love to her, of their night together.

What was about to happen to her had *nothing* to do with the lovemaking they'd shared.

Rayne was jerked backwards and would've fallen if it wasn't for the man behind her holding on to her so tightly. He dragged her to the filthy mattress and flung her down on it. The chain around her ankle clanged loudly in the room. She kicked and struggled against the men, but their hold on her was too tight. As her other leg was chained to the bedframe, and her arms were wrenched over her head, the damn voice kept on describing what was about to happen.

"First, Moshe will take you on your back, so he can look at your face. This is step one, and will most likely be quick. Most boys are quick to release their first time they get inside a woman. The second and third times will be from behind, so you can understand he has all the power, and you are like a dog. Worthless, good for only taking what he gives you. The fourth time he will release inside your dark hole. This is the transition time. If he cannot hold out for one hundred strokes, he will be seen as less than a man in the eyes of his father, uncles, and holy men who are here to witness his transition to manhood."

Rayne whimpered, thinking about how badly a hundred thrusts into her untried back hole would hurt.

"Then you will take him down your throat for the fifth time. The sixth will be against the wall, and the seventh will be again with you on your back. By the time the seventh time comes, you will be slick with his release and your blood, and will be ready for him and will take him easily and without fight. The goal is for him to make you find your womanly release that last time. If he can hold on and not release until you do, he will have succeeded and will be a man. If he cannot make you release, he will have failed. And will have to start again on another day."

Rayne couldn't believe what she was hearing. After being raped seven times, if *she* didn't orgasm, she'd have to go through this again? It was obviously a setup so they could rape women over and over again, all in the name of their custom. It wasn't as if any of them really gave a shit if the women they were with orgasmed or not.

She wasn't sure she'd survive being violated once, let alone seven times, and Rayne knew she'd die if she had to go through the barbaric ritual more than once. She'd find a way to kill herself before suffering through it again. These people were insane.

Rayne kept her mouth shut, knowing nothing she

could say would make these monsters change their minds.

She glanced over at the men sitting in the chairs, waiting and watching. Some were related to the boy; and that made the fact they were there and supporting this awful ritual a hundred times worse. They didn't look like old wise men, they looked like lecherous middle-aged men who got off on observing a woman being raped and tortured.

"The more blood that flows, the luckier he will be in manhood. The more you struggle and fight, the more of a man he will become."

Rayne couldn't hold back her words, finding the courage she'd been lacking up to this point. What did it matter if she pissed them off now? If they killed her? It was actually probably better. Maybe if they got mad enough they'd just slit her throat or something, although that probably wouldn't keep Moshe from raping her. The thought of him violating her dead body made her want to throw up, but she didn't let it stop the words that spewed out of her mouth.

"Shut up. Just shut up! You're all sick. This is rape! This is wrong. You can't honestly believe the shit you're spewing. Let me go, I don't want your little penis anywhere near me!" She frantically thrashed in her cruel bindings as the boy came up beside the mattress and looked down at her and smiled.

Rayne looked at him in the hopes of seeing the person who'd nodded at her shyly back in the other room. He wasn't there. He'd been replaced by a boy on the cusp of manhood who wanted to impress the elders sitting and standing behind him, and who had nothing but lust-filled thoughts of fucking for the first time.

He stood there and watched her struggle for a moment, then turned and said something to the men behind him. There was laughter and agreement.

Of course the man who spoke English was there to translate for her. Rayne knew she'd hear his heavily accented voice in her nightmares for years to come. "Moshe says he is pleased. You are round and ripe and your skin ripples as you struggle. Already your blood flows from your wrists and ankles. He says he will be the luckiest man this ritual cycle."

Rayne closed her eyes as the boy brought his hands up to his pants. This was happening. She couldn't believe it. She *had* to believe it.

Rayne forcefully brought Ghost's image to her mind to block out everything around her. His face, his hands, his scowl as he took a picture of the nasty taxi driver's license when they were in London, the words inked on his side…quiet professionalism.

If she was going to die, the last thing she wanted to see in her mind was Ghost.

Chapter Nineteen

D UDE AND HOLLYWOOD worked together as if they'd always been teammates. The SEAL and Delta Force member eased in and out of the shadows as though they belonged there, setting charges at strategic points along the perimeter of the building.

Blowing out holes in the walls of the government building probably wasn't the Egyptian government's first choice in tactics, but after watching a bomb explode in a corner room that had to have killed all of the women inside, the teams were done waiting for permission. They were sent in to take care of business, and that's just what they were going to do. No other Americans, or any other hostages, were going to die on their watch. They couldn't just sit there and do nothing. That's not what they'd been trained to do and now was the time to act.

They had to get inside and get the remaining hostages out...and if that meant some, or all, of the militants were killed in the process, all the better. Thirteen men against an unknown number of tangos might seem like an uneven fight to a lot of people, but Hollywood knew they weren't just any thirteen soldiers. They were SEALs and Delta Force. They were trained for this shit. They were a part of the two most lethal groups of Special Forces soldiers the United States military had.

Hollywood spoke into his throat mic. "B to base. All is go."

"Ten-four, B. Ready for flight," came the quiet response through the radio.

Hollywood and Dude backed away from the last charge they'd set. As soon as they were a safe distance away, they'd give the high sign to Truck, and he'd simultaneously set off all of the charges at the same time. It should create enough chaos inside the building for the teams to sneak in and, hopefully, escort any remaining hostages out.

The men were paired up, a Delta with a SEAL. Typically the SEALs would stay teamed with their own and the same with the Deltas, but since they'd worked together briefly in the past, and trusted each other, they decided to split up the teams to capitalize on their strengths. It was highly unusual, but neither of the groups typically worked by the book.

"B to base. Countdown to flight," Hollywood informed Truck tonelessly.

"Prepare for takeoff," the other man returned immediately.

Dude and Hollywood crouched down against a wall in an alley not too far from the building, covered their ears, and waited for all hell to break loose.

RAYNE TRIED TO concentrate on her memories, but that damn voice kept forcing itself into her consciousness. She heard one of the men speaking faintly, presumably to the boy, and the asshole who spoke English felt the need to translate every single fucking word.

"He is telling Moshe to make sure your legs are spread as far apart as possible so he can get as far inside you as he can go."

Rayne felt the baby-smooth skin of Moshe's thighs against her own. She felt him scooting up and forcing her legs farther apart in the process. Her legs had already been spread, but as much as she resisted Moshe, he was still able to push her legs obscenely wide. The chains on her ankles pulled taut as Moshe spread her thighs farther than what was comfortable, tearing the flesh around her ankles. She was still wearing her underwear, but knew the barrier it was currently providing would soon be only a memory. She squirmed against her bonds, despite knowing it was futile. No, this couldn't be happening.

The fucker kept up the blow-by-blow of her imminent rape.

"Now they are telling him what it will feel like when he gets inside. You'll be dry, which provides more friction for his root. They are trying to get him to explode before he gets inside, holding off will prove he's man enough to resist temptation."

Rayne was going to throw up. All over Moshe and all over herself. This was horrific and she needed to be somewhere else, anywhere else. She couldn't hold back the whimper that sneaked out of her throat. Her hands fisted in their bindings and she trembled, every muscle in her body tense, readying itself for the invasion about to come.

Just as she felt Moshe's soft, boyish hands touch her upper thighs and squeeze painfully, an explosion ripped through the room.

Rayne screamed in terror like a cornered dog, not understanding what was happening. She'd been ready for her body to be violated, but instead the bed shook under her as the walls crumbled. Rayne watched as large cracks appeared in the ceiling above her head.

She glanced over at the men who had been leaning toward the bed in anticipation of Moshe's initiation and first foray into manhood, and saw that they were no longer sitting with lust in their eyes staring at her, but had stood up and were all trying to push out of the room at the same time. Running like the cowards they were deep inside.

A hand gripped her breast, hard, and Rayne gasped at the sensation. Looking up into Moshe's eyes, she saw no trace of the boy she'd thought to try to gain sympathy from. He was pissed his initiation was being interrupted. He cruelly squeezed her breast through her bra once more and hissed something at her in his own language before springing off her and quickly pulling his pants back up, holding them closed with his free hand, not bothering to tie them shut.

As he was leaving the room, he turned back and said in perfectly understandable English, "I'll be back. I *will* become a man today," and he ran out the door.

Rayne shivered and frantically pulled at the chains holding her to the bed. All her actions did was make her wrists and ankles bleed more.

There was another explosion, closer than the previous one, and the last thing Rayne remembered was watching the blocks in the wall shake and threaten to crumble as she passed out from fright.

THE SIX SPECIAL FORCES teams of two fanned out across the now crumbling complex. It was complete pandemonium, just as the teams had planned and predicted it would be. Knowing the general areas where the hostages were being kept, each team headed for their preassigned area. The plan was to find as many hostages as possible and lead them out and to safety…and to kill any militants who got in their way.

Ghost and Wolf were point and were stationed in the square. They'd direct any hostages who ran out of the now burning and destroyed building to safety. Blade was the odd man out and was waiting at the rendezvous point for everyone to gather.

Watching in relief as small groups of men and women poured out of the building, each guided by a team member, Ghost and Wolf kept vigilant, ready for any terrorist to decide the escaping hostages should die rather than be rescued. After forty minutes, the flow of hostages slowed to a trickle and most of the teams had checked in. Fletch and Mozart and Truck and Benny had joined Blade, and had been transporting the dazed and confused hostages to safer territory.

The teams had come across pockets of militants hunkered down inside the massive building, trying to hide until the initial breach had been completed, but they'd been no match for the SEAL and Delta teams.

Beatle's voice crackled across the radio. "We just sent a group of about fifteen men your way, G. They say there was a group of women, including some of their wives and girlfriends, who had been separated from them two days ago. They were last seen being led to the blast zone."

Ghost knew what he meant. He hoped they hadn't been the women in the room the militants had set the bomb off in. "Ten-four. We'll intercept and see if we can't get more intel."

"We're standing by," was Beatle's response.

Ghost saw the group of men staggering toward them. They looked haunted by whatever had gone on inside the building. Ghost motioned them over, and they gladly ran toward the American soldiers.

"Who had a partner that was separated?" Ghost questioned, all business.

Six hands went up. Wolf passed the remaining men on to Abe, who was waiting to take the last groups to safety.

"Tell me exactly what happened."

A tall, older gentleman said in a broken voice, "We were all being held together for the first couple of days then we were asked to stand in two lines, men in one and women in the other. One man protested and he and his wife were shot. Then those bastards shot another couple just for fun and threw all of them out the window. We were then led to another room, without the women. We've been there ever since. We heard some explosions, but don't know anything about what's going on. Did you get all the women out? Are they safe?"

"We're working on it, sir," Wolf tried to reassure the man. "We'll do our best to find your women, if they haven't already been freed."

"Thank God," the tall man breathed.

Ghost heard Beatle begin speaking through the radio again. "Problem, Ghost. We found another group of hostages. Women. They're busted up, some worse than others, and hysterical. Said they were locked in a room with a bomb."

"They're alive?" Ghost asked incredulously. Simply being alive was a miracle, especially having seen the damage the bomb had done.

"Yeah. Apparently after they were shut in the room, and before the bomb exploded, they hid behind a big-ass piece of furniture. Details are still a bit sketchy as they're obviously traumatized, but they were damn lucky."

"No shit. Jesus." It was the best news Ghost and Wolf had heard all day. They'd thought everyone in that room had been killed.

"Thing is," Beatle continued quickly, "one woman said her friend was dragged out of the room before the explosives went off."

"Fuck," Ghost said fervently. "Okay, get those women out of there. If you have time, see if you can track down the missing woman, otherwise get the fuck out."

"The one woman is refusing to go until we find her missing friend."

"I don't give a rat's ass what she refuses, get her out of there, Beatle," Ghost threatened in a low voice. The last thing they needed was the hostages calling the shots.

"Ten-four." Ghost could tell Beatle was switching to the all-network channel, the one which all of the SEALs and Deltas could hear. "We're going to start on this end of the building and do one last search for the missing American woman. Her friend says her name is Rayne, and when we find her, to make sure we tell her Sarah and the others are all right. She says she'll worry. Everyone be on the lookout for an American, average height and weight, wearing a pair of jeans and a pink T-shirt. She should easily stand out from the terrorists."

Ghost felt his heart stutter in his chest. It couldn't be. No fucking way. "What was the name of the missing woman again?" he barked into his throat mic. He couldn't even follow proper protocol, he had to know.

How many women had the name Rayne? Not very many, and with the way the hair on the back of his neck was standing up, Ghost knew it was *his* Rayne.

"Rayne Jackson."

"Copy that," Wolf answered when Ghost didn't say another word.

"Talk to me, Ghost. What's putting that look in your eye?" Wolf demanded, putting his finger on the trigger of his M-4 rifle and looking around as if the enemy was staring down his sights at them.

"She's mine. The missing woman…she's mine."

Wolf didn't bat an eye and didn't ask any questions. "Well fuck, man, let's get in there, find her, and get her the fuck out this fucking mess."

Ghost nodded once and started toward the building. Ghost had no idea what Rayne was doing in the middle of a coup in Egypt, but at this point, it didn't matter. If the missing woman *was* his Rayne, he'd do whatever it took to get her out and safe. He wasn't thinking about the lies he'd told her or how she'd react to seeing him like this, all he could think about was holding her in his arms…safe and sound. If anyone got between him and his woman, they were as good as dead.

Chapter Twenty

RAYNE YANKED AT her chains, trying to slip her hands out of the metal cuffs, to no avail. The blood on her wrists and ankles from her struggles helped her to almost free herself, but her hands and feet weren't quite small enough to slip out of the shackles, even with the extra lubricant. No matter how hard she pulled and twisted, she was stuck.

She'd woken up, realized she was alone and immediately started trying to escape. She'd gotten a reprieve, but had no idea how long it might last. Moshe and his sick relatives could be back any moment.

The dust was thick in the air, making it difficult to draw in a deep breath, and the rubble from the ceiling and the walls, which had crumbled in places during the explosions, was covering the floor and the bed. The door had come off its hinges and was partially blocking the entryway into the room.

Rayne would've yelled for help, only she was afraid of whose attention she would gain by doing so. The absolute last thing she wanted was to have Moshe show back up to complete his barbaric ritual, and lying there in her bra and panties meant she wasn't exactly dressed for anyone else to see her either.

She lay back and tried to catch her breath. What could she do? How in the hell was she getting out of this one? Her legs were spread open and the iron shackles around her wrists and ankles didn't give her much, if any, wiggle room.

Hopefully the explosions were the results of the good guys. She had no way of knowing, however. The bottom line was that she couldn't do anything but lay there and wait for someone to unlock her chains. She was stuck.

Every now and then, Rayne would hear a faint echo through the walls of her prison. Was it the good guys? Was it the bad guys? She had no idea. Eventually the sounds would fade and she'd be back to feeling utterly alone again.

She was doing pretty good until she heard the gunshots.

Rayne began to panic, once again pulling frantically at her chains. She needed to get out of here—now. She couldn't wait one second more. Her wrists and ankles didn't even hurt anymore, she barely felt the skin tearing further, or the fresh blood that slowly dripped out of the jagged wounds the metal was leaving with every tug. It didn't matter. She was going to die one way or another, and she much preferred it be on her terms instead of the terrorists'.

GHOST HELD UP his hand, letting Wolf know to stop. They'd informed the rest of the teams they were coming in and were assisting in the search for the missing woman. They'd started on the third floor, since that was where the woman, Sarah, had said she'd last seen Rayne. Beatle was on the second floor, clearing the building as he went.

Methodically they'd cleared room after room in the east wing. They'd only run into three people. Two men and a boy. They'd been hunkered down in a room at the far end of the hallway. Ghost wasn't willing to give anyone a chance—not now, not when Rayne's life may or may not be in the palm of his hand.

After the air cleared, Ghost absently noted, as Wolf searched their pockets, that all three were holding rifles and that the young boy's pants were undone. He had no idea what *that* meant, but standing there wondering was only wasting time. Rayne was somewhere in this building and he had to find her. He knew he'd feel jittery and out of sorts until he saw with his own eyes that she was alive and unhurt.

Wolf finished his search of the dead men and he

and Ghost continued down the hall, clearing rooms, some reduced to nothing more than rubble. At the other end of the hall, closest to where one of the last explosives had been set, the men saw a door hanging on to the doorframe by the upper hinge. It was diagonal across the doorway, blocking it so they couldn't make a stealthy or easy entrance.

Ghost looked at Wolf and held up three fingers. Wolf nodded and stood on one side of the ruined door as Ghost took a position on the other side. The men nodded at each other as Ghost counted down on his fingers. Three. Two. One.

They burst into the room at the same time, rifles drawn and ready to take down anyone who might be hiding inside, just as they had for the countless rooms they'd already cleared in the long hallway.

A feminine screech greeted them as they made entry into the small room. Ghost and Wolf turned as one to the bed, rifles aimed and ready to fire. Wolf was the first to raise the barrel of his rifle up and away from the sight before them.

Ghost was only seconds behind him, but had his rifle slung over his back and was on his knees at the side of the bed before Wolf moved.

"Jesus fucking Christ." The words were quiet and heartfelt and something inside Ghost died when Rayne flinched away from him as he got close.

"Don't. Don't touch me, God, please, don't."

Ghost didn't turn toward Wolf, but heard his muttered curse.

It *was* his Rayne. She'd been chained with her arms above her head and her legs spread apart. There was blood staining the mattress under her. A fine layer of dust had settled over everything in the room, including her. She lay on the filthy mattress in only her bra and panties. As much as he hated seeing her barely clothed, Ghost was thankful she was still wearing something. A small consolation, but he was relieved nevertheless.

She was breathing hard, as if she'd just run for miles, and her eyes were fully dilated with shock and terror. The chains holding her prisoner rattled as she tried to jerk away from him when he reached his hand out to her.

Ghost knew he'd never forget the sight of her—chained, bleeding, and helpless—for as long as he lived. He'd dreamed about seeing her again, about what their reunion might be like, but this was something out of a nightmare.

"It's okay, you're going to be fine. We're American soldiers and we're going to get you out of here." For now, that's all she needed to know. He was wearing black from head to toe, and had black face paint on. If she looked closely, she'd probably recognize him, but she was simply too full of panic and adrenaline to know who he was at this point.

Ghost could see his words slowly sink in and saw the second she forcibly stopped herself from giving in to a full-blown panic attack. Whether it was the English words coming out of his mouth, or just plain ol' desperation, Rayne calmed and turned toward him with a blank look in her eyes. Seeing him, but not really seeing *him*.

"Please, get these off me, please. He's coming back. He said he'd be back. Get me out of here. He's coming back to be a man. Please, get them off."

Ghost looked down to see Wolf studying the chains and the cuffs circling her delicate ankles. He didn't understand Rayne's words, but it didn't matter. He *was* getting her the fuck out of there. "No one will put their hands on you. We'll get you out of here, Princess, hang on just a little longer for me. I've got you. You're okay."

Ghost noticed her body go stock-still, but didn't have time to do anything because Wolf said from her feet, "Ghost, I don't have the tools for this on me."

"Fuck, okay, let me see what I've got in my pack."

Ghost reached a hand into the pocket of his uniform pants. They were deep and he always stuffed them full of as much crap as he could, just in case. He'd found over the years the littlest thing could make the difference between life and death. A bobby pin once saved him and his entire team from being slaughtered deep in the heart of some Afghani hellhole.

Ghost was mentally reviewing what he might have that would work to pick the locks on the chains around Rayne's arms and legs, when he heard her disbelieving voice.

"Ghost? *My* Ghost?"

Jesus, her words made his chest physically hurt. Ghost put a hand up to his chest to rub it before he even thought about what he was doing.

Hers. Yes. He was hers.

Blade broke through his consciousness even as he was opening his mouth to agree with and reassure Rayne. His voice came over their radios, low and urgent. "Incoming. Looks as though there are two large groups of tangos on their way in. You've got ten minutes, tops. Then get out of there. Copy?"

Wolf answered even as Ghost continued his search for a tool to pick the locks around Rayne's extremities. "Copy. Found the missing package. It's going to take longer than ten minutes for extraction. Over."

"Negative," Blade insisted. "They've got RPGs and they look pissed."

"Copy." Wolf didn't say anything more, but leaned down to see if he could break the bedframe. They'd worry about the chains later if they had to.

"Oh God, they're coming?" She couldn't hear the

conversation between Blade and the rest of the teams in the building, but she'd obviously inferred enough from Wolf's side of the conversation. "Please, get me out of here, cut off my hands and feet if you have to, just don't leave me here." Rayne frantically yanked on the chains, trying once again to pull herself free.

Ghost could physically feel her panic. Cut off her hands and feet? No way in hell. He put his hands on her thrashing head and held her still. He leaned over her and put his face as close to hers as he dared. "Calm, Princess. We aren't going to leave you here. Got it? We. Aren't. Leaving. *I'm* not leaving."

"Ghost? It's really you? I don't understand. I thought I dreamed you. I was wishing you were here, keeping me safe, and now you are. Am I still dreaming? Am I dying? Shit, you're a hallucination, aren't you?"

"I'm no hallucination. I'm really here. Now, stay calm while we figure this out, okay?"

She nodded and swallowed hard. Ghost's respect for her grew. She was obviously scared out of her mind, but she was trying to control it for now.

Her voice was a bit less panicked but no less serious when she spoke again. "Seriously though...cut 'em off if you have to...I can't feel my hands or feet anyway. I'd rather that than be left here. I'd have already done it if I had a knife and a hand free. I know what an animal caught in a trap feels like now. Remember that story of the guy who was trapped when a rock fell on his arm when he was climbing? I don't remember all the details now, I think they made a movie out of it, but he cut off his arm so he could get out and get some help. I didn't get it…until now. So please, I promise I won't even feel it. Cut them off. Just get me out of here. Please, Ghost, please."

Ghost ignored her except to say, "Shhhhh, we're getting you out of here."

One, he wasn't leaving her, and two, he sure as fuck wasn't cutting off her hands and feet in order to get her out of this hellhole. He couldn't even believe the amount of bravery—and terror—it took to even suggest it in the first place. He hated she was in this predicament. *Hated* it.

He reached into his left pocket and came out with a Swiss Army Knife. He turned to Wolf. "This is the best I got. Damn, I wish Truck was here, he's the locksmith of our team."

"Benny's ours. I'd kill for a pick right about now," Wolf said absently as he leaned over Rayne's feet and quickly went to work on the lock with the knife Ghost had handed him.

Ghost looked at Rayne's wrists closely for the first time. "Oh, Princess…your wrists…you fought them hard, didn't you?"

The cuff and chain the bastards had used to imprison her and to keep her immobile were rusty, and dirty from the crumbling walls and ceiling, and now covered in Rayne's blood. Her struggles had not only ground the rust and dirt into her wounds, it had also caused the metal chains to bite deep into her wrists. She'd obviously been struggling vigorously in her panic for a while, because from what Ghost could see, she'd done quite a number on her skin.

"If you can't get them off, will you leave me a knife before you go?"

"What?"

"A knife—no, wait, I wouldn't be able to use it. Can you please just shoot me in the head before you have to leave? I'd rather die here and now than go through what they had planned for me."

Ghost knew he should be doing something to try to get her free, but he couldn't. Every word out of her mouth tore through his soul. He had no idea what had happened to her in this torture chamber, but whatever it was had made her completely panic. Her only thought was to escape. Rayne didn't look like she'd been violated, her panties were still in place and he couldn't see any blood, but Ghost knew it was certainly still a possibility.

Before he completely lost his cool, he put one gloved hand on her forehead and opened his mouth to speak, to reassure her, when she continued, sobbing.

"Please, you guys need to go, don't get caught here. These guys are crazy; they won't hesitate to kill you. You don't have time to get me loose. It's okay, just go…I lost you once, Ghost. I couldn't bear to watch them kill you. I have to know you're okay."

"Shhhh, Princess. I'm not fucking leaving you," Ghost repeated for what seemed like the tenth time. "We're all going to get out of here." Her thoughts were all over the place, first pleading for them not to leave her then ordering them to go. Ghost knew it was shock and fear, but he hated to see her this way.

"No good, Ghost," Wolf said in a frustrated voice at his feet.

Ghost turned his head and looked at his teammate for the mission.

Wolf held up the knife. "It's not skinny enough; I can't get the pins to turn. I need something smaller."

Ghost stood up and went to the head of the bed. "What if we kicked in the slats and took the chains with us?"

"I thought about that earlier. It's worth a try. If we can't get the locks undone it's the only solution besides taking the entire bed with us."

"We'll take the entire fucking thing if this doesn't work," Ghost muttered under his breath, knowing it would be awkward at best, and incredibly dangerous and stupid at worst, to try to escape in the middle of a terrorist coup carrying a bed with a wounded and terrified woman on it. It'd be like shooting fish in a barrel. They'd be sitting ducks.

"I have something that might work."

Wolf and Ghost turned to look at Rayne incredulously.

"What?" Wolf asked in an impatient tone, finding his voice before Ghost could. Time was running out. Neither of them wanted to look down the barrel of a shoulder launcher at a rocket-propelled grenade. They'd all be on the losing end of that confrontation.

"My barrette. Chase gave it to me. It's full of all sorts of things. A small blade, a screwdriver, and a lock pick. He tried to show me how to use it once, but I was hopeless. I don't know if it'll work or not, shit, it's probably a novelty thing that will break off in the lock, but maybe..." Her words trailed off at the men's matching expressions of disbelief.

Ghost watched as Rayne turned her head awkwardly and he saw an antique-gold barrette in her hair. He reached for it and it unsnapped easily. He pulled it out and examined it. She was right, the prong in the middle opened up into a sharp point.

He handed it without a word to Wolf, who leaned over her ankles with a smile. "Only *you* would find a woman who'd happen to be carrying the exact tool needed to rescue herself, Ghost. Only you. Damn."

Ghost leaned down and placed a quick, gentle kiss on her forehead, ignoring the dirt. "You're amazing. Hang on, Princess, We'll have you out of here in a jiffy."

It wasn't quite a jiffy, but amazingly, the hair clip worked. After freeing her feet, Wolf passed it to Ghost, who made quick work of the locks at her wrists. After he freed her, Ghost quickly replaced the barrette, making sure to clip her hair back so it wouldn't fall into her face as they made their escape.

After being released from the chains, Rayne sat up quickly on the bed and would've stood and run out of the room if not for Ghost's hand on her arm, holding her still. "Hang on, Princess, let's get you a shirt, yeah?"

Rayne nodded and tried not to be self-conscious about her almost-nudity. It wasn't as if Ghost hadn't seen all of her before, and Wolf wasn't even looking at her. He was at the door peering out carefully.

"I can't believe it's really you," Rayne breathed as she watched Ghost quickly shrug out of his bulletproof vest so he could remove the black shirt underneath.

"It's me. *I* couldn't believe when your friend said there was a woman named Rayne still somewhere in the building."

"Sarah? You found her and the others? They didn't blow up? The assholes said they blew up the room."

Ghost nodded. "They did blow it up. But the

217

women managed to get behind something. Some are hurt, but as of now they're all safe."

"Thank God. And the men who were with them?"

"Them too."

"Good."

"Come on, arms up. We need to get out of here."

Rayne did as Ghost ordered and obediently lifted her arms. She didn't even wince when the shirt scraped against her wrists and blood ran down her arms in rivulets.

"I'm sorry if I hurt you, Princess."

"Honestly, I can't feel them, Ghost." At his frown, she tried to reassure him again. "My ankles either. They don't hurt. It's okay."

When he continued to frown, Rayne only shrugged. "Let's get out of here. I'm ready. Please?" Rayne stood up and went to take a step to the door and would've fallen flat on her face if Ghost hadn't been there to grab hold of her. He scooped her up in his arms and strode toward the door.

"I-I don't know what's wrong. I can walk...at least I think I can."

"I've got you, Rayne. Hang on to me and don't let go." Ghost followed Wolf out of the room and into the deserted hallway.

"That I can do," Rayne slurred.

Blade's voice came over their headsets. "ETA? Tangos entering the complex on the west side. Copy? Coming in hot and heavy on the west. Everyone else is out. Over."

"We're east, coming out with the package. Ghost's hands are tied. We'll need backup. Over."

"Copy. Get the fuck out of there. Fletch and Truck are on their way to assist."

Both Ghost and Wolf breathed a sigh of relief. They weren't out of danger by any stretch, but having Ghost's men on the way would make any fight they had to engage in more in their favor. With Truck, especially. The man was huge and no one in their right mind would mess with him. He wasn't pretty, not even close. His nose had been broken several times and he had a scar that he'd gotten courtesy of a pissed-off terrorist that pulled the side of his mouth down into a perpetual scowl.

No, he certainly wasn't a ladies' man, more often than not they ran in the opposite direction when they saw him. He was exactly who Ghost needed right now, however. He needed a mean motherfucker to help them get out of there in one piece.

"How're you holding up, Princess?" Ghost murmured as they made their way through the eerily quiet hallways.

"I'm tired. I'm so tired."

Ghost jostled the precious bundle in his arms.

"Don't fall asleep. You're losing too much blood, you can't go to sleep. Do you hear me, Rayne?"

He felt her try to sit up straighter in his arms, but she didn't have the strength to do it. One of her arms was around his neck and he could feel the blood from her wrist oozing down the inside of his vest against his now-naked back. It was warm against his skin and knowing it was her blood, and not sweat, made him slightly nauseous.

"So I was right about you being a super-spy after all, huh?"

Ghost squeezed Rayne in response, but didn't say anything.

"Wearing all black, no insignia on your clothes...you're either a spy or CIA. No way you can be a normal solider."

Ghost heard Wolf chuckle almost soundlessly through their radio. He'd opened his mic in case he needed to talk to his team while his arms were full with Rayne.

Rayne continued. "No matter what happens, thank you. I'm guessing you weren't there for *me*, you said you didn't know I was there until Sarah told you, but thank you for coming to find me. Thank you for blowing shit up so Moshe couldn't rape me."

"What?" Ghost gritted out softly. Wolf held up a hand for them to stop and motioned for them to duck into a small room to wait out the small band of militants passing by their exit. They were three feet from freedom, but they couldn't rush their escape. The last thing either man wanted was to have to make a run for it once they got outside.

"They'd made up some bullshit ceremony for boys to become men. It involved raping me seven times, including sodomizing me, fucking me from behind, and forcing me to take him in my mouth." Her words were slurring more and more as she continued.

Neither man interrupted her, wanting to hear the entire story to know how to help her get through it, but also wanting to go back and kill every man they'd come across all over again.

"And get this…if he couldn't make me come the seventh time, he didn't succeed in becoming a man and I'd have to go through it all again. As if any woman would orgasm after being raped over and over again…"

"Did he touch you, Princess?" Ghost's words were low and agonized, but Rayne didn't seem to notice.

"No, not like that. He didn't have time. As I said, you blew shit up right when he was about to start. So thank you. But you should know…my last thought was of you. I tried to remember your smell, your hands, and how delicious you made me feel…I wanted that to be my last thought, not of him and what he was going to do to me. I missed you, Ghost." Her voice dropped to a whisper, almost as if she were talking to herself. "I missed you."

Rayne took a deep, slow breath that hitched before she continued, her voice trembling. "He said he'd be back. He looked like a nice boy, but the look in his eyes told me he was anything but. Ghost?"

"Yeah, Princess?"

She was whispering again now, as if saying it out loud would make him materialize from thin air. "He's coming back to finish becoming a man."

"He's not coming back."

"He is. He said so. He turned to me when they were all running out of the room like scared little pricks. I believed him. He wants to be a man."

"He's dead, Princess. I killed him."

Her eyes opened and she tried to lift her head off his shoulder, but couldn't quite manage it. "You did?"

"Yeah."

"Are you sure? You're not just telling me that to try to protect me like you always do?"

Ignoring the immediate thought that he wanted to spend the rest of his life protecting her, Ghost asked in an even voice, "Was he wearing tan pants with a drawstring? Blue shirt?"

"Uh-huh."

"Then I can tell you with one hundred percent certainty he will never be a man. *Ever.*"

"Thank God. Ghost?"

Wolf motioned that the coast was clear and they headed out of the building where Rayne's nightmare had begun a week ago. Ghost was pissed, understanding now why the boy's pants had been undone. The little fucker had gotten way too close to violating Rayne. *Way* too close.

"Yeah, Princess?" Ghost repeated.

"I can't stay awake. I tried. I did. But if I wake up, will you be there? I don't want to wake up to an empty bed again."

Ghost didn't want her to go unconscious, but she'd lost a lot of blood and it might be better if she didn't remember anything that happened as they fled the building. If they ran into trouble, he didn't want that on her conscience as well. He didn't like the word "if" she'd used though. "You *will* wake up, Rayne. We have too much unfinished business for any other outcome. And you better believe I'll be there," he said, his words giving her permission to let go.

Ghost looked down at Rayne after she finally succumbed to unconsciousness and went limp in his arms. It made it tougher to carry her. The good thing was that now he didn't have to worry as much about not jostling her. He couldn't hurt her if she was out. The blood from her wrist continued to drip down his back and the blood from her ankles was dripping on the ground as they continued out into the stifling Egyptian air.

"Wolf," Ghost growled, getting his teammate's attention. When he turned, Ghost nodded his head toward Rayne's bleeding ankles.

Wolf nodded and keyed the mic, "Truck, package needs tape, we're leaving a trail. Coming in fast and hot. Be ready to FedEx the hell out of there."

"Ten-four."

As Wolf and Ghost headed toward the pickup point so they could get out of Egypt and get Rayne some medical attention, Wolf mused in a serious voice to Ghost, "I don't know what happened before today between you two, but you have a wonderful woman in your arms. Figure your shit out and don't let her go."

"It's not that easy," Ghost protested.

"The fuck it's not. Someday I'll tell you the story of my own woman, Caroline. And if there's time, you can listen to the rest of my team tell their stories. We were just like you and your group. Badass Navy SEALs who didn't need women in our lives. We thought there was no way it could ever work, but we were wrong, and so are you. Give her some credit."

"We're Delta."

"So? If anyone gets it, we do. We can't tell our women anything. They don't know where we are or how long we'll be gone. There's no guarantee we'll come home, but they love us anyway."

Ghost grunted, but didn't say anything.

"Don't let her go, Ghost. From what I can tell, she's an amazing woman. She needs you, especially after what happened in there. You, out of anyone she knows, understand and can help her. But more than that, you need *her* too. I can see it."

Ghost had never been so glad to see Fletch and Truck in all his life. He wasn't comfortable with Wolf's words. He wanted the woman in his arms more than he'd ever wanted anything; he just had no idea how to accomplish it. Wolf said it could work, but Ghost had no idea how.

First things first. Rayne needed a doctor and they needed to get the fuck out of Egypt.

After that? Who knew?

Chapter Twenty-One

RAYNE LAY SLEEPING on the makeshift bed Ghost had made for her. Luckily, their escape from the square had been anticlimactic. They hadn't run into any more militants and the Egyptian Army had finally gotten serious about making sure the coup was squashed once and for all. They'd swept into the government building after hearing all the hostages had been rescued and hadn't wasted time trying to negotiate or take anyone alive.

The sympathizers who'd been on their way with their RPGs had been taken out before they were able to set off any of the rockets. For now, the building was secure, but everyone knew that chopping off the arms and legs of the beast wouldn't keep it down for long. The head would have to be cut off for the coup to be fully extinguished. And the likelihood of that was slim. Ghost wouldn't be surprised if they found themselves back in Egypt sooner rather than later. But that was fine with him. He'd gladly take out the fuckers who had hurt Rayne. They might not have physically been in that room with her, but they'd given the militants the firepower to make it happen.

Ghost didn't care about the Egyptian Army at the moment. All he cared about was Rayne and making sure she was safe and healthy. Truck and Fletch had met them in a back alley off the square and quickly wrapped Rayne's ankles and wrists in pressure bandages. Truck had lifted Rayne out of Ghost's arms as if she didn't weigh more than a child, and they'd hurried off to meet the rest of the teams.

Ghost would've protested, but he knew Truck could carry Rayne for miles and not tire…he was that big and strong. Besides, Ghost was hoping they'd run into more militants so he could blow them away to get some revenge for what Rayne had gone through.

They'd met no resistance and arrived back with the teams within ten minutes. Mozart, one of the SEALs, had asked if they were taking Rayne to the Red Cross hospital that had been set up to deal with the hostages, and before Ghost could answer, Wolf spoke up.

"No, she's Ghost's. She stays with us all the way home."

Not one man argued, not one man questioned Wolf's statement. If she was one of theirs, then there was no question that she wasn't going to be let out of their sights.

Ghost looked into the eyes of the SEALs standing

around him. Every single one of the men, who he knew were just as deadly as his own team of Deltas, had looks of compassion and care on their faces. If he hadn't seen it for himself, he never would've believed in the middle of a mission, in the middle of a country on the verge of civil war, a group of badass Alpha men could be touched by the plight of a woman, who certainly wasn't looking her best at the moment.

Besides only wearing his T-shirt, Rayne's hair was covered in dirt and it lay lankly around her face. She had dark circles under her eyes, along with bruises on both cheeks. She hadn't said the assholes hit her, but it was obvious they had. She wasn't a small woman, but lying hurt and dirty in his teammate's arms, she looked small and defenseless.

Rayne stirred in Truck's hold and her eyes opened into slits. She looked up at the large man who was holding her, and instead of freaking out, as some women had done in the past when they'd been confronted with Truck's face, she merely smiled a half smile and mumbled, "I hope you killed the fucker who hurt you," and she passed back out.

The look on Truck's face would've been comical if the situation wasn't so urgent.

They'd set Rayne down and Truck and Mozart got to work on her wounds. They were deep and the two men didn't want to stitch them up without thoroughly cleaning them first. For now, they did the best they could with what little sterile fluid they had in their packs and re-wrapped them tightly. Thankfully, Rayne didn't move throughout what had to be a very painful process.

Ghost stayed by her, with one hand resting on her forehead the entire time. When they were done, Truck picked her up again and all thirteen men made their way to their extraction point.

Now they were on the military plane, headed back to the States. They'd land at Fort Hood first, then the SEALs would be returning to California, to their own base and their families.

Rayne was in the back of the plane on the pallet that had been made for her. She'd go straight to the hospital when they landed in Texas for some advanced medical care. Ghost had no idea what would happen after they landed.

"This reminds me of Caroline, Wolf," Cookie said with a smile as they all got settled, remembering how they'd stolen Wolf's woman away from a "situation" once. She'd lain on a pallet at the back of a military plane, much as Rayne did now.

Wolf smiled in memory, but didn't say anything.

"So, what's the story, Ghost?" Dude asked.

Ghost kept quiet.

Not taking the hint, Dude continued pushing. "She

doesn't know you're Delta?"

Ghost shook his head.

"What're you going to do about it?"

Ghost shrugged. "Nothing."

"Dumbass," Abe murmured under his breath.

"Watch it, Frog," Fletch warned, standing up for his teammate.

"I already gave him the talk," Wolf informed his team easily, not in the least perturbed by the hostility emanating from Ghost's teammate. "Told him he would be an idiot to let her go. You guys know how long it took me to claim Caroline. I didn't want him to have to go through the same shit I did."

Ghost broke in before his guys lost it. The last thing they needed was a SEAL-against-Delta fight at thirty-six thousand feet. He had no doubt his guys would win, but it'd be a tough fight. "Look, we met about six months ago. We had a...thing. A one-night thing. That's all it was."

"You haven't hooked up since then, have you, Ghost?" Blade asked knowing a bit more than Ghost would like.

Hollywood whistled low and long, joining in the conversation. "She got to you."

"Shut it, guys," Ghost warned. "We've been busy. Just because I haven't had the time to fuck doesn't mean I've been pining over Rayne."

"It makes sense now," Coach broke in, ignoring his leader's warning. "You've had time, Ghost. Don't fucking lie. That night a month or so ago when we all went out and that barrack bunny was all over you…couldn't figure out why you didn't take that home and tap it, but now we know."

Ghost did not want to discuss this, but it looked like he wasn't going to get his way. "That's not why, asshole. I was tired and she looked like she'd want to hang on for more than a night."

"Bullshit," Fletch said in an easygoing voice. "She wanted what all barrack bunnies want…one night with a military man. She was as much a sure thing as you could get."

Ghost stayed quiet. They were right. The chick in question *had* been all over him, practically had her hand down his pants right there at the bar. He could've taken her in the back alley, had her suck him off, and been back in the bar within ten minutes. But the second he felt her breath on his neck, all he could remember was Rayne's sweet little nips and sucks against him as she lay exhausted in his arms. He hadn't had a woman since Rayne, and hadn't even missed it.

"It was after that mission in Turkey, wasn't it?" Truck asked. "You had that layover in London. You were a day later than the rest of us getting back because your flight was canceled. That was about six months ago."

"It's fate, Ghost. My advice? Don't fight it," Wolf said with certainty.

Ghost never would've opened up, but he was tired and worried about Rayne, and still felt a bit off-kilter about finding her in the middle of an op. And knowing she'd almost been raped and violated over and over again, all in the name of some fake ideological crap, made him feel raw and even vulnerable.

"I lied to her. She doesn't even know my name."

"She called you Ghost in there," Wolf pointed out easily. "She knew who you were immediately."

"That's not my name though."

"It's who you are," Beatle insisted, repeating what Fletch had told him earlier. "You're Ghost. I'm Beatle. That's Blade and Truck and Fletch. Half the time I don't even remember our given names. You know Coach won't even *tell* us his real name. He goes by his middle name, but hasn't told a soul what his first name is. What did she call out in the middle of her orgasm?"

Ghost glared at Beatle. "I'm not fucking telling you that."

Beatle continued as if Ghost had answered him affirmatively. "Yeah, that's what I thought. You didn't lie about who you were, Ghost. That's what matters."

"I left her in the morning. I didn't even wake her up to say goodbye." Why Ghost continued to tell the guys everything he'd done, he had no idea. All he knew was that he felt guilty as hell, even though he'd done the same thing time and time again with other women, women whose names he couldn't remember.

"Did you promise her you'd keep in touch?"

Damn. Fletch had already been over this with him, but was rehashing for the other guys.

"No," Ghost said, disgruntled.

Fletch continued, "So she knew it was a one-night thing. I'm assuming she agreed."

Ghost nodded reluctantly.

"Sounds to me as if she knew what she was getting into."

Ghost ran his hand through his hair in frustration. "She did, but she didn't. She'd never had a one-night stand before. She's a romantic. She…she expected more. I know she did."

The men were silent for a beat, and then Wolf spoke up. Ghost didn't know Wolf that well, but he could tell he was one hundred percent sincere when he spoke.

"I tried to push my Caroline away. Thought I was doing the right thing. We know our jobs are dangerous. There's no way I'd want any blowback on her. She'd been kidnapped, had the shit beaten out of her, among other things, and after we rescued her, she looked at me as if I was the sun in her sky…and I pushed her away. I thought it was for her own good. I didn't think I was good for her."

When he paused, Ghost said, "And?"

Wolf smiled a bit. "And, it was all bullshit. I wanted her more than I wanted anything in my entire life. She made me happy, she made me feel human. I wanted to steal her away. Make it so no other man would dare look at what was mine."

"So you went to her and now all's well."

The other SEALs laughed at that. Wolf said drolly, "Not quite. Cookie here gave her his trident pin."

Truck blew out a loud, disbelieving breath. They all knew what the pins meant that SEALs earned once they were officially made part of the teams. For Cookie to give Wolf's woman his SEAL pin had to have been a low blow for Wolf.

"Yeah. Pissed me off. Took me quite a bit of time to exchange his for mine. Fucker. I didn't get it away from her until our wedding." Wolf mock-glared at Cookie, who merely chuckled back at his team leader. It was clear the two men were close.

"It wasn't an easy road. She was upset. I was upset, but in the end, she was mine. That's all it was. She. Was. Mine. The thought of any other man putting his hands on her, of looking at her, of giving her the things she needed in her life, made me crazy. Bottom line is, Ghost, if the thought of her snuggling up to another man doesn't make you want to kill someone, then let her go to live that life. She'll find another man to make her feel good, to marry, to have babies with." Wolf was purposely twisting the knife, trying to rile Ghost and make him *think*. "But if you want her...figure out how to make it work because she'll complete you in a way no one else ever has or will."

The men were quiet after Wolf's speech and slowly they drifted off to sleep. Ghost knew he wouldn't sleep, not with worry for Rayne and Wolf's words rattling around in his head. He went to the back of the plane and took a seat next to Rayne's bed. She'd turned, awkwardly lying on her side, facing the back of the plane.

She was still wearing his T-shirt and the sheet that had been placed over her had fallen below her butt as she'd shifted. The tattoo on her lower back that Ghost had admired all those months ago was clearly visible with her movements. He stared at it for a moment, not believing what he was seeing. His first thought was to cover her up so any of the other guys on the plane wouldn't see her, but he was frozen in place, seeing her tattoo that had so moved him again.

When he'd given her his T-shirt in the government building, he'd only been concerned about preserving her modesty and getting the hell out of the room and situation. As much as he loved seeing her naked, that had been the last thing on his mind. When Truck and Mozart had been patching her up, again, she'd been covered from her neck to her thighs by his shirt, and he was more concerned about the wounds on her ankles and wrists than anything else.

But now, seeing the tattoo that had meant so much to him, and the recent alterations, made his breath catch.

She'd added him to her skin.

Oh, he'd already seen himself in her tattoo the way it had been, but now if he'd thought he could deny that their one night meant anything to her, he couldn't anymore. The proof was in front of him in Technicolor—and it literally made him want to cry.

Fletch cleared his throat behind him, thankfully preventing Ghost from bawling like a baby. He quickly grabbed the sheet and brought it up and over Rayne, shielding her from his teammate's eyes. Ghost didn't want anyone seeing what was his.

"Looks like that one-night stand was a bit more intense than you wanted to admit, on both your parts."

Fuck. He'd been too slow to cover her up and Fletch had obviously gotten a good look at Rayne's tattoo. Ghost stayed silent and didn't look up at his friend, not sure what to say.

"Her tattoo looks familiar…much like the one you got on your leg a few months ago."

Ghost still said nothing. There was nothing to say.

Fletch sighed. Then surprised Ghost by admitting out of the blue, "I've met someone. She's funny and amazing and is more stubborn than anyone I've ever known. She's got secrets, and won't let me in. But the worst thing is that she seems to already have a man."

Ghost did look up at that. His friend was standing with one shoulder against the wall, seemingly relaxed, but every muscle in his body was tense and Ghost could tell he was anything but.

"Every time I see them together I want to pound something. She's got an amazing little girl who is scared of this new guy."

"Fletch—"

He didn't let Ghost continue. "I heard what Wolf said, and he's right. I haven't even touched this woman, but if the simple *thought* of her new asshole boyfriend doing anything to hurt her or her daughter makes me this crazy, I can't imagine what you're going through. If she's yours," Fletch motioned with his head to Rayne, "you need to fight for her, Ghost. And it's obvious she's yours. Looks like you inked her on you, and if that little fucking ghost on her skin is any indication, she's inked you on her too."

"But the teams—"

"You think we won't support you? Think we won't protect her as we do you? What do we all have inked on our sides, Ghost? Huh? *Defend my brothers and their women.* We all want someone. Why would we put that in writing on our bodies if we didn't? For Christ's sake, Ghost. Don't let her go again."

Ghost looked back at Rayne. She was huddled under the sheet and her back moved up and down with her deep, sedated breaths. He nodded once and heard Fletch walk away to leave him alone with Rayne.

After watching her sleep, Ghost made his decision.

He'd fight for her, but he wasn't sure if Rayne would fight for him in return. He knew he had a long road ahead of him. He'd rescued her, yes, but he had a long way to go to get her to trust him again. He understood that as clearly as if Rayne had turned around and said the words.

"I swear to you, Rayne. I will never lie to you again. Never." The vow was quiet and heartfelt, and Ghost meant every word, even if Rayne didn't hear it.

Unable to resist, Ghost pulled the sheet back to take another look at her tattoo. Big Ben was new and stood tall and proud behind one of the wings of the huge eagle. The words "Quiet Professionalism" were written in script, like clouds around the tower. The little ghost looked almost alive, flitting around the clock tower, proof that he wasn't a fleeting part in her life. He touched it reverently with one finger.

Rayne shifted at his touch, pressing backwards as if

unconsciously reaching for him.

Without thinking about it, Ghost eased himself onto the small mattress and fitted her to his front, careful not to jostle her wounds in any way. It was a tight fit on the cot. He was fully dressed, even wearing his boots, but he needed to hold her, to be close to her, to keep her safe.

Ghost pulled the sheet back up and over them, wanting to be sure Rayne was warm enough. He gingerly put one arm around her waist, and eased the other under her head.

Feeling content for the first time in six months when Rayne snuggled back into his embrace, he closed his eyes and prayed. Prayed she'd forgive him his lies, prayed they'd find a way to make a relationship work. They had a lot to figure out, but lying there with Rayne safe in his arms, Ghost couldn't think about anything other than how relieved he was that fate had led him to her when she'd needed him most.

Chapter Twenty-Two

RAYNE GROGGILY OPENED her eyes and flinched at the bright light, immediately closing them again. She felt herself being jostled and heard soft voices around her. It took her a moment to remember what had happened, but as soon as she did, she opened her eyes into slits, being a bit more cautious this time.

She was lying on something soft and being wheeled into a building. She turned her head and gasped.

Ghost. It really *was* him.

Slowly, the pieces of her capture and rescue came back to her. Just when she thought she'd die in that building in Cairo, Ghost had shown up as if by a miracle.

He'd been patient and calm, and he and his...partner...whatever the other guy was, had gotten the damn chains off of her and Ghost had carried her to safety. Rayne remembered bits and pieces after that. Swallowing a couple of pills, the pain of her wounds being cleaned, and being held in Ghost's arms as she slept. That last bit she wasn't sure about, since she'd dreamed about being in his arms almost every night since he'd left her in London.

"Ghost?" The word was shaky and rough, and came out more a croak than an actual word, but he heard her.

He put his hand on her shoulder and looked down at her as they continued moving into the building. "Hey, Princess. You're awake."

"Kinda."

He chuckled. "Yeah, those sedatives we gave you along with the painkillers are pretty potent. You're going to be fine." He got right to it. "You're at Darnell Army Medical Center at Fort Hood. You're safe and back on American soil."

"Texas?"

"Yeah. You're back in Texas."

"My stuff?"

"Stuff?"

"Yeah, at the hotel."

Ghost chuckled. "Only a woman would think about her stuff after what you've been through. Your friend, Sarah, was going to see to it."

"My brother?"

"I'll make sure he knows you're here."

"Okay. Ghost?"

"Yeah?"

The gurney stopped in a small examining room and

Rayne felt almost dizzy at the abrupt cessation of movement. She felt her eyes getting heavy again, and closed them. "Are you gonna be here when I wake up again?"

When he didn't answer her right away, Rayne forced her eyes open. If this was going to be the last time she saw Ghost, she didn't want to miss it.

"Yes. I'll be right here when you wake up."

She didn't want to say it, but the word came out anyway. "Promise?"

"I promise, Princess."

"Okay. Ghost?"

There was a smile in his voice this time. "Yeah?"

"Did you cut them off after all? I can't feel them."

Rayne didn't see the harsh concerned look on Ghost's face, as her eyelids had drooped closed.

"No, Rayne. We didn't cut off your hands or feet. They're still there, but they're in bad shape. I swear I'll never lie to you again. You'll have some nasty scars."

"Don't care. Again? You lied before?"

Ghost put his hand on Rayne's forehead and his voice softened. "Yeah, but that will be the last time. You want to know something, ask." He thought Rayne might've been concerned about having scars, but he should've known she wouldn't give a damn about that. He'd taken Wolf's words to heart. He wanted Rayne. It wouldn't be easy, but she was worth fighting for. He felt normal when he was with her, and that alone made him want to be a better person...for her. He'd not let her go without a fight.

"Okay."

And that was that. Rayne was out. The doctor came in and immediately got to work taking off the make-shift bandages to see what he had to deal with. After making sure he knew what he was doing, Ghost went back out to the waiting room to find all six of his teammates there.

"Truck, will you go and keep an eye on Rayne? I have something I need to do."

"Of course."

"Keep me updated."

Truck nodded and headed back the way Ghost had come. It wasn't usual procedure for any of them to be in the room with a patient, but the colonel made a phone call to some high-ranking officer at the hospital, and they were given some latitude as a result.

"Anything we can help with?" Fletch asked.

Ghost shook his head. "No, but thanks. I'll be back in a bit."

His teammates nodded and Ghost left the hospital and headed for the officer barracks. Six months ago when he'd gotten back to Fort Hood, after the night that changed his life, he'd made it a point to look up Rayne's brother. He was a first lieutenant and Ghost had been impressed. He'd graduated near the top of his West Point class, chose counterterrorism as his specialty, and had nothing but glowing OERs, Officer Evaluation Reports. He was shaping up to be a good leader. The kind who cared about the men under his command. He asked questions of the sergeants in his platoons and took their advice. Lieutenant Jackson was up for promotion and Ghost knew he'd make it with flying colors.

As it was eight in the evening, Ghost hoped the man would probably be in his room. He walked up the stairs to the third floor and knocked on the door.

Chase Jackson opened the door almost immediately. "Yes?"

Ghost was still wearing the same clothes he'd been in for forty-eight hours. He wasn't at his best, and there was no indication of his rank or name anywhere on his vest. On missions, and even around Fort Hood, none of the Deltas wore any kind of identifying information on them for their own safety.

"My name is Captain Keane Bryson. May I come in for a moment?"

Chase looked confused, but stood aside anyway and gestured for Ghost to come inside.

Neither man said anything as Chase led Ghost into the small living room of the one-bedroom apartment. Ghost got right to the point.

"I've just returned from Egypt. Cairo, more exact." Ghost watched Chase stiffen in front of him. Yeah, the man knew the significance of where he'd been.

"Your sister was one of the hostages in the coup."

The lieutenant paled and swayed on his feet. For a second Ghost thought he was gonna face plant on the floor. His hand came out and he propped himself up against the doorjamb. He swallowed once, hard, then swore.

"Fucking shit. Is she… Are you casualty assistance?"

Ghost knew what he was asking. Casualty assistance officers were sent to the homes of relatives when someone was killed in action to inform them of what happened. No one wanted to open their doors to them. He quickly reassured the other man. "No. I'm part of the unit that was sent in to rescue hostages. We got her out. She was wounded, but is okay and here at Darnell Army Medical Center."

Chase narrowed his eyes and tilted his head. He wasn't an idiot. "And *you're* here telling me this be-cause…"

Ghost's respect for the man increased. Ghost out-ranked Chase, and even without knowing he was a Delta Force soldier, he was astute enough to realize something else was going on. Maybe Rayne's brother did know he was Delta. He was in counterterrorism; it wasn't as if he didn't know Special Forces soldiers were around—and if Ghost had been over in Egypt, it was likely Chase knew he was more than a simple captain. For someone like Chase, the fact that Ghost was here in his living room wearing all black, with no visible rank, was as much an admission of who he was than if he was wearing a badge that said "Delta Force Soldier."

"Because she's mine." Ghost's words were blunt and to the point. He held up a hand when Chase opened his mouth and quickly broke down his relationship with Rayne for her brother. "I met your sister about six months ago. We didn't spend a lot of time together, but that's done now. I'm going to do everything I can to make it work between us. I'm here because I wanted to talk to you first. She was hurt over there. She's going to be okay, but she's probably going to need to talk to someone about what happened."

"What *did* happen?"

Ghost knew Chase would get back to the "she's mine" statement, but he was glad to see he was more worried about his sister's well-being at the moment than he was about Ghost's arrogant statement. "She's dehydrated and she's lost some weight, and she was almost raped before I got to her."

"Almost?"

"Almost."

"Thank Christ. But she's hurt?"

"They chained her to a bed, and she...struggled."

A wry smile flitted over Chase's countenance before he got serious again. "Yeah, she would."

"That clip you gave her very well might have saved her life."

Chase smiled a real smile that time and he nodded. "I'll make sure she has a lifetime supply of them."

"Her wrists and ankles are torn to shreds. She's getting them stitched now. I know she'd want to see you when she wakes up."

"I'll head over there as soon as we're done here. Now…what makes you think she wants to be with you?"

"You see the addition to her tattoo?"

Chase startled at that. "She added on to that monstrosity on her back?"

Ghost nodded. "Yeah. She added me."

Chase eyed the hard-looking man in front of him. "She hasn't been the same sister in the last few months."

Ghost simply nodded. He hadn't been the same since he'd left her in that hotel room in London either. So he knew exactly what Chase meant.

"Don't hurt her. I know you outrank me and probably have more power than I could ever hope to have, but I swear to God, if you hurt her—"

"I can't guarantee that I won't, we're both pretty stubborn, but she's mine. I'll kill to keep her safe. I'll fight for her. I'm not giving her up."

Chase didn't respond right away, mulling over Ghost's words. Finally, he held out his hand. "It's good to meet you, Keane Bryson."

He shook his hand. "Ghost. It's Ghost."

"Ghost then."

"I'm headed back over to the hospital now."

"I'm coming with you."

Ghost knew he'd say that, so he simply nodded.

"Give me five to change and get ready."

"I'll be out front," Ghost told Chase as he turned to the door.

"Ghost?"

Ghost turned back to Chase.

"Thanks for rescuing Rayne. And thanks for letting me know."

Ghost nodded again and closed the door behind him. He wanted to get over to the hospital and be there for Rayne, but he'd needed to do this. Needed to be the one to let Chase know about his sister and needed him to know where he stood with her. Ghost knew it wouldn't be smooth sailing, but he'd made the first step.

Chapter Twenty-Three

"**C**HASE, FOR THE love of God, I'm fine," Rayne grumbled as her brother fluffed her pillows behind her back for the third time that day.

She'd woken up in a room at the hospital to see Ghost sleeping in a chair next to her bed. She'd watched him for a while, amazed he was actually there. He'd stayed, just as he said he would. Rayne drank him in as he slept, thinking he looked tired. He was dirty, his black boots and trousers covered in a fine layer of dust. His broad arms were crossed over his chest. The only thing that looked clean about him was his T-shirt. It was obviously new, the creases from where it'd been folded inside a package still evident.

She'd shifted in bed, trying to get comfortable, and Rayne had been amazed how one minute Ghost was asleep, and the next he was wide awake, his eyes finding her face seconds after stirring.

"Morning, Princess."

The words had been unexpected, more so because she'd so longed to hear them that morning so long ago.

She'd cleared her throat. "Morning."

Ghost had stood up and arched, putting both hands in the small of his back as if working the kinks out. He'd leaned over and put one of his large, calloused hands on her forehead. She remembered he'd done that the day before as well. "How're you feeling?"

"I'm good," she'd said automatically.

Ghost had cocked his head and asked again. "How're you *really* feeling?"

Rayne had sighed. "Slightly dizzy from too many drugs and not enough food, but I'm alive, not chained to a filthy bed, and not dealing with being raped over and over. I'm good."

Ghost's mouth had twitched, but he hadn't responded to her snarky remark. "Up to a visitor?"

"Aren't *you* a visitor?"

He did smile at that, and ignoring her comment, he'd said casually, "I'll go get him."

Before Rayne could ask who Ghost meant, or any of the other four hundred and fifty-seven questions rattling around in her brain, he was gone.

She'd shifted in the bed uncomfortably. She'd lifted her right arm only to see bandages covering her from her fingers to her elbow. She'd moved her legs under the blanket and could tell they were similarly bandaged. She had wanted to see the damage, now that she was lucid enough to understand what it might mean, but it'd have to wait. Her limbs were still attached, hopefully that meant she'd get to keep them.

The door to her room had opened and Rayne had looked over and bit her lip. For some reason, her brother was the last person she'd expected to walk through the door, but he was the one person she needed to see after everything she'd been through in the last week or so.

They'd hugged each other and Rayne had cried on his shoulder for at least ten minutes, not noticing when Ghost left the room, before Chase pulled back and tugged the chair that Ghost had been sitting in closer to the bed. He kept his hand on her bandaged forearm as they spoke.

Rayne learned that Samantha was flying in that morning and would be there in a few hours. She'd tried to insist she was fine, but Chase just shrugged and said Sam would be there regardless.

The morning had passed quickly. The doctor came in and examined her wounds before her sister arrived. Rayne had watched attentively as he'd pulled back the bandages, but had to look away after a quick glance. She wasn't usually squeamish, but the oozing, pus-filled, infected wounds were more than her stomach could take at the moment.

The doctor informed her that she'd be staying at least another couple of nights, until the infection was under control. They were pouring heavy-duty antibiotics into her body through the IV. Once a few doses of those were given, they'd consider releasing her.

When Rayne went to protest, the doctor reminded her that if she didn't get the proper care for her wounds, she actually could lose all four of her extremities. That was enough to scare her into agreeing to stay as long as the doctor deemed appropriate. She might have told Ghost and his partner to cut them off in the middle of her rescue, but that was the last thing she really wanted to happen.

Samantha had arrived later that morning and the three siblings had a long chat about what had happened to Rayne in Egypt and how she was doing. Chase even had Rayne agreeing to talk to one of the Army psychologists. She thought she was doing okay, but knew later she'd probably have more time to think about what had actually happened…and almost happened.

It was now late in the afternoon and Chase was driving Rayne crazy. She'd convinced Samantha she was fine, and since her sister had an audition the next day, she'd agreed to leave on the next plane out of Austin, as long as Rayne kept her up to date on everything that was going on.

"Seriously, Chase, I'm fine, stop hovering," Rayne complained.

Chase sat in the chair and propped his elbows on

the mattress beside her hip. Noticing her glancing at the door for the twentieth time that day, he said, "I'm sure he'll be back."

Rayne looked up at her brother in surprise. "Who?"

"Don't act dumb, sis. You know who. Keane."

"Keane?"

Chase blew out a breath in frustration. "Yeah, Keane. Ghost? The man who stated to me bold as brass that you were his woman?"

"His name is John, not Keane."

Chase studied Rayne and could tell she was serious. "He told me his name was Keane Bryson."

"And he told *me* it was John Benbrook."

The two siblings looked at each other for a moment, neither saying anything. Chase clenched his teeth together and the muscle in his jaw ticked, as it did when he was pissed.

She thought back to Ghost's words when she was brought in. He'd told her he'd never lie to her *again*.

Damn, she was pathetic. She tried to play it off.

"Whatever, it doesn't matter. I wasn't watching for him."

"I don't care if he *is* Delta, I'm going to kick his ass."

"Delta? What's that?" Rayne asked, completely confused now.

"*Motherfucker*," Chase exclaimed, pushing his chair

back. "I'll be back tomorrow to see you, yeah?"

"Chase! What are you talking about? Why are you so pissed?"

Her brother leaned down and kissed Rayne on the cheek. "I'll be back in the morning."

Rayne watched in confusion as her brother stormed out of the room, mumbling under his breath.

Chase made his way down to the waiting room, hoping to find Ghost to have a heart-to-heart with him. He hadn't known all the facts when the man had come to his door the night before, letting him know about his sister, but now he had a better understanding of what might have happened between him and Rayne, and he wanted to kick his ass.

He didn't know for sure the man was Delta Force, but it made sense. Everything he'd learned about how Rayne had been rescued and what she'd been through made him more and more sure she'd been rescued by a team of Special Forces soldiers; it wasn't as if any old unit would be sent across the world to stealthily rescue American hostages, and the fact Ghost showed up at his door and admitted he'd been one of the soldiers who'd rescued his sister only hammered that fact home all the more.

The waiting room was empty, but Chase knew Ghost was around somewhere. He'd told Chase he'd give him and Samantha the day with Rayne, but that he'd be back by five to be with her in the evening. It was four forty-five.

Chase stormed outside and saw Ghost standing near the building, looking absently out into the parking lot.

Without hesitating, Chase walked right up to the other man and punched him in the face.

Ghost took the hit without a word, going back on one foot, but when Chase went to do it again, Ghost put up a hand.

"I'll give you the first for free, but that's all."

"You son of a bitch. You took advantage of her."

Ghost shook his head. "No, I didn't. She knew going in what it was between us."

"You arrogant prick. She's not one of your barrack bunnies you fuck at every post."

Ghost lost his temper. "Don't you think I fucking know that? Jesus man, I haven't been able to think about anything *but* her since the day we spent together. I haven't wanted any other woman but *her*. Not. One."

Chase looked at the man in front of him incredulously. Keane Bryson was someone who could get any woman with just the crook of his finger, and they both knew it. For him to admit that he hadn't been with anyone since…well, Chase didn't know how long, but since his sister, was huge.

Ghost squatted in the grass and nonchalantly began

to unlace his military-style boot as he spoke. Chase didn't know what he was doing, but didn't interrupt.

"I had no intentions of looking for your sister. I had chalked it up to my one big regret." At the low growl coming from Chase, Ghost continued quickly, "I didn't regret *her*, or our time together, I regretted *leaving* her. Lying to her about my name. Letting the best thing that had ever happened to me slip through my fingers."

Ghost wrenched off his boot and pulled his sock down to his ankle while pulling up the material of his pants as far as he could. He stood up and pivoted, showing Chase his calf. "I got this inked a month after I left her. I was driven to put her mark on me, to have her *this* way, even if I never saw her again."

Chase looked down and pressed his lips together, not really believing what he was seeing.

Inked on Ghost's leg was a replica of his sister's tattoo. It had obviously not been done today, it was completely healed. The eagle's wings wrapped around Ghost's calf much as the one on Rayne wrapped around her sides. Even the damn Army logo was included, as well as the rifle and the lightning bolt. The only difference was instead of a carnation in one of the eagle's talons, it held a magic wand...a stick with a star on top, complete with smaller stars floating around the tip and ribbons hanging off it. Chase wasn't sure what to say.

Ghost dropped his pant leg and bent to put his boot back on. "I swear to you, I had no intention of disturbing your sister. I was resigned, not content, but *resigned* to have her live inside my memories. But then I found out that not only was she inside that fucking country, she was in the middle of a goddamn coup. It wasn't by accident that I was there, Chase. No way will I ever believe that. I might not be a smart man, or even a very religious one, but when God reaches down and puts the best thing to ever happen to me right in my path—twice—I'm not going to ignore it. Not again." Ghost stood up with his hands on his hips, daring Chase to disagree.

"She knows you lied about your name."

Ghost's hands dropped from his hips and he shoved them in his pockets.

Chase continued, "I didn't know you'd given her a different name."

Ghost sighed, but didn't speak.

"I also let Delta slip, although she has no idea what that means. I'm not one hundred percent sure of that, but regardless, you're going to have a high hill to climb there, Ghost. You lied to her. That wasn't cool."

"I know." He didn't try to defend himself.

"But as much as it pains me to say it, I understand."

At Ghost's incredulous look, Chase nodded. "Yeah, man. I get it. I'm not an idiot. I learned a hell of a lot about what guys like you do in my counterterrorism training. If nothing else, it makes me respect you more because you didn't pull my sister into something she didn't understand."

"Thanks, I—"

"I wasn't done."

Ghost nodded for Chase to continue, to get out what he needed to.

"But man to man, I don't care who you know and what you are, if your plans are to get some pussy and then drop her—"

Ghost couldn't keep quiet. "Did you not hear me? Did you not see your sister inked on me? If I wanted pussy, I could've had it fifty times over by now. It's Rayne I want. *Rayne*."

Ghost held his breath, waiting for Chase's approval or not.

Finally the man nodded. "She's waiting for you. She couldn't keep her eyes off the door all day. Although you should know, she's going to have a million questions. Just do me a favor, would ya?"

"Anything."

"Keep her safe. Me and Sam can't lose her. It's only the three of us in our family now, our folks died in a freak accident while they were on a cruise a few years ago. Their sightseeing plane crashed. I swear Rayne is now the glue that holds us all together."

Ghost nodded and held out his hand to Chase, confirming to the other man what he'd already guessed. "She's Delta now. She's got six new brothers who would lay down their lives for her."

Chase shook Ghost's hand, knowing deep in his heart that every word out of the deadly man's mouth was true. "Good. Thank you, Ghost."

"You're welcome. I'll be in touch."

Chase nodded and watched Ghost stalk toward the hospital building and disappear through the automatic doors. He let out a long breath.

Rayne was stubborn, Lord knows he knew that about his sister, but she had no idea what she was up against with one Keane Bryson.

Chapter Twenty-Four

G HOST DIDN'T BOTHER knocking, merely opened the door to Rayne's room and strode in as if it was his own. She turned her head to him. The look in her eyes was a heartbreaking blend of excitement, welcome, and distrust.

He went over to her bed, pulled up the chair and settled into it. Leaning toward her, he asked, "How're you doing, Princess?"

She huffed out a breath. "Would you quit calling me that ridiculous name?"

"No. Now how are you? Are you in much pain?"

Rayne narrowed her eyes at him. "Is your name John Benbrook?

"No. It's Keane Bryson."

She looked surprised that he'd come clean without a quibble. "And you're not from Fort Worth, are you?"

"No. I live here in Killeen and am stationed out of Fort Hood."

"What else did you lie about?"

Ghost could tell she didn't really expect him to tell

her much of anything, but he laid it out. "I never knew a girl named Whitney Pumperfield when I was in middle school and I was never held up at gunpoint."

"And?"

Ghost stood up and settled next to Rayne on her bed. He supported his weight with one hand by her opposite hip and leaned toward her.

"That's it, Princess. Everything else was the truth."

She looked up at him with unhappy, untrusting eyes. "I don't believe you," she said finally, a bit sadly.

"I know you don't. But I told you once, and I'll repeat it as many times as you need me to. I won't lie to you again."

"Why were you in London?"

"I was on my way back from a mission."

"What mission?"

Ghost sighed; he'd known it was coming, but hoped it wouldn't be so soon. "I can't tell you."

"I thought you just said you wouldn't lie to me," Rayne said belligerently.

Ghost brought his free hand up to her face and smoothed her hair behind her ear. "I didn't lie. I'll tell you what I can, but there are some things I simply *can't* share. I know you understand that, Princess. Does your brother tell you everything he does for his country?"

She shook her head reluctantly.

Ghost lowered his voice and leaned closer to her,

deepening the intimacy between them. "I'm Delta Force. I don't know if you know what that means, but we're the most secretive branch of the military. Even more so than Navy SEALs. You are the only person, outside of those in the military who are on a need-to-know basis and your brother, who I've ever told."

He paused to let that sink in for a moment. When her eyes widened, he figured she understood the enormity of it, and he continued.

"We go where the government sends us, when they send us. We were sent in to get the hostages, get *you*, out of the middle of that coup. You think the President wants anyone to know American forces were anywhere near there?"

He could see the understanding in her eyes, and he pressed his point.

"I might *want* to tell you where I'm going, but I won't. I won't *ever* put you in danger for knowing more than you should, Princess. I *was* on my way home from a mission that day. And I was lucky enough to have crossed paths with you."

"It was a one-night stand," Rayne said in a confused voice, obviously still fighting her attraction to him. "What are you still doing here?"

"I thought it was. I told myself it was, but I think we both knew differently."

Rayne shook her head in denial.

Ghost sat upright, reached into the pocket of his pants, and pulled out a cell phone. He put in the password and clicked a few times on the screen. He turned the phone toward Rayne and watched her face as he explained.

"I've never taken a photo of a one-night stand before. I've never wanted to bring a piece of a woman home to look at first thing when I woke up and to be the last face I see when I fall asleep."

Rayne looked in disbelief at the photo on Ghost's phone. If was of the two of them in front of Buckingham Palace. She was in his embrace with her arms wrapped around his waist and was looking up at him and laughing. She remembered the moment. She'd been teasing him about taking a selfie picture. She had no idea he'd taken the picture when she hadn't been looking at the lens.

She looked away from the picture and up at Ghost. "But you left."

Ghost put the phone back into his pocket and leaned down to her again and agreed. "I did."

Rayne didn't know what else to say. Had no clue what he wanted. Everything he'd told her made her think that he was trying to let her down gently. He couldn't talk about what he did, he was Delta Force, he was one big secret. She was so darn confused.

"How're your wounds?"

Rayne shrugged.

"Can I see?"

"Uh, I don't think you're supposed to remove the bandages. The doctor said he'd look at them tomorrow."

"I'll be gentle. Please, Rayne. Let me see what they did to you."

She held out a hand to him, allowing him to unravel the bindings there. "I'm pretty sure I did it to myself, Ghost."

"No," he immediately countered. "*They* did this to you."

Rayne kept her eyes on Ghost's face as he undid the last of the bandage and gazed at her wrist. Ghost looked up at her.

"You seen this?"

"Yeah, earlier."

"Does it look better now?"

"I'd rather not look."

"Why not?"

"It made me feel sick this morning." Rayne felt Ghost's grip tighten on her for a moment before he relaxed.

"I'm sorry, Princess. God, I'm so fucking sorry." He leaned down and gently, oh so gently, kissed the palm of her hand, above the wound. She barely felt his lips whisper against her skin.

She dared to look. Ghost's large hand held her wrist in his grasp. The torn and infected skin looked obscene next to his tanned, calloused palm. She forced herself to look more closely.

"I think it's looking better, actually," she told him. "It's not quite as...oozy...as it was before."

Ghost leaned over to the table beside her bed and picked up a piece of gauze. He carefully dabbed the wounds on her wrist, wiping away some of the pus so he could get a closer look. He even leaned in and sniffed her wound.

Rayne tried to pull her hand away. "Gross, Ghost, quit it."

He held firm and she couldn't pull out of his grasp. "It doesn't smell putrid. The infection is clearing up. The antibiotics are doing their thing, Rayne. It's good."

"Okay, whatever you say. It's still gross."

He smiled at her then, carefully rewrapping her wrist. He gestured to one of her ankles. "May I?"

Rayne shrugged and watched as Ghost went through the same procedures with her ankle as he did with her wrist. Obviously deciding she was healing nicely, he pulled the blanket back up and returned to his position from before, one hand at her hip and leaning over her.

"Do they hurt?"

Rayne shrugged. "A little."

"Do you need another pain pill?"

She shook her head. "They make me feel weird."

"But you're in pain?"

Rayne shrugged again and rolled her eyes when Ghost leaned over and pushed the call button on the side of her bed. When the nurse came in, he told her that Rayne was in pain and needed a pill. The nurse left and returned in a minute or so with a little white pill and a small cup of water. Ghost helped hold the cup while Rayne washed the pill down with the water.

He had spoken with the doctor before he'd left that morning, and explained a bit of the situation. Ghost might have insinuated that Rayne could be in danger and it was in her best interest to have either he or one of his teammates there at all times, even past the ten o'clock end of visiting hours...but he couldn't be sorry for lying. His words, along with the colonel's conversation with someone at the hospital, assured he'd be allowed to spend the night. There was no place he'd rather be other than at her side at the moment. He'd lost her once, he'd be damned if he'd do it again.

"I hope you don't mind some company tonight," Ghost told Rayne.

"Of course not, although don't be surprised if I fall asleep before visiting hours are over."

"Yeah...about that..." His voice trailed off.

"What did you do, Ghost?" Rayne asked suspiciously.

He shrugged. "I might have convinced the Doc that it'd be okay if I stayed in here with you."

Rayne studied him before saying in a soft voice, "Okay."

Ghost brought a hand up to her head and palmed the back of her neck. "You want me here." It wasn't a question.

She nodded anyway. "I think after what's happened, it'd make me feel better if you stayed one night with me...at least until I get my feet under me again. I'm sure I'll be all right tomorrow."

Ghost inhaled deeply. She had no idea what her words meant to him. She might act as though she didn't trust him, that she was upset with him for lying, and she most likely was...but when push came to shove, she trusted him to keep her safe.

"You're safe here with me, Princess."

She nodded, eyelids beginning to droop.

"You're tired. Close your eyes."

"I told you. It's the stupid pill," she complained. "It's why I don't like to take them."

"Ummm." Ghost made the sound in the back of his throat, neither agreeing nor disagreeing with her.

"Will you sleep with me?"

"What?" Her question surprised Ghost.

"Sleep with me. You're very warm."

He smiled, understanding what she meant. For a second he thought she was propositioning him and his body had reacted accordingly. He never would have done anything when she was half-conscious and in the hospital, but his body sometimes had a mind of its own.

Ghost moved his hand from her neck to her cheek as he palmed her face and ran his thumb over her cheekbone. "I don't think we'll fit, Princess."

"We fit on the plane."

"You remember that?"

"Yeah, sorta."

Ghost considered it. Her hospital bed wasn't any smaller than the cot she'd been on while they'd been flying home on the plane. He mentally shrugged. The hell with it. He might get in trouble with the staff, but there was no place he'd rather be than wrapped around Rayne.

He stood up and leaned over to unlace his boots. He quickly removed them and placed them by the side of the bed. He pulled the sheet up to completely cover Rayne, then scooted in behind her, on top of the covers. Ghost carefully arranged her with her back to his front, put her head in the crook of his arm, and wrapped the other arm around her waist.

"God, I love this," Rayne said sleepily. "I missed this. We slept just like this back in London."

"Well, not exactly. We were both wearing a few less clothes."

She chuckled and pushed back farther into him, trying to burrow to get as close as she could. "True."

She didn't say anything else for a while, and neither did Ghost. He knew things had been way too easy so far. Rayne wasn't the type of woman to just let what happened go by without more of a protest. But he'd take what he could get.

"Ghost?"

The word was soft and slurred.

"Yeah, Princess?"

"I was scared."

His heart nearly broke. "I know you were."

"I was really glad to see you."

"Uh-huh."

"But I'm still mad at you."

"Okay."

"I don't trust you."

"You might not trust me, but you know I'll keep you safe."

"Yeah."

"Go to sleep, Rayne. We'll talk more tomorrow."

"Mary's coming tomorrow."

"Mary?"

"My best friend."

"Ah, the one you sent my picture to when we were in London."

"Um-hum. She tried to find you for me."

"She did?"

"Ummm. She's pissed."

Ghost kissed the back of Rayne's head. "As any good friend should be."

"*Really* pissed."

Ghost's voice got serious. "I'm glad you have a friend like Mary looking out for you. But I swear to God, Princess, this time is different. I'm in this for the long haul. We're going to figure this out. Please give me a chance. Don't let your friend drive a wedge between us. She can be pissed, but please, don't let her talk you out of giving me the chance to show you how much you mean to me."

Rayne was silent for so long Ghost thought she was finally asleep.

Her sleepy voice broke the silence of the evening. "I want to believe you."

"If you believe nothing else, believe that I'm not letting you go. You'll never wake up and wonder where I went again. Okay?"

She didn't answer him with words, but she turned in his arms and cuddled against him, her chest to his. Both arms curled up in front of her, her fingertips resting on him. Ghost could feel her hot breath against him. He felt her nod once, before she finally drifted off into the sleep of the drugged and exhausted.

Chapter Twenty-Five

"**Y**OU HAD BETTER not be that fucking liar John-bullshit-Benbrook."

The harsh words woke Ghost up early the next morning. He carefully extracted Rayne from his arms—neither of them had moved from their positions the night before—and eased out of the bed without waking her up. He didn't say a word, but bent down and grabbed his boots and gestured with his head to the hallway.

It looked as if Rayne's friend, Mary, had arrived and she was pissed, just as Rayne had warned him she would be. Sometime between her brother letting the cat out of the bag, so to speak, and him arriving last night, Rayne had spoken to her friend and told her what she'd found out.

As soon as the door closed behind them, Mary lit into him. "You have some nerve showing your face here. She's been in a funk for six months. *Six months.* You obviously didn't even care enough to try to see her before, but here you are. All touchy-feely and wanting to stay by her side. Where were you four months ago when she tripped stepping off a curb and twisting her ankle? Or two months ago when she was trying to break up a fight on a flight and got elbowed in the face? I know she agreed to sleep with you, she told me all about it, but you still shouldn't have done it. She told me about your conversation about how she's a romantic. No matter what she said, you should've known after spending the day with you in London she would've read more into sleeping together than you would. She doesn't do one-night stands, assclown. You shouldn't have taken advantage of her like that, she—"

Mary's words were cut off by a large hand covering her mouth from behind. Ghost looked up to his teammate, Truck, with amusement.

"If you think that's gonna stop her from saying what she wants, I think you're sorely mistaken."

"It's early, she's too loud. People are trying to sleep." Truck shrugged, easily controlling the now-struggling woman in his arms. "Maybe you should take this outside."

Ghost stood up after tying his boots. "Good idea." He looked at Mary, who was shooting daggers out of her eyes. "Shall we go and talk about this rationally? Or will my friend, Truck, here have to carry you outside?"

She mumbled something behind Truck's palm and nodded. He lowered his hand and stepped around

Mary to introduce himself.

He held out his hand. "Truck. Good to meet you."

She glared at him, seemingly ignoring his scary countenance, refusing to shake his hand. She poked his chest with her finger as she spoke. "Whatever. If I find out you had anything to do with him," she pointed her thumb at Ghost, "ignoring my friend, you're in just as much trouble as he is." With that, she stomped down the corridor, obviously expecting Ghost to follow her so she could finish speaking her mind.

"Looks like you have a fan, Truck," Ghost told him teasingly.

He shrugged. "At least she didn't seem to care about the ugly mug."

"Wanna come with me and play backup?" Ghost asked.

"No way, Ghost. You're on your own there."

They both chuckled as Mary hissed from the other end of the hallway, "You coming?"

Ghost made his way toward the slender woman standing with her hands on her hips, knowing he had to appease Rayne's best friend before he could even begin to make any more headway with Rayne herself.

They headed outside to a set of picnic tables. Ghost sat on the tabletop and rested his forearms on his bent knees.

Before Mary could light into him again, he said

quickly, "First things first, I haven't slept with anyone since her."

That seemed to take the wind out of Mary's sails, but she climbed up next to him and asked only slightly less belligerently, "Why should I believe you? You lied about your name, it'd be easy to lie about something like who you've slept with."

Knowing nothing he said would get through to Rayne's friend as well as show-and-tell, Ghost leaned down to untie his boot for what seemed like the millionth time in twelve hours. He'd found showing his tattoo to Rayne's friends and family was the quickest way to make them believe his sincerity.

"I never expected to ever find a woman who fit me. Who 'got' me like Rayne did. But by the time I realized what I had, I'd already lied to her. If it makes you feel any better, I've been struggling against what I know I *should* do versus what I *wanted* to do for the last six months."

Mary didn't look moved in the least. She merely raised her eyebrow as if to say, "So?"

Ghost wrenched his pant leg up and tilted his calf towards Rayne's friend. "I got it three weeks after I got back from London." He heard Mary's in-drawn breath at the sight of his tattoo. Figuring she got the meaning, he lowered his pants and set to work putting his boot back on…again.

"She tried to tell me it wasn't a big deal, but I knew better." Mary's voice was less caustic now, but still accusatory. "It was a shit thing to do."

Ghost was getting sick of being accused of being the bad guy. He knew he screwed up, but he'd suffered just as much as Rayne had. "Look, cut me some slack, all right? She knew going in I was a one-night kind of guy. Shit, I told her enough…and she agreed. I never would've done it if she hadn't."

"But you pushed."

"I did, but you know as well as I do that I didn't have to push very hard. Rayne's refreshing and I knew she was something special. Mary, her favorite part of our trip around London was looking at a fucking balcony."

Mary chuckled, loosening up for the first time. "Yeah, she made me look at the pictures of that damn thing a million times."

They shared a smile before Mary got serious again. "She's my best friend in the world. I'd do anything for her. She was by me every step of the way when I had cancer. When I got depressed, she pushed and pushed until I sucked it up. I think she was happier than I was when the doctor's said it was in remission."

"I'm very glad you kicked cancer's ass, Mary. You're the kind of friend I want Rayne to have. Loyal to a fault and protective as all get out," Ghost told her honestly.

"Thank you. When the airline called her emergency number, and got me, and I found out she was neck-deep in whatever was going on over there in Egypt, I panicked. I don't know what I'd do without her. I miss my old friend, Ghost. I miss her laughter and her easygoing ways."

"I'll be honest with you, Mary—"

"That'd be a first."

Ghost ignored her snarky interruption and continued, "I wasn't going to come after her. She deserves more than I can give her. I won't be able to tell her where I'm going or what I'm doing. I could be gone for weeks at a time, it depends on our missions." Before Mary could interrupt him again, he quickly continued, paraphrasing what he'd told Rayne's brother.

"But...finding out she happened to be one of the hostages I was sent over there to rescue changed my life. I mean, what are the odds? There had to be some sort of divine intervention and I'm not an idiot. I'll protect her with my life, I'll keep her safe from others who might want to take advantage of her. I'll be her friend and her lover. I'll do whatever I can to make it work between us."

"Is she moving down here to Killeen?"

Ghost shrugged. "I have no idea. I haven't even talked to *her* about this shit yet. But you obviously need reassuring and I'm not going to do anything to get between you two. She's gonna need you when I'm gone on missions. It won't be easy being with me, but I hope to Christ she's willing to at least try."

"Have you seen her tattoo? I mean the additions to it?"

Ghost nodded solemnly.

"I think she's willing to try."

"I mean it, Mary. Whatever you guys need, I'll do it." Ghost looked Mary in the eye.

"Do you love her?"

"I don't know," Ghost replied immediately. "I think it's too soon for that."

"Good answer, slick."

"I wasn't trying to be slick, but I've only been with her for about twenty-four hours. But I can tell you this, she's touched me deeper than any woman ever has before. The thought of her being sick, or wounded, or what almost happened to her over there makes me want to kill someone. Fuck, I *did* kill someone for her."

Ghost regretted the words as soon as they left his mouth. Shit, he knew better than to talk about his mission, but apparently it was the right thing to say.

"Good. Fuckers. I wanted to ask her about it, but was afraid it would bring up bad memories for her. I only talked to her for a little bit yesterday when she called, and I'm sure I'll hear more details later, but if you killed the motherfucker who was going to become a 'man' after raping her, all the better."

Ghost nodded.

"As much as it pains me to say this, because I was all ready to hate you for lying to my best friend, I think I like you...whatever your name really is."

"Keane Bryson."

"No wonder you go by Ghost." Mary's words were said as an aside.

Ghost chuckled but didn't respond.

"Anyway, as I was saying, I *think* I like you...but I have to say, my feelings could still swing the other way, so watch yourself, Keane Bryson."

Ghost nodded. "Now that we're done with this little heart-to-heart, can I please get back inside to Rayne before she wakes up and doesn't see me there and panics, thinking I left her again?"

Mary immediately hopped off the bench. "Shit, that's exactly what she'll think. Why didn't you say something sooner?"

Ghost shook his head as he followed Mary back into the hospital. She was a prickly thing, but dammed if he didn't like her too.

LATER THAT AFTERNOON, Rayne was sitting up in her

bed, laughing at the tension between Mary and Truck. Ghost had been at her side when she'd woken up that morning, along with her best friend. Surprisingly the two had seemed almost chummy, when Rayne was sure Mary would've ripped him a new one. She'd been pissed the day before when they'd spoken over the phone and Rayne told her about Ghost.

Ghost had left that morning not much longer after she'd woken up, saying he had "shit to do," but that he'd be back later in the evening. But he hadn't left her alone. Apparently his teammate, Truck, was on babysitting duty, and at first it irritated Rayne, but now she loved the entertainment he and Mary had provided all afternoon.

They'd argued about what to get her for lunch, they'd argued about what to watch on television, they'd even argued when Mary told him to scat because she wanted to talk girlie shit with Rayne. Truck refused to budge, saying that if Ghost wanted him here, watching over his woman, then that's where he was going to stay.

Truck was as intimidating as anyone she'd ever seen. The nurses didn't waste time when they came in to see how she was doing or if she needed more pain pills. With Truck sitting in the corner, arms crossed over his chest, his natural scowl on his face, they made a quick retreat.

But Rayne didn't mind him being there, he was

actually comforting to her, no matter how scary his countenance might be. And Mary wasn't intimidated by anyone; she took him on, figuratively, toe-to-toe.

"When can we get you out of here and back home?" Mary asked Rayne.

Rayne shrugged. "I'm not sure when I'll be discharged. The doctor said my wounds were looking better this morning, but he still wants to keep me at least one more night, maybe two."

"You can stay here, with Ghost," Truck said.

"No way, Trucker," Mary argued immediately, grinning when he narrowed his eyes at her nickname for him. "She can go home with me."

"She isn't up for traveling yet," he returned.

"Why not? You're not her doctor; we'll wait and see what he says."

"Guys," Rayne protested, holding up her bandaged arms. "Stop, please. You've been fighting all day and while it's amusing as hell, it's getting pretty annoying."

Mary huffed out a breath and relented. "Okay, but I'm still not sure why he's even still here."

Both women looked at Truck expectantly.

"As I already told you guys, Ghost asked that I stay and keep an eye on Rayne, to make sure there was nothing you needed until he got back."

Rayne tried not to think it was really sweet of Ghost, but failed. It was very nice to be on the receiving end of such attention. Especially after no interaction with him for so long.

She had no idea what she was going to do when she was discharged. Most likely she'd go back up to her place in Fort Worth. She'd called her boss at work and had been granted three weeks or so of leave and she planned to take every second of it. The thought of getting on a plane and resuming work held no appeal for her whatsoever. And if she was completely honest with herself, the thought of flying into another foreign country was even less appealing.

Why Ghost would even want her to stay with him was beyond her. They didn't know each other. There was no way she'd stay with him...was there?

As if their conversation about Ghost conjured him up, the man confidently strode into her hospital room. "Thanks for staying, Truck. Any issues?"

"What issues could there have been?" Mary griped, standing up with her hands on her hips. "We're in a public hospital on an Army base, for cripes' sake."

Rayne giggled. Mary had always been a bit brash, but it was amusing to see her standing up to both Ghost and Truck as if she could make them do something.

"Calm down, Mary, just wanted to make sure Rayne was good." Ghost came up to her bedside, leaned over, and kissed her on the forehead. Looking into her eyes, he asked, "You all right? Not in too much pain?"

Rayne shook her head in bemusement. "I'm good."

He studied her for a moment, as if trying to decide if she was telling the truth or not, finally murmuring, "All right."

Truck got up to leave and shook Ghost's hand. "Same time tomorrow?"

"Nope, got everything I needed to get done today. I'm off tomorrow. I'll be here."

"Sounds good."

"The colonel will be talking with you tomorrow though," Ghost warned his teammate. Since he'd taken the day to go over what had happened in Egypt, it would be Truck's turn to say what went down as well. It was procedure for the colonel to talk to them all separately, to make sure he got all angles of the mission for his final report.

"Gotcha. No problem." He turned to Rayne. "It's good to see you up and alert. Can't say carrying you out of that fucked-up situation was my idea of a good time."

"Mine either, but thanks, Truck. Seriously. I don't remember all of it clearly, but I do remember feeling safe in your arms."

Obviously pleased, but not wanting to make a big deal out of her words, Truck turned to Mary. "Want to get some dinner?"

She looked shocked for a moment before recovering. "Sure, why not? It'll be amusing, if nothing else."

Truck smiled, and held out his hand toward the door. "After you."

Mary went to Rayne's bedside and gave her a quick hug. "You'll be okay? I'll see you in the morning?"

"Of course, I'll be fine. Go on, you've been here all day. Get out and get some fresh air. You're going home tomorrow, right?"

Mary made a face. "Yeah, I have to work. I couldn't get out of my shift. But I'm free the next two days after that so I can come back and get you if the Doc discharges you. Just let me know when you're being released and we'll make arrangements."

"I'm sure Chase can bring me home."

Mary waved her hand. "Whatever is best for you, Rayne." She hugged her again, a bit longer and harder this time. "I'm very glad you're all right. Take it easy and don't let this guy take advantage." She gestured to Ghost as she straightened up.

Rayne laughed. "Okay. See you tomorrow before you go?"

"Definitely."

"Have a good dinner."

Mary smiled with an evil look in her eye. "Oh, I'm sure it'll be entertaining."

Rayne rolled her eyes and watched her best friend leave the room with Truck.

She turned to Ghost. "Your friend is in big trouble. I hope he knows what he's doing."

"I think he can take care of himself."

"Don't say I didn't warn you."

Ghost sat down in the chair Mary had been occupying for most of the afternoon and leaned his elbows on the bed.

"You really doing okay? How's the pain? And be honest."

"It's much better than yesterday. I don't have shooting stabs of fire going up my arms and legs anymore."

"Have you taken any pills?"

Rayne shook her head. "No, I've graduated to taking just Tylenol, thank God."

"Let me know if it gets worse."

Rayne studied Ghost carefully before asking in a serious tone, "What are you doing here, Ghost?"

He cocked his head but didn't say anything.

So Rayne continued, "I mean, we had a one-night thing. You said you didn't do relationships. But here you are, putting a guard on me for whatever reason, spending the night here, sleeping next to me…I don't understand. I thought you would make sure I was all right, then get on your way again. You rescued me, thanks for that, but we're at the same place we were six months ago. We met as strangers and we're strangers still."

"You don't feel like a stranger."

Rayne tried to reject Ghost's words, but he was right. He didn't feel like a stranger to her either. At least in some ways. "In a couple of days, maybe tomorrow, I'll be out of here and back home in Fort Worth. You're here. I'm there. What do you want out of this? Another night of fucking?" She made sure her words were shocking; she was feeling raw and confused and wasn't sure what was going on.

As soon as the words were out of her mouth, Ghost was leaning over her. "What we did was *not* fucking and you know it. We made love in that hotel room. We worshipped each other."

Rayne tried to control her wildly beating heart. "I'm sure you've worshipped lots of women since then. I'm nobody special."

Ghost looked her in the eyes and willed her to believe him and told her what he'd confessed to both Chase and Mary. "I haven't been with anyone since you, Princess. Any orgasm I've had has been with my own hand and memories of you."

Rayne's mouth hung open, but he continued, not letting her speak.

"All I have to do is remember your taste and the

feel of your hot body clenching mine as I made you come all over my dick and I lose it as if I'm a teenager. Every time, without fail. As for what I want out of this? You. I want *you*. I regretted leaving you as soon as the door closed behind me, hell, even before that, but I honestly didn't see a way I could make it work. But now? Seeing you again? Seeing you lying on that fucking cot scared out of your mind, feeling how you clung to me and trusted me to make it right for you? I'm willing to do whatever I can to make it work between us."

"What if that's not what I want?" Rayne managed to ask, honestly floored this virile, tough-as-nails man was laying it out like he was.

"Then I hope I can change your mind."

Rayne didn't know what to say to that, but Ghost continued, not waiting for her to reply.

"You've got some sick time coming to you...right? Why not spend it here in Killeen with me? My colonel is allowing me to take some time off and I want to spend it with you. Stay with me, at least for a while. I have a guest bedroom. It's all yours for as long as you want it. Let's get to know each other, and I don't mean in the biblical sense. If we decide we can't stand each other out of the bedroom, at least we'll know. But, Princess...if you decide to stay, I expect you'll give us an honest chance. I'm not taking this lightly."

Rayne was floored. She hadn't expected this. "But I live in Fort Worth."

"I know. I didn't say there wouldn't be some challenges we'd have to work out. But let's not put the cart before the horse."

"I don't know...you hurt me, Ghost. I...this will be worse if you—"

"It's different now, Rayne. Swear. I'll do whatever I need to in order to take care of your heart."

"Can I think about it?"

"Of course," Ghost answered immediately. Then ruined his seeming generosity with, "You have until you're discharged."

"Ghost!" Rayne admonished. "That's not really that much time to think."

"If I let you go back up to Fort Worth, I'm afraid I'll lose you. You'll start second-guessing what I want, and what you want, and you'll let others talk you out of it. Then you'll go back to work and it'll just become harder and harder. You won't have the time off, and I'll be going on missions. Give us this, Rayne. Give us time to see if there's anything between us other than the awesome sexual chemistry we have going on."

"You have a guest room?"

Knowing she was going to say yes was such a load off him, Ghost let out a huge breath. "Yes."

"And when I want to go home, you'll let me?"

Ghost swallowed, not wanting to agree, but doing it anyway. "Yes."

"Then okay, I'll stay with you...for a couple of days and see how it goes."

Ghost picked up her hand, careful not to hurt her, and kissed the fingertips peeking out from the bandages. "Great. Now scoot over, let's see what's on TV."

"What?"

"You aren't ready for bed yet are you? It's early, and I've ordered our dinner, it should be here in thirty minutes."

"Ghost! You can't order dinner into a hospital."

He shrugged. "Okay, you got me. I didn't order it in, but Fletch is bringing it by in thirty minutes."

"What're we having?" Rayne asked with interest this time. She'd only been there a day or so, but she was so ready for some real food.

"Burritos from Moe's, and some of their chips and salsa."

"Oh my God, are you kidding?"

"No."

"I *love* Moe's! Their chips are the best! They've got those big salt granules that are so good. Wait, what kind of burrito did you get me? Because I don't like beans, and I don't—"

"Veggie burrito, extra rice, no meat, no beans, extra tomatoes and pico. Sour cream, lettuce, cheese, and a side of hot salsa."

Rayne looked at Ghost incredulously. "How in the world—"

"I bribed Mary to tell me what you liked."

"Thank God. I think you and me might get along all right, after all."

Ghost pulled Rayne into his side. He didn't gloat, but simply said, "Yeah, I think so too."

Chapter Twenty-Six

RAYNE ROLLED HER eyes for what seemed like the millionth time. She was finally allowed to leave the hospital and she'd been dealing with not only her brother and Ghost, but all six of his teammates as well. They were hovering and driving her absolutely crazy. It should be illegal to allow so much testosterone in one room at the same time.

"You know you can come and stay with me," Chase told her for the third time.

"We've talked about this, Chase. We'd probably kill each other within a day. Your place is too small, and besides, you'll be working. Ghost has the next week off. It'll be fine."

She watched as Chase glared at Ghost and he smirked back. For the millionth and one time, Rayne rolled her eyes.

"Fletch," Ghost called and flicked his keys through the air toward his friend, "bring my car around."

Fletch caught the keys easily and nodded before heading out of the room.

"Beatle, want to see where the doc is? He should've been here by now," Ghost asked.

Rayne sat in the chair in the corner of the room where Ghost had plunked her ten minutes ago. She'd tried to tell him she was fine to walk, but he'd simply told him he liked having her in his arms and proceeded to pick her up and put her where he wanted her.

The doctor had been impressed with how her wounds were healing, and while walking wasn't the most fun thing at the moment, she could do it. Slowly but surely the pain was lessoning. She'd be stiff for a while, okay a long while, but she was mobile.

Finally, a nurse stepped into the room, pushing a wheelchair. "All right, Ms. Jackson, it looks like—" Her voice cut off abruptly at seeing the bevy of huge men in the room. She cleared her throat and tried again. "It looks like you're all set to get out of here. The doctor signed your discharge papers and regrets he couldn't be here to let you know himself. He knew you were anxious to leave, and when an emergency came up, signed the papers to free you."

She handed Rayne a stapled set of papers. "Here's your instructions about those wounds. Come back in a couple of days and get the stitches checked out; if they look okay, they should be able to come out not long after that. Try not to get them soaked, only quick showers, no baths, and keep the bandages on. He's written you a script for painkillers if you need them, and make sure you fill the antibiotic prescription so you can start on those tonight. Do you have any questions for me?"

"What kind of physical activity is she cleared for?" Ghost asked with a straight face.

"Oh my God, you did *not* just ask that," Rayne hissed and smacked Ghost lightly on the arm. She wanted to hit him harder, but it would've hurt her wrist. He was sitting on the arm of the chair next to her and he simply turned his head to her and smiled. Rayne blushed a deep red, embarrassed that not only his teammates, but her brother had heard the question.

The nurse smiled indulgently. "I'm not suggesting she should go out and run a marathon, but pretty much whatever she feels up to, she can do." The nurse addressed her next words to Rayne directly. "Just don't overdo it and if anything changes with your pain levels or with how the wounds look, come back in immediately."

Ghost nodded as if he'd expected her answer. "I'll be sure to monitor her carefully."

"Seriously, just kill me now," Rayne muttered, putting her head in her hands.

Ghost laughed again and scooped her out of the chair. Rayne screeched and grabbed hold of his T-shirt at his chest with frantic hands.

"Easy, Princess. I wouldn't ever drop you. You're safe."

"Warn a girl next time, would ya?"

Ghost winked at her. "You got it." He placed her carefully in the wheelchair and put a duffle bag in her lap. It held the few outfits Mary had brought down with her and some of her, "girly shit," as Chase had called it. Ghost put his hand on her shoulder as the nurse pushed her out of the room and down the hall toward the sliding glass doors at the front of the building.

The other men trailed behind her as if they were in some sort of weird military parade or something. Rayne smiled at the second and third looks all of Ghost's friends were getting as they made their way to the exit.

Finally, the nurse stopped just short of the doors. Ghost went to pick her up, but Rayne put her hand on his arm. "I want to walk. Please?"

Ghost nodded, but motioned for Hollywood to stand on her other side, just in case she needed either of them.

Everyone held their breath as she hobbled toward Ghost's car, now idling at the front of the building thanks to Fletch. Chase wrapped her in a big hug before she got in. "Take care, sis, and call me if you change your mind and want to stay with me or if you need *anything*."

"I will. Thanks, Chase. I love you."

"Love you too, Rayne. I'll talk to you soon."

Rayne nodded and smiled as Ghost carefully helped her into the front passenger side of his car. He shut the door behind her and she watched as he fist-bumped and gave a chin lift to his friends. Before too long they were on their way.

"Finally." She breathed the word on a sigh.

"Long day?" Ghost asked.

"Not really, but dealing with all of you guys and your over-the-top macho bullshit is exhausting."

Ghost looked surprised for a moment then laughed. "Yeah, I guess we can be a bit much all at once, but it's because we care for you."

Rayne looked at him with a question in her eyes. "Your friends don't know me."

"Yeah, but they know you're important to me. Since you're important to me, you're important to them. And since you're important to them, they care about you."

"I don't get it."

"You will."

"God, I hate it when you talk in riddles," Rayne mock-complained, crossing her arms on her chest, careful not to jostle her wrists. The thought that all of Ghost's men liked her simply because Ghost did was startling, but felt good. After the last day and a half of all of them visiting her in the hospital, she'd begun to think of them like brothers.

Fletch seemed to be the closest with Ghost. They joked with each other, but she could see the genuine respect between the two of them. Fletch was tall, maybe a couple inches past six feet, and had colorful tattoos on both arms, but it was his clear blue eyes that really made him stand out.

Coach was quiet and reserved, but Rayne thought he was actually the most dangerous of the group. There was just something about him that made her think he was constantly looking for a threat, and that he'd easily be able to neutralize it if one did arise. Hollywood was gregarious and outgoing and loved to tease her unmercifully. If she hadn't known he was a part of Ghost's top-secret team, she never would've guessed he was able to kill a man with his bare hands.

Beatle was the shortest man of the group, probably around five-eleven or so, and was their nautical expert and knew everything there was to know about sailing and the ocean.

Blade was tall and skinny, like his namesake. When she'd remarked that she saw why he'd received his nickname, everyone had laughed. They'd told her he wasn't named Blade because of his build, but rather because of his skills with a knife. Rayne hadn't asked any more about it.

And then there was Truck. He was huge, and if Rayne was being honest with herself, he wasn't that attractive, not like the other men on the team. But it had only taken being around him for a little while to see he was self-conscious about his looks, but tried to play it off. And of course, watching him and Mary go at it like two little kids who liked each other but didn't want to admit it, so they instead picked at each other, was entertaining enough to forget that the man could squash someone as if they were a bug if he so chose.

"I like your friends," Rayne told Ghost as they pulled into traffic and headed toward his place."

"I'm glad."

"Where do you live again?"

"Belton. It's just off I-35. Close enough to the base, but not so close as to have to deal with all the crap that comes with living near a military base."

"What kind of crap is that?"

"Pawn shops, tattoo places, strip joints, pay-day loan stores…that sort of thing."

"And you have an apartment?"

"No, it's a small house. Built in the seventies. It's not the fanciest place, but it's clean and in a good neighborhood with families. I didn't want to live in an apartment this time. I enjoy the quiet."

Rayne nodded. Suddenly unsure as to what she should talk to him about. It'd been easy joking and laughing with him when they were in the hospital together. But now that they were alone, it seemed weird.

"Are you up to stopping on the way to get your prescriptions filled, or would you rather get home to nap and I can go out later and pick them up?"

"I'm okay with stopping now. It feels good to be up and about. I'm sure I'll be tired later, but for now, I'm enjoying being free."

Ghost chuckled. "I bet."

They were silent until Ghost pulled into the drug-store parking lot and made for the drive-through.

"I'd like to go in," Rayne told him.

Ghost frowned. "I'm not sure you should be on your feet yet, Princess."

"I need stuff."

"I can get what you need later."

"Tampons? Can you get me tampons? And deodor-ant?"

Without missing a beat, Ghost responded, "Yeah, Princess. I can get you tampons without spontaneously combusting."

"Have you ever bought them for anyone before?"

Ghost sighed and pulled into a parking space. He turned to Rayne, who was glaring at him. "No. I've never made a midnight run to the store for tampons or maxi pads or any of the other mysterious feminine products you might think up. But even though I've never done it, I'm not scared of it. Especially not for you. If you need them, I'll gladly buy them. But Rayne, I don't think it's a good idea for you to be pushing yourself so fast. You just got out of the hospital. It hasn't even been a week since I found you strapped—"

Ghost cut himself off, mentally smacking himself in the head. The last thing he wanted to do was remind her of what had happened.

Rayne sighed and looked down at her hands in her lap. She wanted to clench them together, but knew it'd hurt. "I don't have any of my things. Mary brought me some, but it's not the same. I feel…I feel out of my element. I just wanted to walk around a store as if I was normal again. I want to try to get back to doing everyday stuff and not think about…*it*. I'm sorry about the tampon thing. I didn't mean anything by it."

Ghost put his finger under Rayne's chin and gently tugged upwards, imploring her to look at him. "I'm sorry for reminding you. It's too soon, I know. Come on; if you lean on me, I'll walk you through the store and you can get whatever you want. Hell, buy twelve boxes of tampons and three bottles of prenatal vitamins. That'll confuse the clerk for sure."

Rayne smiled. Ghost was funny, and being sweet and understanding made her like him all the more. "Thanks."

"But I should say," Ghost smiled mischievously, "I won't look twice about you buying tampons if you won't be embarrassed if I buy condoms. That will *really* confuse the poor person who checks us out."

He watched as Rayne blushed. Ghost leaned forward and kissed her lightly on the lips, wanting to prolong it, desperate to have her taste on his tongue again, but he forced himself to pull back. "Come on, Princess. Let's see what we can find to make you feel normal again."

Chapter Twenty-Seven

GHOST'S HOUSE WAS just as he said it was. Smack-dab in the middle of a small neighborhood. It had three bedrooms and was just big enough not to feel stifling. The first two days, Rayne had done a lot of sleeping. Ghost had slipped her a nighttime aspirin the first evening and she'd slept for fourteen hours straight.

She'd woken up feeling much better. Ghost had made a huge lunch and they'd sat around the table talking for at least two hours. She hadn't slept as long the next time, but still managed to sleep through the entire night without budging.

They'd fought for the first time when Rayne had wanted to take a shower. Ghost had reminded her the doctor said not to get the stitches wet, and Rayne countered that he'd said not *too* wet.

Rayne knew Ghost was just trying to take care of her, but she felt disgusting and needed that shower like she needed air to breathe. The sponge baths she'd received at the hospital, while refreshing, weren't the same as being able to fully wash herself.

Finally just walking away from Ghost, she stomped—as well as she *could* stomp with her still-aching ankles—to the bathroom. She thought about locking the door, but felt better about Ghost being able to get to her easily if something *did* happen.

Stepping under the hot water was one of the best feelings in the world. She swore she could literally feel the Egyptian dust sluicing off her.

After the way-too-short shower, she sat on the toilet seat with a damp towel wrapped around her body and examined her ankles and wrists for the first time.

Rayne wasn't vain, she'd never been the kind of woman men immediately hit on when she went out, but she wasn't hideous either. She had curves in all the right places, too many for some men, but she'd been asked out enough to know men generally found her attractive.

But staring at her torn and scarred skin, seeing the black stitches in her skin and remembering how she'd gotten the wounds, was...upsetting to say the least.

She recalled every moment of her time on that mattress. How humiliated she'd felt, how desperate and helpless...how scared. Seeing the result of her futile struggles, and remembering how the man translating her torture session had said the more her blood flowed, the better man Moshe would be, was simply too much. For a moment, she swore she could hear the heavily accented English in her brain, describing in detail how she'd be raped over and over and over again.

Rayne cried. She cried for herself. She cried for the two women she didn't know who'd most likely gone through the same thing she had, but worse, because whatever boys were doing the rituals had probably had time to go through it with them. She hoped with everything inside her that they'd been rescued as she had. Even if they'd been violated, they could get help and hopefully live their lives far away from the monsters who'd hurt them.

After a while, Rayne didn't know why she was crying, just that she couldn't stop.

In the middle of her breakdown, Ghost suddenly appeared. Rayne would've been upset, but she was so glad to see him, to have him wrap her in his arms where she felt safe. Rayne latched on to him as he picked her up carefully without a word, and she buried her face in his neck.

Ghost's stomach clenched at the sound of Rayne's anguish. He'd been waiting for her to break down for two days, and while he hated that it had happened, it was also a relief. She was strong, one of the strongest women he'd ever met, but he knew she had to deal with what had happened sooner or later.

She'd had the distraction of being in the hospital and dealing with her pain and wounds, and then her brother and Mary, then moving in with him temporarily...but she'd finally had enough time to think, to remember what had happened.

Careful not to jostle her wounds, Ghost carried her into the living room and sat on his couch, settling Rayne in his lap. The towel she'd been wearing had come loose and he pulled it free. It was damp and it wasn't as if he hadn't seen and examined every inch of her body before. He pulled a soft, fuzzy throw blanket from the back of the sofa over her and tucked her into his chest and rocked, letting her cry.

It took about twenty minutes, but finally Rayne's tears began to subside and she lay docile in his arms, sniffing every now and then.

"Need a tissue, Princess?"

Ghost felt her nod against him and reached over to grab a couple from the box next to the couch. One of her arms came up from where she'd held the fluffy blanket against both their chests and she not-so daintily blew her nose. Without lifting her head or saying a word, she held the used tissue out, as if she were the princess he called her, and Ghost took it with a smile, dropping it on the small table to throw away later.

She settled back against his chest. Finally, she murmured, "Am I naked?"

Ghost smiled. "Yup."

"Is that a banana in your pocket or are you just glad

to see me?"

He outright laughed that time. "Princess, you're sitting in my lap without a stitch of clothing on. Of course I'm happy to see you." He sobered and asked, "Feel better?"

He liked how she took a minute to think about his question before answering.

"Yeah. I do. I just...I looked at my wrists and ankles for the first time...really looked, and remembered. It just kinda hit me."

"I'm not surprised. You've been dealing with a lot of other stuff...other than what happened to you."

Rayne nodded in agreement in his arms. "Did you really kill him?"

Ghost hadn't expected the question, but he supposed he should've. She'd been hurt and panicked when they'd been escaping and had the conversation. "Yeah, I'm ninety-five percent sure I did."

"Can you tell me?"

He appreciated her asking, and not demanding. If nothing else, it boded well for their future. She probably didn't realize the significance of what she'd done, but he did. "When Sarah and the other women you'd been held with were rescued, Sarah mentioned you and was frantic to let us know you'd been taken away from them. We began a search in the area where the other women were found. You were in the last room on the hallway, very close to where one of our explosives was set."

"That's what scared them all away. The room started crumbling in and they all ran like little girls."

Ghost chuckled and squeezed Rayne affectionately. "I swear to God, Rayne, I'll never forget entering that room and seeing you there. I was relieved you were okay, then pissed at the way you were trussed up."

Realizing Ghost needed this as much as she did, Rayne didn't interrupt, but let him talk.

"Anyway, before we got to your room, we were searching all the other rooms in the hall. We entered one and there were three people inside. The youngest raised his rifle, probably thinking we wouldn't kill him because he was a kid."

"But you did." Rayne's voice was low and Ghost couldn't read it.

"Yeah. We did."

"What was he wearing?"

Ghost realized that even though they'd had this conversation when they were bringing her out of the building, she obviously didn't remember it. "A blue shirt and tan pants."

"When we were all being held together, he came in and he seemed so nice. He wandered over to us and I smiled at him, trying to be friendly, trying to make him see that we were people. Innocent, unarmed humans. I knew it probably wasn't smart because Chase had always told me never to do anything to stand out, and even the littlest thing could put me in the crosshairs of a bad guy if I did. He wasn't wrong, obviously."

Rayne sighed, loud and long. Ghost didn't interrupt or otherwise rush her. She'd tell the story in her own time and at her own pace. Whatever she needed, he'd give her.

Finally she continued, "He smiled back. I thought he was shy. I thought maybe I'd remind him of his sisters or mother. I thought he'd go back to the other two men and tell them not to hurt us." Rayne paused then continued sadly, "But he didn't. It was a selection. Because I smiled at him, he chose me."

"It's not your fault, Princess."

She shook her head against him and finally picked her head up far enough so she could look Ghost in the eyes. "I thought I was going to die. He was crouched over me, his penis in his hand, stroking himself, getting ready to rip off my panties and rape me…while all those other men looked on and cheered. I was scared, Ghost."

Jesus fucking Christ. Ghost didn't think he could handle hearing any more, but he would. For her. He shifted under Rayne until he was lying supine on the couch, his head propped up on the arm of the sofa. He adjusted the blanket until it covered all of Rayne and he held her to his chest. "I know you were. Anyone would've been scared."

"But you know what?"

Her words were muffled against him, but Ghost could still easily hear her. "What?"

"I was pissed too. Pissed that he'd ruin my memories of us. Ruin sex for me forever." She shrugged awkwardly in Ghost's arms. "It's stupid. I knew I was going to die, but I didn't want to remember *him* doing that to me. I wanted my last memory to be of us."

"You're safe now, Princess. He's dead and can't do it to anyone else. You're here with me. And I swear to you, whenever you're ready, we can make more memories to block out the bad ones."

She nodded and lay still. Ghost didn't say another word, but let Rayne work through her memories at her own speed.

"I like this." Her words were strong and firm.

"Me too. You feel good on top of me."

Rayne picked her head up at that. "You know, we didn't do it this way back in London."

Ghost smirked, glad her mood had changed...at least for now. He had no doubts the memories would creep in again, but he'd be there for her. He'd listen to her relive what had happened over and over again if that's what she needed.

"Yeah, we didn't quite make it that far, did we?"

Rayne put her head back down and Ghost felt her fingers flex against his upper chest. "What are we really doing, Ghost?"

This he was expecting sooner or later. "We're getting to know each other. Dating. Seeing each other. Going steady...whatever you want to call it."

"I'm having a hard time getting over the lies."

Ghost loved how honest Rayne was with him, even if her words sliced through him deeper than any enemy's blade ever could.

"I'm sorry I caused you pain, but, Rayne, I couldn't have done anything different. I'd just come off a mission and was flying incognito back to the States. I had no idea I'd meet the woman made just for me when that flight was canceled."

He heard her indrawn breath, but continued on, "I'd offered that one night before I realized you were *it*. Somewhere between lunch and that damn balcony, I figured it out, though. I knew if I was ever going to settle down, if I was ever going to spend the rest of my life with one woman, it'd be you. But I still lied to you. I spewed out that fucked-up story about Whitney Pumperfield. I'd already told you I was John Benbrook. I was selfish. I knew if I told you I was lying, you'd disappear and I'd never get a chance to hold you in my arms. To see what it was all about."

"See what *what* was all about? It's not like you'd

never had a one-night stand before, Ghost."

"To see if caring about someone made a difference in bed."

Rayne was silent for a moment then tentatively asked, "Did it?"

"I think you know the answer to that."

She did.

"And then I saw that third tattoo."

Rayne propped herself up on his chest, careful not to dig her elbows into him. "Yeah, what was up with that?"

He laughed a little at the interest on her face. "You have no idea what that did to me."

"I have a little idea," she teased, obviously remembering how he'd taken her from behind and pulled out and exploded all over her ink.

Ghost smiled and brought his hand up and tucked her hair behind her ear. "It was as if you had *me* drawn on you."

"What? I don't understand. I didn't even know you before that night."

"I know, and that's what made it even more amazing. Every single thing on that tattoo, besides the flower, was me. It was as you were marked as mine before you even *knew* me. The eagle...the symbol of the United States and all it stands for. The Army logo and the rifle...I know it was for your brother, but it epitomizes *me*. Even the damn lightning bolt. Did you know the Delta Force crest has a lightning bolt in it?"

By the look of surprise in her eyes, he could tell she didn't.

"Yeah. So it was a bit of a shock seeing that on your back. I should've known then, it was a big enough sign, but I still didn't believe it."

"I didn't know."

"I know you didn't. Look to your left, Princess."

At the weird shift in topic, Rayne did as Ghost asked without thought.

"Look at the third shelf down."

Rayne gasped at the picture Ghost had on his bookshelf.

It was them. It was the picture he'd shown her at the hospital, of her in his arms, laughing up at him. Even though she'd been at his place for two days, she'd slept most of that time, and the rest of the time she'd either been eating or hanging with Ghost in his kitchen. She hadn't really checked out his place at all.

"Now keep looking around. Do you see any other pictures? Anything else in this room that shows I have an ounce of personality?"

Rayne smiled at his self-deprecating comment, but did as he asked. There wasn't a single picture anywhere, not even of his team. There were no pictures on the walls, only a huge-ass television set and books upon books on the shelves flanking it.

Ghost took Rayne's head in his and turned her back to him. "I lied to you back then. I'm sorry. But honestly, I'd probably do it again the exact same way. I'm Delta, Rayne. To the marrow of my bones. I will protect my country and my team with everything I have. Before you, that meant not letting anyone in. My parents died a long time ago, and I don't have any siblings. I'm not close with my aunts and uncles and have no idea if I even have cousins out there somewhere. This team is my family. The Army is my family. I'd die to keep them safe."

Rayne understood what he was saying. It sucked, but he was right. It wasn't as if he could've come right out and told her he was a top-secret soldier and here's his address if she wanted to look him up. But he had a picture of them in his house. It was one thing to have it on his phone still, another entirely for him to have gone to the effort to get it printed up and framed. She meant something to him. That, in turn, meant everything to her.

"I have something else to show you."

"Oh Lord, there's more?"

Ghost chuckled at her tone. "One more last revelation, then we can get on with whatever it is we're doing. Okay?"

Rayne nodded.

Ghost sat up with Rayne in his arms, and she barely bit back the girly screech at the sudden movement. He stood up and then immediately turned around and sat her back down. The cushion was still warm with his body heat. Rayne clutched the blanket around her, making sure none of her girly bits were hanging out.

She was more than confused when Ghost lay on his belly next to her and put his legs in her lap. Did he want a massage? What the hell was he doing?

"Pull up the right leg of my sweats, Princess."

Rayne had no idea why Ghost wanted her to look at his leg, but did as he asked, then gasped as the tattoo there was revealed.

She quickly pushed the material all the way up to his knee and traced the beautiful colors with her fingertips. Holding the blanket to her chest with one hand, she bent over his leg to see it closer.

"I took a picture of your tattoo before I left that morning. It was probably a dick thing to do, but with all the other dick things I did that day, what was one more? You were lying on your stomach and I couldn't resist. I edged the sheet down just far enough so I could get a shot of your tattoo. I couldn't get it out of my head. You had me inked on you…and I wanted the exact same design on my skin to remind me of you. Every day I wanted to see it and remember how beautiful you were. How you looked, how your tattoo looked, as I took you from behind."

Some people might think his words were crude, but Rayne couldn't bring herself to care. To her, they were beautiful.

"I came home and within a month, had you on me, Princess. Less than a month."

"It's perfect. But doesn't the Army logo blow the whole 'no one knows I'm a badass top-secret military soldier' thing?"

"Yeah, it does." He didn't even sound sorry.

Rayne processed that for a moment. "You could've left it off."

"Then it wouldn't have been like yours."

Rayne's lip wobbled, and she frantically tried to hold back her tears.

"As you can see, the only difference is the princess wand."

At Ghost's words, Rayne lost it. She couldn't hold back the tears anymore. He might've left her in that hotel room in London, and maybe would've never tried to find her or contact her again, but he hadn't used her. The tattoo staring her in the face proved he cared.

She was back in Ghost's arms before she took in a second heaving breath.

"I didn't show it to you to make you cry, Princess," he cajoled.

"I-I-I know," she hiccupped. "You've seen the additions to mine?"

Ghost nodded against her head. "Yeah, I saw it on the plane on the way back from Egypt. And I have to say *now* your tattoo is fucking perfect. I thought it was before, but you adding our Big Ben and me flitting around the top? Perfect."

"I did it three months ago."

Ghost kissed her temple and they sat on the couch without a word for a while.

With one last sniff, Rayne said. "Can I have another tissue?"

Ghost smiled and handed one to her, smiling again when she used it and simply held it out to him to take from her.

"I need to get dressed."

"Don't do it on my behalf."

Rayne halfheartedly swatted him. "Perv."

He chuckled. "Okay, Princess. You go get dressed and I'll re-bandage those for you."

Rayne held one of her hands out. "Do you think it looks like bugs are peeking out from my wrists?"

"Uh…no?"

"Oh come on, Ghost. Look! It's as if their little black antennas are peeking out."

"Ew, that's gross."

"You've never had stitches before?"

"Oh I've had them, just never thought of it that

way before…and now, thanks to you…I won't be able to think of anything else."

She giggled before looking back down at her wrists. "It looks like I tried to kill myself."

Ghost turned her head with a finger under her chin. "The scars will fade, but, Rayne, the scars only show the world how tough you are. You shouldn't be ashamed of them." He then brought her hand up to his mouth and kissed each and every mark on her wrist. Then did the same to the other one.

When he shifted as if to get on his knees and do the same to her ankles, Rayne said, "Okay, okay. They're badges of honor. Get up, seriously."

When Ghost looked up into her eyes and smiled, Rayne knew she'd never be the same. She had no idea where they were going or what would happen between them, but at that moment, she knew she was a goner. Whatever this man wanted, she'd bend over backwards to give it to him.

Chapter Twenty-Eight

"THERE'S SOMEONE I'D like you to meet," Ghost told Rayne at breakfast the next morning. They'd watched movies the night before and Rayne had no idea how to tell Ghost she thought she was ready to sleep in the same bed with him again. She'd missed him the last few nights, remembering how safe she'd felt when he'd snuggled up to her in the minuscule hospital bed.

"Yeah?"

"Her name is Penelope. I can't really tell you how the guys and I know her, but she lives down in San Antonio and comes up here to Fort Hood every now and then.

"Ooookay."

"I think it'd do you both some good to talk."

"You're gonna have to give me more than that, Ghost. I'm not good with small talk. You can't just shove some random woman at me and say 'talk.' It doesn't work like that."

Ghost pushed back from the table, gathered their

plates and took them to the kitchen. He came back, sat down, and leaned on his elbows. "Do you trust me?"

Rayne nodded. Amazingly enough, even after all the lies he'd told her when they'd first met, she did. From the second she'd seen him in her prison in Egypt, she'd trusted him with her life. That hadn't changed.

"Then go get some clothes on and we'll go."

Rayne just shook her head in exasperation. "Okay, give me ten minutes and I'll be ready."

An hour later, Rayne was sitting in a small conference room on the base, waiting to meet the mysterious Penelope. Ghost didn't tell her anything more than he already had, just made small talk about nothing in particular on their way to Fort Hood.

After a few minutes, the door opened and a small blonde woman, maybe only a couple inches taller than five feet, walked in. Rayne had no idea why she looked familiar, she knew they'd never met, but she did.

"Ghost! It's so good to see you!" Penelope exclaimed and came across the room and hugged Ghost tightly. "I know we've talked on and off in the last couple of months, but it's so good to actually *see* you."

"You too, Tiger. How are you?"

"Good."

"Things back to normal at home?"

"As normal as they could be, I suppose. Cade's still driving me crazy, being all overprotective and shit."

"And the rest of the guys?"

"They're figuring out that I'm still the same ol' person I was before."

"And Moose?"

Rayne watched as the young woman blushed.

"He's being a bit more hardheaded, but he'll figure it out eventually too."

Ghost turned to Rayne and held out his hand. "I want you to meet Rayne. Rayne, this is Penelope Turner. She's a firefighter down in San Antonio, and a former Army Reserve sergeant."

Rayne held out her hand. "It's good to meet you, Penelope."

They shook hands and Penelope turned to Ghost. "You didn't tell her, did you?"

Ghost shook his head. "Figured it was up to you to share what you wanted."

"Fine, then scoot," she said with a teasing smile.

Ghost turned to Rayne and hugged her tightly. "Don't overdo it. If you get tired, let me know and we'll go home."

Rayne rolled her eyes. "What do you think we'll be doing in here, Ghost? Running obstacles? Pushups? Cripes. I'm assuming we'll just be talking. I'm sure I'll be fine."

"Oooh, I like her, Ghost. She doesn't put up with your overbearing protective bullshit."

"Shut it, Tiger."

Penelope and Rayne grinned at each other, and Rayne felt at ease for the first time since arriving. Maybe it wouldn't be so bad trying to have a conversation with this stranger after all.

Ghost kissed Rayne on the lips; he'd been doing that a lot the last twenty-four hours after their talk on the couch and the tattoo show-and-tell. "I'll be back in a bit."

As soon as the door shut behind Ghost, Penelope sat and said, "So here's the quick rundown. About nine months ago, I was kidnapped by ISIS over in Turkey. A SEAL team came over and stole me back, we got shot down, and Ghost and his crew came and got us all out. That's how I know him. I never hooked up with him or anything."

As Penelope spoke, Rayne realized why the woman looked so familiar. "Oh my God, I saw you on TV. You're the Army Princess! I was so happy when I heard you were rescued!"

Penelope smiled. "You and me both."

Rayne put two-and-two together. "You were rescued six months ago, right?"

"Uh-huh."

"That's around when I met Ghost. He must've been on his way home from that mission."

"He'll probably never tell you for sure, but setting

319

this up is his way of letting you know the stuff he can't tell you. He knows *I* can tell you, but he can't...and won't."

Rayne understood. "And you're really okay? You were held a long time."

"About three months."

Rayne didn't know what else to say. She wanted to ask so many questions, but didn't want to be rude.

"I wasn't raped."

Jeez, Penelope didn't pull any punches. She just laid it all out there.

"Oh, they beat the shit out of me, and I was scared for most of the time I was being held, but they didn't rape me for whatever reason, thank God. Ghost tells me you were over in that thing in Egypt and that it was a close call for you."

Rayne nodded.

"Sucks being a hostage, doesn't it?"

Rayne smiled. Penelope summed it up nicely. It was refreshing to be around someone who didn't sugarcoat things. "Yeah. It does."

"Here's the thing. I like Ghost. I like *all* the guys on the team. We aren't buddy-buddy. I'm not their confidant or anything and we don't go out for tea when I come up here. But Ghost obviously is into you, because he set this up. Guys like him...they aren't the flowers-and-candy type. He probably won't take you out to a romantic dinner. I don't see him renting a plane and having it fly a banner declaring his love for you."

Rayne giggled and nodded in agreement.

"But if you pay attention, you'll see the signs that he cares. A hand against your back. Asking if you need anything. He'll make sure you eat before him. He'll walk on the outside of the sidewalk, making sure you're away from traffic. The signs will be there, but they won't ever be the big romantic gestures most women crave."

"He wraps my wrists and ankles every morning. He took my nasty snot-filled tissues yesterday without making a big deal out of it. He let me have as much cream cheese on my bagel this morning as I wanted, even though it meant I used most of it and he only had a little bit."

Penelope nodded. "Exactly. They'll swear until they're dead as a doornail that they aren't romantic, when in reality, what we see in the movies and on TV as 'romance' is just smoke and mirrors. I don't know about you, but I'd much rather have their brand of romance than Hollywood's."

"He's intense."

"Yeah, they all are," Penelope agreed.

"He's bossy."

Again, Penelope agreed. "I'm guessing if you think

about it, he's bossy when it comes to your well-being. Yeah?"

"Mostly."

"And I might be overstepping, but I bet he's bossy in bed too. And that might be a harder one to take, but again, I'll repeat what I said before...he's bossy when it comes to what you need...to your well-being."

Rayne thought back to their night in London. Penelope was right. He'd been bossy, moving her this way and that, ordering her on her knees, but he'd taken care of her every time. He'd held off his own orgasm until he'd satisfied her.

"So while you might be unsure about him, and while he might seem too intense, remember what it is they do for a living. He flew into Iraq and he and his team snatched me and six SEALs out of the mountains as if they were going out for groceries. I'm assuming he strode into that fucking building in Egypt and plucked you out of whatever situation you were in and made it seem easy doing it. Am I right?"

"Yeah, pretty much."

Penelope leaned forward toward Rayne. "I come up to base every month or so for counseling. I might seem as though I'm tough, that I can deal with what happened to me, but I have my bad days. I saw some shit over there that I know I'll never forget for the rest of my life. I've seen enough firefighters and soldiers try—

and fail—to get through the shit they've experienced without help, and it doesn't work." Penelope cleared her throat, obviously pushing through extreme emotion. "I haven't met many people who have been held hostage like me, especially not by a foreign terrorist group. Us women have different things we have to be worried about than men do. I wouldn't mind if, when I come up, we could...talk. That is, if you wanted to. If you felt comfortable."

For the first time, Rayne saw a different side to the woman in front of her. Gone was the bold, brash firefighter who could obviously hold her own in a male-dominated field. Looking into her eyes, and seeing the vulnerability there, made Rayne realize how much she needed this woman. Mary might be her best friend, but she'd never understand what she'd been through. And as much as she loved her brother, he couldn't relate to her either.

Somehow Ghost had known both she and Penelope needed each other. Damn, she was falling for him all over again.

"I'd like that. I hadn't realized until just now that my friends, and even Ghost and his team, would never understand."

Penelope nodded in agreement. "Yeah, it took me a while too. I was mad at everyone, and it didn't help that the media wouldn't stop hounding me for my story. But when I finally bit the bullet and came up here to talk to the counselor, she suggested that it might do me some good to find a support group, with other victims. While I did that, and it helped, none of them had been through exactly what I had. A lot of their experiences paralleled what we went through…the helplessness, the terror, the uncertainty, but it just wasn't the same."

"There are groups?"

Penelope reached a hand out, and Rayne put hers in it without hesitation. The connection felt right.

"Yeah, there are. Down in San Antonio, I met the most amazing woman. Her name is Beth. She moved out here from California after a horrible experience. She was kidnapped and tortured by a serial killer, but managed to survive. We've connected in a way that we hadn't been able to with others, simply because we'd both been held hostage. I'm sorry to say I can't help her with dealing with being violated, since I wasn't, but I'd love to introduce you guys if you're ever down my way."

Rayne nodded. "I don't think I'm quite ready for that yet…but if you give me time…"

"No pressure. Seriously. It took me quite a while before I was ready to talk to anyone about what happened." Penelope sat back and smirked. "So…is Ghost as good in bed as it seems he'd be?"

Rayne blushed and said nothing.

"Ha! I knew it. Those guys are so fucking beautiful it should be illegal. Oh, don't worry. I'm not jonesing for your man or any of the guys on his team. I've got my own guy I have my eye on back home, but you have to admit they're some awesome eye-candy."

Rayne laughed and agreed. "Yeah, I swear sometimes I feel as if I'll have to get out a stick and beat the women off when we're out and about."

"He's got eyes only for you, woman. Never doubt it. When guys like him fall, they fall hard. They're exclusive and would kill anyone for even thinking about putting their hand on you."

"I'm beginning to see that."

There was a knock on the door and both women turned as it opened and Ghost stuck his head in. "All good?"

"We're fine, get your ass in here and take care of your woman. I have an appointment to make." The bold and brash Penelope was back, any sign of the vulnerable woman underneath the harsh façade gone.

Ghost strode in and leaned down and kissed Rayne. He put his hand on her shoulder. "You girls have a nice visit?"

Penelope rolled her eyes. "Oh good Lord, Ghost. Yes, it was fine. We chatted, Rayne understands that you're a Neanderthal, but one that has her best interests at heart. She knows who I am, and we've made plans to meet again. That answer all your questions?"

"Yup. You're the best, Tiger."

"Whatever. Come on, give me a hug and let me get out of here. I'll see you next time I'm up."

Ghost gave the slight woman a huge bear hug, lifting her feet up off the floor in the process. Rayne watched, loving seeing this side of Ghost...the protective-older-brother side of him.

"Don't be a stranger. I'll get the team together next time and we'll do lunch or something."

"Sounds like a plan. See you later, Rayne. Remember what I said."

Rayne pushed her chair back and stood. "I will. It was nice meeting you."

"You too. Glad you're safe."

Rayne looked up at Ghost after Penelope had left the room. "Thank you."

He didn't even pretend to not know what she was talking about. "You're welcome."

"I don't know how you knew I needed that when I didn't know I needed it myself, but thank you. She's amazing."

"So are you, Princess."

"I was only held about a week. I can't imagine what she went through."

"Don't compare yourself to her or anyone else. You

went through your own nightmare. It wasn't any less horrible than what she went through. Give yourself some credit. You're one hell of a woman. Got it?"

Rayne smiled, thinking about what Penelope had said about bossy men. "Got it."

"Come on, let's get you to the doctor and see what he says about those stitches. Then we'll go back home and I'll make you some lunch and we can watch a movie."

"*The Notebook*?"

"Fuck no. I've seen you cry enough for one week."

Rayne smiled, having known he'd veto it. "Okay, Ghost. Whatever you want to watch."

"Come on, woman. I'm feeling the need to spoil you."

"Far be it from me to protest that."

Rayne smiled as Ghost put his arm around her waist and walked with her out the door and into the hot Texas morning.

Chapter Twenty-Nine

RAYNE WOKE WITH a cry and shoved at the arms holding her down. Moshe was there and wanted to be a man, but she'd be damned if it would be with her.

"Jesus, Rayne. It's me. It's Ghost. I've got you, you're okay."

The words barely penetrated her sleep-fogged mind, her only thought was escape. "No! Get off me. No!"

"Rayne!" Ghost's voice was harsh, and just what she needed to realize she wasn't in Egypt. She wasn't being held captive, and it wasn't Moshe with his arms around her, it was Ghost.

Rayne looked up at Ghost and swallowed hard. "Sorry, I'm okay. I'm okay."

"Christ, Princess. I wanted to *help* you by introducing you to Penelope, not make you regress. I'm so sorry."

Rayne buried her face into Ghost's chest and let him move them so they were once again situated on the couch, where they'd been earlier that evening while watching *Under Siege*. The doctor had said her wounds were looking good and he'd gone ahead and taken out the stitches. He'd given her a mild painkiller and they'd come back to Ghost's house and he'd put in the movie.

Obviously her talk with Penelope and dealing with the stitches had brought the memories of her captivity to the forefront of her mind.

"It's fine, Ghost. I'm okay, I just…I need to deal with it, and not thinking about it isn't working. Will you just…will you hold me?"

"All fucking night, Rayne. Just relax. I got you."

"Can I sleep with you?" Rayne felt Ghost's muscles tighten under her. "I mean," she tried to backpedal, "it's not a big deal, I can—"

"Yes. I want you with me. I was waiting for you to give me a sign you wanted to. You have no idea how much I wanted to go into your room and carry you to my bed."

"Why didn't you?"

"Because I wanted you to be there because *you* wanted to be there. Not because I coerced you into it."

"I want to be there. I haven't slept that great since the hospital, when you were there with me."

Ghost carefully squeezed Rayne against his body. Christ.

Later, he carried her to his room, and after she got

ready in the bathroom, helped her to the bed.

"Wow, this is quite a bit bigger than the hospital's, isn't it?" Rayne tried to joke.

"It might be bigger, but we won't be taking up any more space than we did in that tiny bed," Ghost returned, settling Rayne on her side and pulling her against him. He wrapped himself around her as he'd done in the past, and as he'd thought about doing the last few nights. Ghost buried his nose in her hair and inhaled her scent. He'd missed it. He'd missed her.

"Go to sleep, Princess. I've got you. I'll be here when you wake up. Promise."

He felt her nod against him. He lay there holding her tight long after she'd drifted into a comfortable sleep. Thanking God again for putting her in his path and giving him one more chance to do the right thing. To do what they both needed.

The next morning, Rayne shifted, feeling better than she had in a long time. She froze when she felt Ghost's calloused hands on her back. She was lying on her belly, head turned to the right, arms at her side. Ghost was kneeling next to her, massaging her lower back. She raised her head and turned so she could see him. "What—"

"I wanted to see it fully."

Rayne realized he was looking at her tattoo. Half the time she honestly forgot it was there. She blushed.

Even knowing he'd already seen the additions to it, it was still a little embarrassing. She nodded and relaxed in his hold.

Ghost tugged Rayne's shirt up, and helped her raise her arms until he could remove it. Before she'd even settled back down, he'd straddled her hips and had both hands on her tattoo. He traced the words "Quiet Professionalism" with his fingertip, the touch light and almost ticklish against her back.

"Why two-thirty?" Ghost asked in a reverent tone.

"It's the last time I remember looking at the clock that morning."

"That last time. When I took you from behind," Ghost said with certainty.

Rayne nodded but didn't speak. She felt him lean down and brush his lips over the ghost. She'd thought it appropriate to have it hovering around the iconic clock since he'd told her he'd once climbed the stairs all the way to the top.

"It's absolutely beautiful, Princess. And knowing our time together meant as much to you as it did to me is priceless. You have no idea what you've given me with this. It's better than anything you could ever say to me, or buy for me. Swear to Christ, I'll do everything in my power to treasure you. To treat you right. I can't promise I won't fuck up because, well, I'm a guy and I'm not used to this. But know that I'll never do anything on purpose to hurt you."

"Okay, Ghost." She felt him move his lips across her back, kissing every part of her tattoo.

"And this is probably the wrong thing to say, and I'm probably a dick for even thinking it, but I swear to God I hope you like taking me from behind. I have a feeling it's going to be my favorite position with you. Seeing me inked on you. Seeing this eagle ripple as I pound into you from behind…yeah, I've had you once and couldn't get the memory of this tattoo out of my head. But now that you've purposely added *me* to it? You might as well have stamped 'Property of Ghost' across your back. Because you're mine. Hear me, Rayne? Mine."

Rayne shifted and pushed her ass up into him. Jesus, every word out of his mouth made her wetter and wetter. She honestly hadn't planned on going there with him this week. She wanted to get home and really think about it, but she couldn't resist him anymore. She wanted him more now than she did six months ago…if that was even possible.

"I'll take it any way you want to give it to me, Ghost."

"Oh fuck." The words were uttered in a tortured voice, as if she'd just broken through the last of his restraint.

Rayne heard a flicking sound and looked back to

see Ghost reaching for her panties with a wicked-looking Swiss Army Knife in his hand. "Hold still, Princess. I have to get these off of you. I can't wait to see you. I'd rip them off, but unfortunately, that only works in romance novels."

Rayne held her breath and felt the elastic around her waist give way. Before she could think about what to do or how to move, she felt her hips in Ghost's hands. "Don't put any weight on those wrists. Let me do all the work."

Rayne thought briefly about what Penelope had said...realizing this was one more way Ghost was taking care of her. He remembered her wounds and didn't want her hurting herself further.

Ghost held Rayne's hips in his hands and licked once from her clit to her ass, reveling in the wetness he encountered along the way. "You all right? No bad memories?" He wanted to shove himself as far inside her as he could get, marking her as his, but he didn't want to hurt her either. It hadn't been that long ago when she'd thought she was about to be raped. He'd rather cut off his own arm than hurt her physically *or* mentally.

"More, Ghost. Oh God, *more*."

Smiling, Ghost leaned down and did it again, slower this time. Relearning her taste and feel. The angle was a bit odd and he couldn't reach her clit as easily as he could if she was on her back, but he hadn't lied. Seeing her tattoo as he ate her from behind was as close to Heaven as he knew he'd ever reach from Earth.

He leaned over and grabbed his pillow, easing it under her hips. Seeing it wasn't going to be enough, he ordered, "Yours too, Princess. Give me your pillow."

She gave it up without a word, staying down but moving her arms up to rest beside her head.

"Oh yeah, I've imagined this in my head so many times I can hardly believe you're here in front of me. You have no idea how beautiful you look with your ass in the air for me. Spread your legs more. Yeah, that's it. Christ, Princess. Fucking mine. All mine."

Ghost leaned down and took her with a passion he hadn't shown before. He sucked and licked, and ate at her like a man starved. When she started to moan and shift under him, he held her still for his mouth. Ghost finally added one finger, then two, easing into her tight sheath as he concentrated on flicking his tongue as fast as he could against her clit.

Hooking his fingers and stroking the small bundle of nerves on the inside at the same time as he moaned against her clit, he sent Rayne flying over the edge into oblivion. She bucked against his hold, shivering and shaking and crying out his name. Ghost didn't let up until he felt her pull away from him slightly. Knowing he'd pushed as far as he could, that his touch was now more painful than it was erotic, he backed off. Enjoying the sight of her juices on his fingers and dripping out of her as he pulled away.

He pulled up to his knees and didn't take his eyes off her. He ran both hands over her back, spreading her wetness onto her, being sure to trace the words that represented him with his quickly drying fingers.

He leaned down and once again kissed the image of the ghost on her back. "Can you take me, Princess? Are you okay?"

Rayne groaned and he felt her push up against him. "Yes, please, Ghost. Please, I need you. I want you inside."

Ghost leaned over to the table next to the bed and pulled out a condom. He'd bought them on the way back from the hospital, enjoying the shit out of Rayne's blush as he set them on the counter and smirked at her lecherously.

He quickly sheathed himself, and brought his hands back to Rayne's skin. "Can you get up on your elbows without hurting yourself?"

Before the words were completely out, Rayne was up. The position brought her ass up to just the right height for him to plunge inside. "Let me know if this is painful for you, Rayne. I mean it. I don't think I'm going to last all that long, I've imagined this for six long months, but I still don't want you to have a moment of pain. All right?"

"Um-hmm," Rayne moaned, pushing back toward him.

Ghost held himself away, wanting to make sure she understood. "You hear me? Tell me you understand."

"I hear you, Ghost. I'll tell you if it hurts, but dammit, it hurts not having you inside me. I need you."

Her words pushed him past his breaking point. He fit his blood-engorged cock to her tight sheath and slowly pushed inside.

They both moaned at the same time. "God, it feels like coming home," Ghost told her as he held himself still inside her. He could feel her clenching around him and could literally feel her hot juices coat his cock as they both acclimated to the feel of him inside.

"You feel huge this way," Rayne told him, pushing back against him.

"Yeah, I can get farther inside you in this position," he told her, not sure what he was saying. He held her hips still as he pulled back then slowly, inch by inch, pushed inside her again.

Ghost watched as she arched her back and the wings on the eagle rippled with her movement. "I wish you could see this, Princess," Ghost told her, moving his hands from her hips to her ink. "Every time you push up against me it looks as though this eagle wants to fly right off your skin."

"It really does something for you, doesn't it?" Rayne asked breathlessly.

"Yeah, it does. But it's more than just the tattoo. It's that it's *your* tattoo. And it's on *your* back, and I'm buried inside *your* body watching it move and flex for me. Don't think I'm getting off on the tattoo itself. I'm getting off on knowing what it means to you, and that you had me on you before you *knew* you had me on you."

"Jesus, Ghost."

He smiled a bit at the urgency and desperation in her words.

"Move. Now."

"Yes, ma'am. My pleasure."

Ghost kept a steady pace, plunging in and out of Rayne with measured thrusts. When he felt her trying to get up on her hands, he pushed down on her upper back. "No, Princess. Stay down."

"But...I need—"

Realizing she was on the edge and not caring if she hurt herself or not, she only wanted to get off, he ordered, "Touch yourself. Balance on your shoulder and touch yourself."

She immediately did as he asked, and brought one hand down to where they were joined. Ghost felt her frantic movements on her clit as he continued to thrust inside her. He leaned over and tugged on the nipple of the breast he could reach as he caressed her back with his other hand.

"That's it. Rub yourself, take yourself there. You're so hot and tight, I can feel you grip my cock as you get close. Take what you need, take yourself over."

Ghost felt her hand speed up and she began to buck back against him more frantically. He pinched her nipple roughly and thrust into her harder and harder. Feeling her muscles tense as she finally flew apart, Ghost let himself go. Holding on to her hips with both hands again and watching as he pushed inside her once, then twice, then he held himself tightly on the third stroke and felt himself explode as Rayne continued to buck against his firm hold as she came down from her orgasm.

"Jesus, Ghost," Rayne murmured after several moments had passed. "If it's like that every time, you're gonna kill us."

"I can't think of a better way to die." Ghost reluctantly pulled out, groaning along with Rayne as he slipped from her. He put his hand on her folds and massaged lightly, loving the feel of how hot and wet she still was.

"Mmmmmm," Rayne murmured, shifting under his caress.

"Don't move, I'll be right back."

"Umkay."

Ghost hurried to the bathroom and took care of the condom. He ran a washcloth under some warm water and wrung it out before returning to Rayne.

She'd taken his words literally and lay in exactly the same spot he'd left her. Her ass propped up by the two pillows, her arms resting limply by her head, and a satisfied smile on her face.

Ghost ran his hand gently from her shoulder blades to her ass, caressing her, petting her. He placed the warm washcloth against her folds and tried to control his hard-on when she shifted under his ministrations.

"That feels awesome," Rayne breathed, opening her eyes and watching his face as he cleaned her.

He finished up and tossed the wet cloth on the floor, not caring where it landed. He'd deal with it later. "Lift up."

Rayne lifted her hips and let Ghost pull the two pillows out from under her. She watched as he kept the one that was directly under her for himself and handed the other one back to her. She shifted onto her side and waited for Ghost to settle before she moved into him. He gathered her close, turning on his back and letting her use his shoulder as a pillow.

She smiled as he groaned when one of her legs bent and brushed against his semi-hard shaft. "Are you ready to go again? Already?" she asked incredulously, slurring her words with exhaustion.

"No. But if you give me thirty minutes or so, I will be."

Rayne groaned, but gamely replied, "Okay, maybe I'll nap until you're ready then."

Ghost smiled and pulled her closer. "You do that, Princess. Sleep. I've got you."

Rayne's last thought before she fell into sleep was that she loved how Ghost always told her he "had her."

Chapter Thirty

THE NEXT COUPLE of days were full of resting, relaxing, and relearning each other's bodies. Ghost had taught her the reverse cowgirl position, and Rayne thought she might even enjoy that better than when he took her from behind. She loved being able to have some control, and even torture Ghost a bit by controlling the pace of their lovemaking, and he certainly loved being able to watch her tattoo.

He taught her the joys of shower sex, and bathtub sex, and semi-public sex when he took her out on his porch one night. Rayne had been afraid the neighbors would see—or hear—her but Ghost had allayed her fears by asking if she really thought he'd do anything that would humiliate her. When he'd put it like that, she'd let go of her inhibitions and allowed Ghost to lead her where he wanted to take them.

When she had another nightmare, Ghost had stayed up with her and listened as she finally described in detail what had happened to her. He hadn't said a word, but had let her get it all out. And after she was done, and after she'd cried and snotted all over him, he'd simply held her for the rest of the night, with no pressure to do anything else.

She felt loved. She had no idea how it had happened so fast, or if what she was feeling was even right, but there was no other word for it. Ghost had blown past all of her barriers and made her feel like the most cherished thing in his world.

The two of them had even gone out and met the rest of his team for lunch one day, something Ghost had sworn afterwards he'd never do again. He'd been disgruntled that the rest of the guys were purposely trying to rile him by flirting with her.

Rayne made sure she made it up to him when they got home by dropping to her knees and convincing him she only had eyes for him.

Today was the first day Ghost had gone into work since she'd gotten out of the hospital. His week of leave was up and he had to go back in. He'd woken her up with his head between her legs and had taken her so hard she had no doubt he'd rather stay in bed with her for the rest of the day than go to the base.

Ghost had finally left her with a kiss and told her to make herself at home. She'd wandered throughout his house, able to look around freely without feeling self-conscious for the first time since she'd arrived. Ghost's taste in books ranged from old westerns to the autobiographies of famous military leaders. He had protein powder in his kitchen cabinets along with ramen noodles. There were no romantic comedies in his collection of DVDs, but his tastes were eclectic there too, ranging from sci-fi to historical documentaries, along with the war movies she'd expected to find.

After eating lunch, and growing bored, Rayne called Mary. She knew her friend had the day off since they'd spoken briefly every day. Mary didn't quite trust Ghost, and wanted to check in frequently to make sure Rayne was all right.

"Hey, Mare. How are you?"

"Good. How are *you*?"

"Great. Ghost went back to work today."

"Ah, left you alone in the house, huh? What'd you find?"

"What? Nothing!"

"Bullshit. Does he have a stash of *Playboys* in his bedside drawer?"

"I didn't look there! Jeez, Mary. I only scoped out the food, book, and movie situation."

"Girl, get your ass in his room and see what he's got in his drawers then!"

"Mary!"

"Don't 'Mary' me. You know you want to."

Rayne hesitated for a second then mentally shrugged. Her friend knew her too well. "All right, I'm going."

Mary laughed at her and waited to see what she'd find.

"Okay, I'm opening one drawer...nothing interesting...socks."

"He keeps socks next to the bed? Weird. What about the other side?"

"Don't get your panties in a twist, give me a second." They both laughed as Rayne moved around to the other side of the large mattress. "Ooooh, okay. The condoms he bought the other day are in here, and a tube of lube."

"Lube? Girl, he had better not be needing that, otherwise he's not doing something right."

Rayne giggled. "No, I can honestly say we haven't needed any lube thus far, but...oh!"

"What? What is it? *Playboy*? A *Playgirl*?"

"No...um...a small vibrator, nipple clamps, and those ball things."

"Ball things?" Mary asked, and Rayne knew if she could see her she'd have a shit-eating grin on her face.

"Yeah...you know...those things that women put inside them and when they rub up against each other they chime or something? I think they're Chinese."

"Ben Wa balls?"

"I guess."

"Holy shit, Raynie...you've got yourself a kinkster."

Rayne could feel herself blush. She closed the drawer. "It's not that big of a deal. At least I didn't find whips and chains or something."

"There's still time to look around, girl."

Rayne wandered back into the other room and plopped down on the couch. "I'm bored, Mary."

"Bored huh? Had enough of your forced vacation?"

Rayne nodded. "Yeah, I think so. I mean, I didn't mind when Ghost was here. We were busy all the time."

"Busy…yeah…that's what you're calling it?"

"Hush, you sex fiend. I meant we went out to eat, or to my doctor appointments, or watched movies…we were busy. But now that he's back at work and I'm stuck here…I'm bored."

Mary was silent for a moment. "You ready to come home then?"

"Yes. No. Shit. Maybe. I don't know," Rayne complained. "I love being with Ghost, but I don't like sitting around feeling useless."

"You ready to go back to work? I'm sure your boss would let you come back early."

"No!" Rayne's negative answer was swift and emphatic.

"So you don't want to stay there, you don't know if you want to come back here, you're bored, but you don't want to go back to work," Mary summed up without inflection.

Rayne buried her face in her hand. "I'm a mess."

"Yeah, you kinda are," Mary agreed.

"I thought you were supposed to stick up for me, make me feel better."

"I'm sorry, you must have me confused with a Stepford friend or something," Mary intoned. "Look, this is only the first day Ghost has gone back to work, right? Give it some time. Read a book. *Relax.* You've always had a hard time sitting around and doing nothing. I'm sure you're still healing. Don't rush it. But, Raynie, know that the second you're ready to come home, I'll be there to get you."

"I know you will. I love you, Mare."

"Why don't you ask Ghost if you can borrow his car while he's at work? You can check out the area. See what you think. I know you. You're falling for him. Eventually, if you want to make this work, you're going to have to move down there."

It was so like Mary to be blunt and say what Rayne was thinking. "I don't want to leave you."

"Babe, I work in a bank. It's not as though my job isn't mobile."

"You'd move down here with me?"

"Hell yeah I would. I love you, Rayne. You're my best friend in the world. You were there for me when I needed you the most. I know we can't live together for the rest of our lives. Eventually our lives might take us in different directions, but if I can support you and help you find the man of your dreams and make it work, and can be at your side while you do it...why wouldn't I?"

"Jesus, Mary."

"No! No crying! I can't handle it. Just tell Ghost you want to borrow his damn car and do it. Find out if there's a decent mall, if there's a Starbucks nearby, if there's a good country and western bar where I can pick up men...you know, all the important stuff."

Rayne gave a watery chuckle at her friend. God, she had no idea how she'd lucked out in finding Mary. "Okay, I will. Good idea."

"Of course it was."

"I'll call you tomorrow and report in?"

"You better."

"Love you, Mare. Thanks for always making me feel better."

"Love you too, Raynie. Seriously, I'm happy for you. I wasn't sure about Ghost at first, I saw how much he hurt you. So far he's doing all right by you, but I'll reserve judgement until he proves it once and for all. Okay?"

"Okay. Talk to you tomorrow."

"Bye."

"Bye."

Rayne hung up the phone, feeling better now that she had a plan. She'd been worried about leaving Mary behind. It was stupid, but they'd been through a lot and had lived near each other for a long time. Rayne was closer to Mary than she was Samantha, and couldn't imagine not being able to pop over to her place for a drink and a movie whenever the mood struck.

LATER THAT NIGHT, lying boneless on top of Ghost after having jumped him the second they'd gone to bed, Rayne tried to ask as nonchalantly as she could, "So...have you used those Ben Wa ball things before?"

Shrieking in surprise when Ghost flipped her abruptly on her back and loomed over her, she held on to his arms and looked up at him.

"You been going through my drawers, Princess?"

"No...well...yeah. You weren't here. I was bored."

"I've never used them personally, but have seen them used."

"Seen?" Rayne wrinkled her nose at Ghost.

He chuckled. "Not in person, in a video."

"Porn?"

"Yeah, Rayne. Porn. Does it surprise you that a career military guy like me has seen porn?"

"Um, no, but…"

"It was extremely hot…I'm sure the woman's reaction was way faked and over the top, but I couldn't stop thinking about what they might feel like for you and how when you wriggled and squirmed, they'd chime inside you. I know they can't actually give you an orgasm, or at least I think that's right, but imagining them inside you while we go out to eat and how they'd get you wet and excited so I could fuck you the second we got home… Yeah, I decided maybe we could give them a try."

"Me?"

"You, what?"

"Inside me, specifically? Or inside a woman in general?"

Ghost understood her question and kneed her legs apart so he could push up against her core and she could feel him lengthening.

"You, Princess. Before London, the only thing in that drawer was a copy of *Playboy* and that bottle of lube. But after you, I watched some videos, got off, and immediately bought those clamps and the balls off the Internet and kept them in my drawer. It was stupid, I had no intention of doing anything with them, but just the thought of them there and the image of what they'd look like on and in you was enough to make me so hard I could pound nails."

"Uh…"

"Want to try them out?"

"What? Now?"

"Why not?"

"Because we just had sex?"

"Just because I just made love to you doesn't mean you can't orgasm again. It might take me a bit longer, but I can guarantee seeing how much you enjoy my toys on you will do the trick in no time."

Rayne moaned as Ghost leaned over and reached for the handle on the drawer. She leaned up and nibbled on his shoulder as he moved above her. She had no idea what it was about Ghost that made her so uninhibited, but she loved it. She loved him.

Chapter Thirty-One

T HE NEXT WEEK and a half went by quickly for Rayne. She spent the days driving around the Killeen/Belton area and reporting back to Mary, and her nights being loved to within an inch of her life by Ghost.

It was almost time for her to get back to work. She'd spoken with her boss and he'd agreed to keep her on the Dallas/Fort Worth-London route for a while until she'd gotten her bearings. Then she'd be back in the regular International rotation again.

The thought made her want to puke, but Rayne sucked it up. It was her job; it was what she had to do.

Rayne heard Ghost open the door to the house and when he didn't immediately appear, went looking for him. She found him standing in the laundry room, staring at what she saw was simply a load of dirty clothes she hadn't yet put into the washer. Ever since she'd asked to borrow the car while he was at work the last week or so, Ghost had been picked up by Fletch and dropped off after work by one of the other guys on the team.

This was the first time she could remember him coming into the house through the garage, and thus through the small laundry room.

"Ghost? What are you doing? Are you all right?"

He looked up at her. "You're doing our laundry."

"Yeah? So? It was dirty. You didn't want to walk around in nasty, smelly clothes did you?" Rayne had no idea what his deal was.

Ghost dropped his duffle back on the floor and came toward her. "You're doing our laundry."

"Yeah, Ghost. I am," she repeated.

"Ours. *Our* laundry."

"Did you hit your head today? I'm seriously worried about you."

Ghost picked her up by her waist and set her down on top of the washing machine. "I fucking love coming home and walking into my house and seeing your panties mixed up with my boxers. To come home and know you're here. Waiting for me. You have no idea. None."

Chills broke out on Rayne's arms and legs at Ghost's words, but he didn't stop.

"This is what we fight for. This is what we're willing to die for."

"For me to wash your dirty clothes?" Rayne had no idea what he was getting at. She wasn't trying to be snarky, her question was genuine.

Ghost leaned his head against hers and closed his eyes. She could feel his hands squeeze her waist and move up under her T-shirt to her lower back, where he stroked. She knew he understood exactly what he was doing. He wasn't absently caressing her; he was running his hands over her tattoo, over *their* tattoo.

"All my life, since I've worked with the team, we've rescued people, we've killed, we've gone into any and every situation, no questions asked. And every time I've come home to an empty house. I've done my own laundry, cooked my own food, cleaned my own space. I fucking *love* coming home to you, Princess. You make everything I've done, every sacrifice I've made, worth it."

"Ghost—"

"I love you. I know it's fast. I know people will call me pussy-whipped, but I don't give a shit. You're mine. I left you once, I won't do it again. You were given to me to cherish, to protect, and to love. I'm not fucking that up again."

"Oh my God."

"I'm not asking you to marry me. I'm not even asking you to move in with me, although I've loved every second of you being here."

"Even when I used your razor to shave my legs and you cut yourself to shreds when you tried to shave the next morning?"

Ghost smiled briefly then got serious again. "Any-time you want to steal my razor, go for it. I don't give a shit. But yes, you're not perfect, and neither am I, but you don't get on my back for the stupid stuff I do. I love that about you. It's one of the million things I love. But you know what I love the most?"

"No," Rayne whispered, wrapping her legs around Ghost's waist while she waited for his answer.

"That I can tell you're trying. I know you're bored, Princess. I know you'll never be a housewife who waits for her man to get home. But you're trying, for me. For us. And that means more to me than you'll ever know."

Rayne swallowed through the tears in her throat. She'd thought she'd been hiding it from him. She should've known Ghost was too observant to let something like that slide.

"It's almost time for you to get back to work, right?" he asked, against hitting at the heart at what Rayne had been stressing about.

She nodded. "I have the DFW-London rotation starting this weekend."

"You ask for that?"

"Um-hum. I'm not ready for anything else yet."

Ghost pulled back and put his hands on either side of her head. "I love you, Rayne Jackson. I couldn't take it if something happened to you."

Rayne could only nod, trying to swallow back the lump in her throat.

"You'll stay here until you need to go back up to Fort Worth, right?"

She nodded again.

"Okay, here's the thing. Sometimes I'll be able to tell you when we have to leave for a mission, other times we might not get that much advance notice. When we left for Egypt, we knew about forty-five minutes before we had to be at the airport. But this time we got advance notice. We're leaving for a thing tomorrow morning."

"Tomorrow?"

Ghost nodded. "It's actually pretty good timing. You're ready to go back to work and have to go home to Fort Worth. I want you to stay here, in my house...in our bed, until you have to. All right?"

"What time?"

Ghost moved his hands, scooted Rayne's butt closer to him, and lifted her up. Her legs clamped tighter around his waist and she held on as he walked to the other room and the couch. "Early. Probably around three."

"Will you wake me before you go?"

"Absolutely. I'll never sneak out of our bed again, Princess. No matter what time it is, I'll wake you up to say goodbye."

Rayne sniffed once, trying to hold her tears at bay. This was what he did. He was a super-solider who had to go and save the world. She couldn't be a baby about it. "Okay," she whispered. "You hungry?" She watched as a grin moved over his face.

"Starved."

Her lips quirked up in a smile at his lecherous response.

"I meant for food."

"I could eat."

"Good. I made us some tacos. It's nothing fancy, but it was easy and I wasn't sure when you'd be getting home."

"Sounds perfect. You should know...after we eat?"

"Yeah?"

"I'll be taking you to bed and making you come so hard you'll be sore, making sure you won't forget about me."

"Lord, Ghost, seriously?"

"Oh yeah, seriously. I'm gonna need to tide us over until I return."

Ghost helped Rayne stand up and smirked at the blush that moved across her face. He leaned down and kissed her chastely on the cheek. "Come on, Princess. Let's eat so we can go and have dessert."

Chapter Thirty-Two

RAYNE WRUNG HER hands together as she sat in the jump seat. The flight from DFW to London had been tough. It wasn't the flying that was the hard part—it was knowing she had an overnight layover waiting for her that was the problem.

The airline had put her and Sarah on the same flight, obviously thinking, correctly, that they might like to see each other and that it might be good for them after what had happened. Rayne had hugged Sarah tightly and their coworkers had been polite enough to ignore the tears they'd shed at their reunion.

The flight had gone off without a hitch. They didn't even have anyone try to become a member of the mile-high club, which was somewhat unusual. Feeling no need whatsoever to tour the city, especially since it held such wonderful memories of Ghost and he wasn't there with her, Rayne had stuck like glue to the two pilots and the other flight attendants as they'd made their way to the airport hotel.

She and Sarah shared a room and had talked much

of the night about their experience and how happy they were to be alive and well.

Now she was on her way back to the Dallas/Fort Worth area after getting the passengers settled in for the long ten-hour flight back to Texas.

Rayne took a deep breath. She'd done it. She'd gotten over the hurdle of her first trip, akin to getting back on the horse after it had bucked her off.

The only thing that would've made it better was to be able to talk to Ghost after she'd gotten to the hotel while in England. But Rayne knew she probably had quite a few instances in her future of wanting to talk to Ghost but not being able to, because he was off saving the world.

TEN DAYS LATER, Rayne stuck her keys in her purse and dropped it on the little table inside her apartment. She wheeled her small suitcase back to her room and left it there, deciding to deal with it later. Kicking off her shoes, and sighing at the relief of having her feet free from the heels she hadn't worn the entire time she'd been convalescing, she plopped down on her sofa and put her head back against the couch.

She had one day off, then she'd be back on the plane heading over to London again. She'd be on this run for another week, then she'd have to decide what to do. Her boss had hinted that her next rotation would be the DFW-Paris-South Africa rotation, but the thought of having to step foot on the continent of Africa made her break out in hives. Intellectually, she knew South Africa wasn't Egypt, but emotionally, it was way too close for her way of thinking.

It'd been almost two weeks since she'd said good-bye to Ghost, and she hadn't heard anything since. Ghost had warned her that he wouldn't be able to talk to her at all while he was gone. However, hearing him say it and experiencing it were two completely different things.

While she'd relaxed in Ghost's house after he left, she'd watched the news for the first few nights he was gone, and had called Mary completely freaked out over a story about a terrorist bombing in a subway over in Japan. Mary had, luckily, talked her off the ledge and told her to shut off the damn television and quit imagining the worst.

Mary had come to get her from Ghost's house the next day, even though Chase had promised to take her back up to Fort Worth whenever she was ready. Rayne needed some Mary time, and it had been more than worth it. They'd chatted all the way home and by the time Mary had pulled up in front of Rayne's condo, they'd decided that the news was off-limits. All it did was stress Rayne out and make her have nightmares.

Rayne knew she should get up, get ready for bed, eat…something, but it felt so good to just sit and relax for a moment, she couldn't move.

The next thing she knew, her cell phone was chirping next to her.

She looked around in confusion. Her condo was dark except for the light she'd turned on in the hall as she'd come in earlier that evening.

Looking down at the phone, Rayne saw it was two in the morning. The incoming call was from "Unknown." Hastily swiping the screen to answer, she wondered if this could be Ghost…finally. "Hello?"

"I'm looking for Rayne Jackson," the voice on the other end of the line said with a slight Texan drawl.

Rayne's heartrate sped up and she sat upright on the couch. Was this someone from the Army? Who had her number and would be calling her at this hour? She didn't think it was any of Ghost's teammates, she didn't recall any of them having an accent like this man did.

"Who is this?"

"Is this Rayne?"

"Who is *this*?" Ghost had given her a short lecture before he left about how he never wanted the dangerous stuff he did to leak back on her, and while it *shouldn't*, he urged her to always be careful about what she let slip about herself, him, the two of them, and what he did for a living.

The man on the other end of the line chuckled. "I see Ghost has taught you well. My name is Tex. I'm a friend of his."

Rayne frantically thought about what to do. Did she believe him? Did she not? If she hung up on him, would she miss learning something about Ghost and when he'd be back? She decided to err on the side of caution. "And?"

"I also see Ghost hasn't told you about me."

"No, he hasn't."

"Okay, as I said. My name is Tex. It's really John, but everyone calls me Tex. I also know Wolf and his team...you met Wolf a couple of months ago in Egypt, yeah?"

That surprised her. First, she wasn't sure who knew the SEAL team and the Delta team were in Egypt, and because of the way Ghost got her out of the country, she wasn't sure many people knew *she* had been over in Egypt in the middle of all that had gone down.

"Yeah, I met him." She still purposely kept her answers vague.

"Good girl. Not telling me anything."

Rayne flushed at the pleasure she got from his words. She didn't know this man, but it still felt good that he was acknowledging her attempts to keep information close to her chest.

"Look, here's the deal. You like Ghost, right?"

"What are you, matchmaker-dot-com?"

"I'm pretty sure you do." Tex ignored her snarky remark. "This was his first deployment since you've been together and he thinks he's doing the right thing, but my wife and I talked, and we don't think he is. Hence this phone call."

Now Rayne was feeling uneasy. "What?"

"Two days ago, Ghost and his team arrived back at Fort Hood. Ghost was admitted to the hospital for wounds he sustained while on a mission. It's my understanding he's still there, and should be released sometime in the next two days."

Rayne's thoughts were all over the place. "What? Is this a joke?"

"No, Rayne. There's no way I would joke about this. Call your girl, get in the car, drive *safely* down there. The team should all be at the hospital when you arrive."

"Is he okay?" Rayne's voice was low and frightened.

"He will be. And Rayne?"

She was already on the move, heading to her bedroom to throw on a pair of jeans and a T-shirt. She had to call Mary, then her boss; she'd have to figure out who to switch with at work so she could—

"Rayne." Tex's voice was deep and commanding

now, as if he knew how on edge she was.

"Yeah?" Rayne stood stock-still in the middle of her hallway, gripping her phone and pressing it hard to her ear.

"Don't let Ghost give you shit. He gives it to you, you give it right back. You're the best damn thing that's ever happened to him, and if you let him push you away, you'll both suffer for it. Got me?"

"Yeah, okay."

"I mean it, Princess. I've never seen Ghost so…settled as I have since you came back into his life."

It was his use of her nickname that made it sink in that the man was most likely telling her the truth. He knew Ghost and he was back from the mission…and hurt. "You've seen him?"

"Well, no, that's a figure of speech. But I keep tabs on all my brothers…and sisters. I know you met Tiger a few weeks ago."

"Tiger?" Rayne couldn't think.

"Sorry, Penelope. But now's not the time. Go to Ghost, Rayne. He's going to be fine. Swear."

"Okay. Thanks for letting me know."

"You're welcome. Now go call Mary. I'll talk to you later."

Rayne took the phone from her ear when she heard nothing but silence on the other end. That was extremely weird, but she didn't have time to really think about it. She quickly dialed Mary as she hurried into her room.

They were on their way within twenty minutes. Mary had answered on the first ring and had rushed over to Rayne's condo, even though it was the middle of the night. She'd helped Rayne pack, throwing way more clothes into Rayne's suitcase than she would've thought to herself, and they'd jumped in Mary's car and were on the road.

Luckily, this early in the morning, traffic around the Metroplex was light to nonexistent, so they were able to get on I-35 and head south with no issues.

When Rayne finally had some time to think, she told Mary apologetically, "I'm so sorry, you were supposed to be working today, right?"

Mary shrugged. "I called and left a message for David and told him I'd been up all night with diarrhea and I wouldn't be in."

Rayne wasn't in the mood to laugh, but Mary could always say just the right thing. "You did not!"

"Oh yeah, I did. That man has no idea how to deal with all us women who work for him. All we have to do is hint that we're having some womanly problem or something else that he doesn't want to even *think* about, and he's shoving us out the door. It's pretty humorous really."

"Will he be short-handed today if you're not

there?"

Mary looked over at Rayne, who, while she sounded okay, looked as though she was at the end of her rope. "Raynie, I work at a bank. Remember? It's fine. If someone has to wait an extra five minutes to get a cashier's check or to deposit money, it's not the end of the world."

"Yeah, all right. I just don't want you to get in trouble."

"I wouldn't care if I *did* get fired. If you need me, I'm there for you."

That was it. That was all it took for Rayne to lose it. She'd been holding in her tears and hearing her best friend's words broke the dam. Dammit, she'd never been the weepy type and it seemed as if all she'd done lately was cry.

Mary didn't stop the car, knowing Rayne wanted and needed to get to the hospital down at Fort Hood, but she patted her friend on the shoulder and kept her hand on her in support. Finally, after ten minutes, Rayne composed herself enough to stop her tears.

"What do you think happened? Why didn't he call me?"

That was the big question floating around in Rayne's brain. Why did this Tex person have to call her and let her know Ghost was back in the country? Why didn't one of his teammates contact her? Why didn't Ghost himself? Was he sorry he'd hooked up with her again? Was he trying to end it with her? All Rayne had were questions, and no answers.

"Hey, stop it," Mary ordered as she calmly drove south. "Beating yourself up with all those questions I know you have flitting around that brain of yours isn't going to solve anything, because I sure as hell don't know the answers. We'll get there and you can ask Ghost himself. If he won't answer, I'll corner Trucker and get him to tell me what the fuck is going on. Okay?"

Rayne nodded. "Yeah, okay. Truck likes you, so that should work."

"What? Truck doesn't like me."

Rayne looked over at her friend, sorry she couldn't see her that well in the dim early-morning light trying to peek over the horizon. "Uh, yeah, Mare, he does. And I think you like him back."

"You're wrong. He's a big ol' ugly jerk. I'm looking for Tom Cruise, not Quasimodo."

"Mary Michelle Weston! That was a horrible thing to say," Rayne scolded, honestly shocked. Mary was known for telling it like she saw it, but Rayne hadn't ever heard her be so cruel before.

"I'm sorry," Mary apologized immediately. "I didn't mean that, but he drives me crazy. He's just so…I don't know."

"Strong? Virile? Commanding?" Rayne suggested coyly.

"Annoying," Mary decided.

"You only spent one day together, I don't understand how you can feel so annoyed with him. You don't really even know him that well," Rayne mused, more to herself than Mary.

"I know," Mary sighed in frustration. "I don't either. But I swear he said things he knew I'd get riled up about, *just* to see me get pissed. Guys don't usually do that around me, and it confused me."

"You guys are cute together. Just don't...don't do anything that would mean you wouldn't want to see each other. He's on Ghost's team and you're my best friend. You'll most likely be seeing a lot of each other...if this works out."

"*If* this works out? Rayne!"

"Well? I would've thought Ghost would've called me the second he was back. And even more so if he was hurt. And if he couldn't do it because of his injuries, he'd have one of his friends call. So until I know what's going on, I just..." Her words trailed off.

Even Mary didn't have a comeback for that one. The miles flew by as Mary confidently drove her best friend to see her lover. The man Mary knew Rayne had come to love more than life itself. If the man thought he'd scrape her friend off like goo he'd gotten on the bottom of his shoe, he had another thing coming.

Chapter Thirty-Three

MARY AND RAYNE burst through the hospital doors, making it from Fort Worth to the Army base in record time. Rayne had no idea what room Ghost was in, surprisingly Tex hadn't felt the need to impart that information to her, so she stalked up to the reception desk.

"I'm here to see Ghost…um…Keane Bryson."

"Visiting hours don't start for another hour," the woman informed Rayne, seeming not to notice the frazzled state of the woman standing in front of her…or not caring. "You can wait in the waiting room over there," she pointed vaguely down the hall, "with all the others."

Wanting to argue, but knowing it'd be futile, Rayne started down the corridor with Mary. She figured "all the others" the woman had mentioned meant all the other relatives and friends of other people in the hospital, but when she walked through the door of the little waiting area, she realized she'd meant all the others who were waiting to see *Ghost*.

They were all there. Fletch, Coach, Hollywood, Beatle, Blade and Truck, and even Wolf and Penelope were there. Seeing all Ghost's friends looking worried put the fear of God into her. Was Ghost hurt more than Tex had let on? Was that why no one had gotten ahold of her? She was so confused, and worried, and stressed out, she couldn't think straight.

Fletch came over to them. He took Rayne by the elbow and led her to a chair. "What are you doing here, Rayne?"

Before Rayne could open her mouth to answer, Mary had done it for her. "What's she doing here? Are you high? She's here because her *boyfriend*, who she hasn't seen for over two weeks because he was off to who-knows-where doing who-knows-what, was *injured* and she *just* found out about it even though he's apparently been here for a couple of *days*."

"How did you find out?"

That question didn't go over well with Mary at all, either.

"Oh, this is rich," she hissed. "You're all here to support your guy, but not one of you had the balls to call and let Rayne know he was here? That you were back?"

Rayne decided she'd better cut in, otherwise Mary would probably get them all kicked out. Her voice had risen and was way too loud for a hospital at this time of the morning—hell, for any time.

"Are you guys all okay?" Her small voice cut through the tension in the room, and successfully brought Mary's tirade to a halt.

Hollywood answered, "Yeah, we're all okay."

"And Ghost?"

"He's going to be fine too," Hollywood said vaguely.

Rayne sat awkwardly, looking around at Ghost's teammates, not knowing what to say. She had a pit in her stomach that wouldn't go away.

Mary harrumphed, and announced she was going to go find some coffee. Rayne sat quietly watching the clock, waiting for time to go by so she could see for herself that Ghost was "fine" and to get some answers as to what was making his teammates act as though she'd seen the Watergate burglar or something.

Finally, after an hour, Rayne stood up without a word and headed to the door. Turning, she asked quietly, "What room is he in?" to nobody in particular.

Fletch stood up. "I'll come with you."

"Me too," Mary declared, but was stopped short by Truck's hand on her shoulder.

"Let her go."

The last thing Rayne heard was Mary pitching a fit over Truck not letting her leave the room. It would've made Rayne smile, but she was beyond that at the moment. Fletch led the way to room 227 without a word. Knocking once, he opened the door.

"Hey man, you have a visitor."

A visitor? She would've preferred being called "your girlfriend," but didn't hold it against Fletch too much. Rayne stepped inside the room, noticing that Fletch came in too, but he stood by the door rather than nearing the bed.

Ghost was sitting up with three pillows behind his back. His left arm was resting on a fourth in his lap and was covered from his wrist to his upper arm with bandages. He wasn't wearing a shirt, or one of those hospital gowns, and his muscular chest was bare in the warm room.

His brown hair had been singed off on one side of his head and it made him look lopsided. His lips were mashed together in a straight line, and if he'd had the ability, fire would've been shooting out of his eyes.

Rayne had seen Ghost many ways. Laughing, worried, concentrating, lost in his release, content, but she'd never seen him as angry as he was right this moment.

Knowing she'd come too far to back out now, she said tentatively, "Hey, Ghost."

He didn't even look at her. His eyes were trained on Fletch. "What the ever-loving fuck?"

Fletch didn't look perturbed in the least. He

lounged against the door and shrugged. "She showed up here this morning with Mary."

Rayne refused to step back, but the look Ghost leveled on her made her quake a little bit in her shoes. "How did you find out I was here?"

"Tex called me." Rayne didn't even think about lying. He was that pissed.

"Fucking Tex," Ghost said under his breath, looking back at Fletch. "Get her out of here."

"Wait a second," Rayne protested, but she felt Fletch's hand on her arm. She tried to wrench out of his grasp, but all that did was hurt her. She yelped and ordered, "Ow! Let go!"

"Fletch…" Ghost's voice was low and hard—and full of warning for his friend.

Rayne had no idea if he was warning Fletch to get her out of the room, or not to hurt her. Either way, Ghost had already hurt her himself. She straightened and glared at him. "I don't understand. Ghost, talk to me."

But he'd already turned his head to look out the window in the room, dismissing her.

Fletch led her out of the room and back down the hallway to the waiting area, not letting go of her arm until they were inside.

Rayne didn't know what he thought she'd do. Make a break for it and go running back to Ghost's side? As if. The man had made it very clear what he thought of her showing up to see him. Crystal clear, in fact.

Mary came up to her and the other guys all stood when they entered. Rayne saw Fletch shake his head at his teammates in some sort of silent communication.

"What happened? Is he okay? What's going on?" Mary demanded.

"He didn't want to see her," Fletch remarked calmly.

"What?" Mary screeched, looking ready to go head-to-head with Fletch.

"Sit down, Mary," Rayne ordered, settling herself on a chair and crossing her arms in front of her belligerently.

"Rayne?" Mary drew out her name as if she were asking four questions with just that one word.

"If Ghost thinks he's done with me, he's smoking crack. What an asshole. I can't believe he just did that." Rayne was on a roll, and didn't see the worried looks change to smirks on the faces of Ghost's friends. "I don't know what his problem is, but I'm not going anywhere."

"But Rayne, he kicked you out," Mary said in confusion.

"Yeah, he did. But I'm assuming he also kicked all of *these* jerks out too, otherwise they'd be in the room with him, or at least taking turns," Rayne complained, motioning to the men in the room with her head. "He's too stubborn. I might not have been with him long, but I *do* know that about him. He's probably got some fucked-up idea that he doesn't want to hurt me or some such bullshit and thinks he's protecting me or something. Screw that. Asshole." Rayne looked up for the first time at the men in the room.

Fletch could see the devastation in her eyes, but was proud as he could be that she was sticking to her guns and not letting Ghost run her off.

"How—"

"You know we can't talk about the mission," Beatle said, cutting off her question.

The muscle in Rayne's jaw ticked as she clenched her teeth. "I. Know. That," she clipped out evenly, obviously leaving the word "asshole" out of her sentence. "I was *going* to ask, how is he doing?"

Fletch answered for the group. "He's fine."

"Fine," muttered Rayne. "It's like getting blood from a stone." Raising her voice, she asked the question again a different way. "It looks like he's been burned. How badly?"

It was Coach who took pity on her and gave her what she wanted. "Mostly second-degree. Some third-degree on his arm. The explosion came a bit too close for comfort, but he calmly stopped-dropped-and-rolled and got us the fuck out of there."

"Skin grafts?"

"Yeah, they took some skin from his leg and patched up his arm from there."

"His leg?" Rayne asked, panic sounding in her voice for the first time.

"His inner thigh. Not his calf," Fletch reassured her, knowing exactly what she'd been worried about. Doctors don't use tattooed skin for grafts.

Rayne sighed in relief. If they'd had to mess up his tattoo, that would've been bad. "Okay, so what? You guys are rotating going in to piss him off? Is that the plan?"

Penelope smiled at her from across the room and piped up for the first time. "Pretty much. Did Tex call you too?"

Rayne nodded.

"Yeah, same here. I swear that man loves to meddle."

"Was it bad, Rayne?" Blade asked from his position leaning against the wall.

Rayne knew what he meant. "It certainly wasn't the welcome home I was expecting, I can tell you that."

"Thank fuck you didn't run off crying," Beatle said. "Seriously. He ordered us not to call you, and as much as it sucked, we obey orders. But that man needs you. The first thing he bitched about when we were…safe, was how this was going to kill you."

"This isn't going to kill me," Rayne protested. "What was he thinking?"

"Not sure, but seriously, we'll do what we can to help you, though he's not happy you're here," Fletch told her.

"No shit, Sherlock," Rayne mumbled. Then said in a stronger voice, "And I'm not happy he's here, but it's not going to kill me. And I'll tell you one thing, I'm not going anywhere."

"Aren't you supposed to be heading out to London tomorrow morning?" Mary asked, always the voice of reason.

Rayne slumped in her chair. "Oh. Yeah. I forgot. Damn."

"I'll take care of it," Truck assured her, heading for the door.

"What? How?" Rayne protested as he disappeared without another word. She looked at the other men. "What's he gonna do?"

Hollywood shrugged. "No clue. But if Truck says he'll take care of it, he'll take care of it."

Rayne knew she should probably protest a bit more, but honestly, it was really, really nice not to have to worry about that at the moment. She'd been shocked and hurt by Ghost's words and actions, but she kept remembering what Penelope had said to her and what she'd thought all those months ago when Ghost was trying to tell her he would never be a romantic kind of man.

These men would never be romantic in the fairy-tale sense. Ghost would never shower her with presents and sweet words. Oh, he could *be* sweet, but it was more in a rough, tough sort of way. Ghost was protective of her and would rather cause *himself* pain than her.

So with all that rattling around in her brain, his words and actions made a sick sort of sense. She didn't like it, and she'd be telling him later that he needed to take more care with her, but deep inside, she knew he was protecting her.

He hadn't called her because he didn't want her to see him like he was. Hurt and wounded. Their relationship was still new, and Rayne figured he didn't want her to worry about him. He was protecting himself as much as he was her. At least she hoped that was it.

While it pissed her off, she got it. When she'd been in the hospital, there were times she'd wanted to shove Ghost out. She wasn't at her best, felt like shit, and she hadn't wanted him to see her that way. It had to be twenty times worse for a man like Ghost. Feeling helpless and defenseless wasn't in his psyche.

So...she'd wait him out. She'd hang out here with the guys and Penelope, and wait until Ghost was discharged. Then she'd make him see that he was being an idiot. If he thought she was going to go away just because he'd ordered it, he obviously didn't know her very well.

Chapter Thirty-Four

LATE THAT NIGHT, Rayne snuck down the hall to Ghost's room. The nurses at the desk ignored her horrible attempt at being stealthy, either because they felt sorry for her, or because one of Ghost's teammates had sweet-talked them into letting her by. She didn't care one way or the other, as long as she got a chance to see Ghost.

His burns were coming along nicely, and he'd be going home the next day. Fletch had driven her over to Ghost's house earlier and let her take a shower and put her stuff there. She'd told Fletch to come back in two hours and she'd cleaned up as much as she could before he came back.

The house was pretty much exactly how she'd left it a couple of weeks ago, but Ghost's duffle bag had been sitting in the breezeway. She'd unpacked for him and started a load of laundry. She changed the sheets, so they were fresh and clean, and scoped out the grocery situation, reminding herself to ask Fletch to stop at the store before he brought her back.

Rayne pushed open the door to room 227 and peeked in. Ghost was in much the same position as he'd been when she'd seen him that morning. Sitting up in bed with his injured arm resting on a pillow in his lap. His eyes were closed and his breaths were slow and even.

Not wanting him to wake up and rip her a new one, Rayne tiptoed to the chair at the foot of the bed. She picked it up carefully, so it didn't make a sound, and gently placed it next to Ghost's mattress on his uninjured side. She pulled the chair as close as she could to the bed and sat quietly.

She watched Ghost sleep for a while, memorizing his face all over again. She'd missed him so much and just being by his side made the butterflies inside her gut settle for the first time since he'd left.

His rhythmic breathing put Rayne into a sort of trance and she swayed in her seat. Carefully, trying not to jostle the mattress or the covers—or more importantly, his injured arm—Rayne rested her head on the mattress beside Ghost's hip. She'd just close her eyes for a second. She'd been up for way longer than she was used to and had experienced several adrenaline highs and lows throughout the course of the day. She was exhausted.

Ghost knew the second Rayne fell off into sleep. He opened his eyes fully and looked down at the woman he loved. He'd clocked her the second she'd entered his room. Not only could he smell her delicious shampoo, but she wasn't nearly as stealthy as she thought she was. Besides, he was Delta. It was highly unlikely anyone could sneak up on him, wounded or not.

Rayne looked exhausted. She had dark circles under her eyes and her face was paler than Ghost remembered it being. He raised his hand to push her hair out of her face and froze. He put his hand back at his side and sighed. She shouldn't be there. She'd told him already, but Coach had reminded him that it'd been Tex who had called both her and Penelope to let them know he was back and in the hospital. Damn the man.

There was no one Ghost wanted to see more than Rayne, but it wasn't fair to her. He didn't want to worry her, and getting wounded on the first mission after they'd gotten together wasn't the way to keep her from worrying. His plan had been to wait until his wounds had healed then brush them off as nothing serious when he saw her again. He'd tried to tell himself it wasn't a lie, but looking at Rayne now, he knew he'd fucked up again. He'd promised not to lie to her ever again, and he'd gone and done it; granted it was by omission, but a lie was a lie. The first time he'd been tested.

He'd been an asshole that morning. But the shock of seeing Rayne standing in his room when he hadn't been prepared for it, looking more beautiful than he'd remembered, was too much. He didn't want her seeing him wounded and hurt. He wanted to be whole for her. To be her rock, the indestructible man who'd always be able to protect her.

"She was something to see this morning."

Ghost looked up from Rayne's sleeping face to see Fletch standing in the doorway. His words were soft, barely audible to the normal person, but Ghost heard him just fine.

Ghost looked back down at Rayne. Not able to resist, he took a lock of her hair and rubbed it between his fingers, loving how soft it was.

"I'd thought you'd broken her. You were such an asshole. I was ready to defend you, to comfort her, to let her cry on my shoulder, but damn if she didn't march down to the waiting area and plunk herself on a chair and decide she wasn't moving. She's got your number, Ghost. She's your perfect match."

Ghost stubbornly kept his mouth shut.

Fletch continued as if he was having a real conversation with his team leader instead of a one-sided one. "I took her to your house today as well, at her demand, of course. She took a much-needed shower, since she'd jumped out of bed when Tex called her early this morning without any thought to herself. She washed your shit, and made a grocery list for later. Full of healthy crap like chicken noodle soup and orange juice. I even saw she put condoms on it."

Ghost looked up at that and saw his friend's lip curl in derision. "Yeah, fucker. You treated her like dog shit and she's still got your best interests at heart and wants to be with you. I know you didn't want her to see you in the hospital, but she has. Get over your snit and apologize. After talking with Mary, it sounds as though she's got more crap she's trying to deal with in her life than just you. Pull your head out of your ass and talk to your woman. Help her, Ghost. Her job is weighing on her and she's struggling with it. You trying to push her away isn't helping. Stop being a dick and take care of what's important. She's right there in front of you."

Not giving him a chance to defend himself—not that Ghost would've, every word out of his friend's mouth was the God's honest truth—Fletch turned and left the room.

Ghost looked back down at Rayne. She was hunched over his bed, her hands in her lap, sleeping the sleep of the exhausted. She could've gone to a hotel, or his house. She should've fled that morning after he'd been so horrible to her. Honestly, it was what he'd expected she'd do. But here she was. Sleeping at his side. For some reason she wanted to be with him, even if she thought it was when he didn't know.

He was proud as all get out that she hadn't run off in tears, but he'd hurt her, and that gutted him. He'd only wanted to protect her from this side of his job. But she wasn't an idiot. She'd been in the middle of one of his missions. She knew, better than most anyone, what he did and the risks he took.

He groaned softly under his breath. He'd fucked up. Big. He had a lot of making up to do to his woman. He hoped she'd let him, but the fact that she was here, next to him now, made him think he had a chance.

Ghost lay his head back against his pillows and tried to block out the throbbing of his arm. Third-degree burns hurt like hell. Refusing to push the button that would allow the mind-numbing drugs into his system through his IV to ease the pain, he closed his eyes. Rubbing Rayne's hair through the fingers of his uninjured hand soothed him. She was here. His Princess was here.

The next time Ghost opened his eyes, it was to look over and see Mary's brown eyes glaring at him. He looked around, hoping to see someone else, anyone else, but it was only him and Mary. She didn't give him even a moment to get his bearings.

"She called me at two-thirty in the morning frantic to get down here to you. She was going to drive herself...and probably get herself or someone else killed with the state she was in. She's supposed to be at the airport right this second getting ready to fly...you know...her *job*? But instead, she's running around trying to make sure you have what you need when you get home, and she doesn't even know if you'll be nice to her when you get there or not. She's been badgering the doctors and nurses, telling them to get in here and give you pain meds so you won't hurt anymore, and I know she's got a grocery list a mile long for later this morning, when she makes one of the guys take her so she can fill up your pantry. If you think for one second your assholeness scared her away, you're wrong."

Mary took a deep breath and leaned toward Ghost, not taking her eyes off him. "She loves you, you big jerk. I have no idea why, right this moment, but she does. This is still new between you guys, and I have to tell you, I'm inclined to warn her off of you every chance I get. She might worship the ground you walk on, and you might have your team eating out of your hand, but you have a long way to go to convince me you're right for her."

"You're right."

"And if you think I'm going to let you mentally abuse her and…" Mary's words trailed off as Ghost's words sank in. "What?"

"I said, you're right. I was an asshole. I was going to wait until I was out of the hospital and better to call her. Actually, I was going to go up to Fort Worth and surprise her with the fact I was home."

"That might have worked with other women, but it will never work with Rayne," Mary informed him.

"She'd know you were injured and she'd worry. She'd think you were hiding something from her and she'd probably end up pushing *you* away, thinking you were trying to get rid of her."

At the confused look on Ghost's face, Mary laughed, but not in a ha-ha kind of way. "Yeah, it's messed up. But Rayne has been in love with you for seven months. She'd never admit it, but she's loved you since London. She has a tendency to do more for others than she'll let them do for her."

"That's gonna change."

"See? You say the words, but your actions don't match."

"Go find me a doctor, Mary. I'm getting the fuck out of here."

Mary stood up and she and Ghost locked eyes for a moment before Mary nodded. "I said it once, but it bears repeating. The jury's still out as far as I'm concerned. Treat my friend right and you'll have no issues with me. But if I get one *hint* that you're belittling her, making her feel guilty about something, or just plain making her sad, I'll haul her ass away from you so quickly you won't know what's going on."

"You'll have no worries about me from here on out. You have my word as a man, and as Delta."

Mary nodded again and went to find a doctor.

Chapter Thirty-Five

"FLETCH? IS THAT you? I'll be right there!" Rayne called as she quickly tried to put away the last of the cans in the cupboard. "Did you hear anything? Will Ghost be coming home today?"

When Fletch didn't answer, Rayne twirled around to call out again, anxious to know if Ghost would get released from the hospital. She knew he was probably going stir-crazy. She still had to decide if she was going to be at his house when he got home or not. She wasn't going anywhere until she'd had it out with him, but if he was in pain and needed a day or two, she'd gladly give it before they had their confrontation.

She stopped in her tracks when she didn't see Fletch, but Ghost himself standing on the other side of the counter.

"Oh, Ghost. Did you get out?"

Ghost smirked at her question, as it was obvious he'd been released since he was standing right in front of her. "Yeah, Princess. I didn't exactly have to have the guys enact a covert recon to get the doctors to release

SUSAN STOKER

me from the hospital."

A blush moved up her face.

"Good, yeah, that's good. I, uh, got you some stuff, so you're good to go. You didn't have much to eat. I cleaned everything out before I left the other day. Your laundry is all clean and put away. You have, uh—"

Rayne's words cut off abruptly as Ghost stalked toward her. She took a step back for Ghost's every step forward until her ass hit the counter and her backward momentum was stopped.

Rayne wasn't exactly afraid of Ghost. Even though he was bigger than she was, and she knew without a doubt he could hurt her, she also knew he'd never put his hands on her. It was his words that made her nervous at the moment. He could slay her with them, and she wasn't ready for them yet. She'd been building herself up to tell him off for making her feel like shit, but now that her chance was here, she was totally chickening out.

Ghost saw the fear in her eyes and hated that he'd put it there. "Princess. God. I'd never hurt you."

"Yeah, I know that." She said the words but wouldn't quite meet his eyes.

"When I woke up yesterday I was in pain, and was already second guessing my decision not to let you know I was back. It seemed like the right thing to do when we were flying home. But the second the words were out of my mouth, the second I saw your reaction, it was as if I might as well have reached out and punched you in the face."

"Ghost, I—"

"I was frustrated, hurting, and sick inside that I couldn't jump up and follow you."

Rayne stayed silent, listening. Ghost continued baring his soul.

"I love you, Rayne. And those aren't just words for me. I've never said them to any other woman in my life. I told you when we were in London that I suck at relationships. And I think right now, you'd have to agree. But never, and I mean never, no matter what shit I might spew or what I might do, think that I don't love you."

"They didn't mess up your tattoo, did they?"

The words were so not what Ghost was expecting, it took him a moment to wrap his brain around them. "No. The graft was taken from my inner thigh. I threatened every doctor and nurse who came near me that if they touched one millimeter of my ink, their lives were in danger."

Rayne turned her head as if contemplating what he said. "You need to get off your feet then."

"Rayne…"

She shook her head. "Go. You can sit on the couch if you want, but that leg has to hurt. I know you had some third-degree burns and Lord knows why the doctors let you out already, probably because you're annoying and pigheaded. But if you were this determined to get out of the hospital, you're going to have to deal with *me*. So go sit."

Ghost did as Rayne asked and backed away, not losing eye contact until she turned to the cabinet to reach for something. He sat in the middle of the couch and watched as she puttered around his kitchen.

"Are you hungry?" she called out.

"No."

"Thirsty?"

"No."

"Well, there are some sandwiches in the fridge for later if you need something. You don't want to overdo it and mess up that arm any more than it already is."

Ghost so wanted to stalk over to Rayne and pick her up and carry her to his bed—to *their* bed—and throw her down and shut her up the best way he knew how, but he wasn't sure what was going on in her head. And he had to know that before he did anything else that might damage their relationship.

At last, she'd finished with whatever it was she was doing in his kitchen and sat on the sofa next to him. Not touching, but at least she hadn't chosen the chair on the other side of the room.

"Don't do that again."

Ghost wasn't sure which "that" she was talking about, but he agreed immediately. "I won't."

Rayne was smarter than anyone he knew. She immediately called him on it. "What won't you do?"

"Any of it. Swear at you. Scowl at you when I'm really just pissed at myself. Not tell you the second I'm back in the States. Not greet you with a kiss when I see you again."

"What about hurting me?"

Ghost sighed. "Unfortunately, Princess, I can't promise that. I'm a dick. You know this. I'll most likely say and do stuff in the future that will hurt you. But I *can* promise not to do it on purpose. If you'll call me out when I do it, I'll do my best to curb it."

She didn't say anything for a bit, then finally said in a quiet voice, "My first thought when you and Wolf burst into that room in Egypt and I realized it was you—not just any soldier, but *you*—was to tell you to get out. As much as I wanted to be rescued, I was embarrassed that I was so vulnerable. I wanted you to remember me as you last saw me...on my knees in front of you, enthusiastically taking everything you had to give me."

Her words made Ghost's cock stir, but he sat quietly next to her, letting her get out whatever it was she needed to say.

"But instead you had to see me tied down and helpless…and half naked. I was humiliated and embarrassed, and I'd dreamed that when you saw me again, it'd be when I felt sexy and beautiful. So when you told me to get the fuck out of your room and you stared at me with nothing but ice in your eyes, I swear to God I saw the same thing in you that *I* felt in Egypt."

She looked at him, willing him to understand. "I get it, Ghost. I know why you did it. I do. But what *you* need to understand is that you'll always be my super-secret spy. The guy who can slay dragons and nasty taxi drivers with a look. Just because you're hurt doesn't mean you aren't still my über-masculine spy. I know you're a badass. Anyone in their right mind knows that by looking at you. Please don't shut me out. If you do, this won't work. You'll slowly kill me day by day, because I'll know you're keeping a part of you from me."

"Come here, Princess." Ghost put out his good arm and held his breath, hoping against all hope she'd do as he asked.

Rayne hesitated a moment, then threw herself into Ghost's side. She snaked one arm around his stomach and shoved the other behind his back against the cushion. She snuggled her face into his chest and squeezed.

Ghost had barely moved his injured arm out of the way before she'd landed on him, and held back a grunt of pain. Having Rayne in his arms was heaven. Better than any medicine the doctors could give him. "I love you. I'll never shut you out again. I swear."

Rayne nodded. She knew she was maybe being an idiot for forgiving him so easily, but she loved him. It was a stupid thing for him to have done, but she got it. She really did. "I love you too, Keane."

"Ghost. Call me Ghost."

Rayne smiled against him. "I love you, Ghost."

"God, Princess. I'm so sorry, I—"

"Enough. We've discussed it, you've apologized, it's done. Okay?"

"Okay."

"I'm reserving the right to bring it up again if you do anything remotely similar, so you've been warned. Maybe that'll be some incentive for you to not be a bonehead again in the future. Now…how's your arm? Does your leg hurt? What do I need to do to make sure it stays clean? Are you allowed to get it wet? What does—"

Ghost covered her mouth with his to shut her up. When he finally lifted his head, he reassured her, "I'm fine. I have to go in every day for the next week for them to change the bandages and do something horribly painful to the dead skin on my arm. I'm not supposed to submerge my arm, but my leg should heal up pretty quickly. Tomorrow night I'll be able to shower and not worry about it."

Rayne put her hand on Ghost's cheek. "You need to be more careful next time. Avoid those nasty fire-storms. Okay?"

"You got it, Princess."

"Come to bed?"

"Hell yes, I thought you'd never ask."

"No hanky-panky though, mister. You're not up for it."

Ghost laughed. "I'm *always* up for it where you're concerned."

"Whatever. Come on, I put some clean sheets on our bed, you'll sleep so much better here than in the hospital."

"I like that."

"What? Sleeping?"

"*Our* bed."

Rayne smiled and helped him up.

When they were lying in bed not too much later, after Rayne had helped him get his shirt off and gently kissed the bandages over his arm, Ghost said quietly, "We have a lot to talk about, Princess."

"I thought we were done talking."

"We were…about my dumb-ass decision. But we need to talk about us. We have a lot to work out."

Rayne nodded against his chest drowsily. "Not really, me and Mary already figured it all out."

"You did?" That made Ghost really nervous, since Mary wasn't his biggest fan at the moment.

"Uh-huh." She paused for a huge yawn then continued. "We're both moving down here. Me to be with you, and Mary because she loves me and says she can get a job at any ol' bank. I don't know if that's true or not, but I'm pretty sure she can get transferred or whatever."

"You're moving to Belton?"

Rayne obviously didn't realize how big of a moment this was for Ghost, because she simply murmured, "Uh-huh…"

Ghost shifted and rolled Rayne until she was on top of him, and predictably, she immediately tried to scramble off.

"I'm going to hurt you."

"No you aren't, scoot up here."

"What?"

Ghost put his good hand on Rayne's ass and pushed her toward his face, careful to keep his injured arm out of the way. "I need you, Princess."

"You can't! Ghost, you're gonna hurt yourself."

"Not if you do all the work. I need to taste you. I need those gorgeous folds in my mouth. I can't lie on my stomach, so you're going to have to crawl up here and kneel over my face. Just watch my arm as you go."

"Ghost! I'll suffocate you."

"No you won't. Promise."

Rayne hesitated for a moment more, but finally eased up toward his face. She hadn't worn any undies to bed, only one of his large Army T-shirts. She could feel her wetness smearing on his chest as she went.

"God, you're beautiful. I can't believe you're mine. You have no idea what it means to me that you're willing to move down here to be with me." Ghost looked up Rayne's body as she stopped, kneeling over him. He could smell her arousal, and he could see her chest rising and falling with her quick excited breaths. "I love you. You have no idea how much. Now come on, get to work, woman. I want to feel you all over my face."

Rayne looked up in embarrassment, but moved to where Ghost wanted her. Far be it from her to deny Ghost what he wanted...especially when she'd be the recipient of his generosity.

Epilogue

RAYNE KNEW TRUCK was waiting downstairs and Fletch would be there any minute, but the second Ghost walked out of their bathroom in his jeans and tight T-shirt, she had to have him. She didn't even give him a chance to fight; she dropped to her knees and went to work on his belt and zipper.

"Rayne? We don't really have time—"

"I'll be quick."

Ghost put one hand on her head as she pulled down his boxers and freed his cock. "Princess, seriously—"

That was all he got out before Rayne engulfed his entire length in her mouth and moaned.

"Jesus. Yes. Take it. God, yeah."

Rayne hadn't always been confident in making love to Ghost this way, but not only had she been a good student, she'd discovered how much she loved taking his cock down her throat. She'd told him once that she got the biggest kick out of reducing her man to a pile of goo.

Ghost took control of her actions by putting one hand on the back of her head and the other under her chin. He gently thrust in and out of her mouth, being careful not to hurt her in the process.

"You love sucking me off, don't you, Princess?" When Rayne moaned, he felt it all the way to his toes. "Are you wet for me?" She nodded in his grip, but didn't stop licking and sucking as her head bobbed up and down on him.

"As soon as you finish me off, take off your pants and get on the bed. Spread your legs so I can tongue you until you come. Yeah?"

Rayne moaned around him once more. Ghost had no idea what it was about taking him this way that turned her on so much, but it did. He never knew when she'd get a wild hair and want to take him down her throat. He'd never let her do it where they might be caught, but she never ceased to surprise him when she'd lean over in their car or when they were in a semi-public spot.

Groaning, Ghost felt the come churning up from his balls. "I'm close, Princess. Almost there... Oh yeah, right there..." He felt Rayne's soft hand grab hold of his balls and give them a tight squeeze before fondling them not quite gently. It was all he needed.

He let go of Rayne's head, never wanting to force her to do anything she didn't want to do...namely, swallow his come if she didn't want to. He laced them together behind his head and arched his back as he exploded.

When he no longer saw stars behind his eyelids, Ghost opened his eyes and looked down at the woman he loved more than his own life. Rayne sat at his feet, caressing his softening cock, as she lovingly licked him clean.

"What set you off that time?" he asked, genuinely curious. He'd just come out of the bathroom after brushing his teeth and she'd jumped him.

"You."

He smiled and ran his hand over her hair, enjoying the after-effects of his orgasm and Rayne's hands on him.

"I could smell the cologne you put on. And you don't wear jeans a lot…you're just…hot."

Ghost smiled again. She was so fucking cute, and all his. He reached down, tucked himself back into his pants, and got to work belting himself back up. "Go lie on the bed, Princess. Your turn."

"But, Fletch and Truck—"

"They'll just have to wait."

"But they'll know…" Her voice trailed off, but she went to the bed as he'd asked her to.

"You should've thought about that before you attacked me."

Ghost watched as Rayne smiled and blushed, but popped open the button on her shorts and pulled the zipper down.

"Don't take them all the way off. Just to your knees."

"But—"

"Hush. Do it."

Ghost got on his knees on the floor and pulled Rayne's legs up until they were around his neck. Her panties and shorts at her knees made it so she couldn't spread open. While it was more of a challenge for him, Ghost knew it would be super frustrating and exhilarating for Rayne.

He leaned in and licked her once, loving how wet she was. He'd never met a woman who loved giving head as much as she did. She'd protested that she'd never enjoyed it before, that it was only him, and that made him feel ten feet tall.

Rayne moaned as he moved one finger to her opening and pressed in, not giving her a chance to prepare for his invasion. She was soaked and he could feel her muscles pulling at his finger. Wishing he had more time—he could eat her out for hours, but Fletch and Truck really were waiting for them downstairs—Ghost got to work pleasing his woman.

Within five minutes, Rayne shivered with her second orgasm. He'd plundered her clit, not giving her any chance to pull away or to come down after her first quick orgasm. She lay limp under him as he pulled his finger out of her warm body. He leaned down and ran his tongue up her slit, catching the wetness that seeped out with the removal of his finger.

"You're gonna be wet for a while, Princess."

"Ummm."

"Do you think you'll be able to refrain from pulling my cock out for a few hours while we hang with the team?"

"As long as you don't do anything sexy…maybe."

Ghost laughed and turned to kiss her inner thigh. He ducked and lifted her legs back over his head. Pulling her up farther on the bed, he leaned over her as she worked to get her clothes back in order.

"I love you," Ghost murmured against her lips, knowing she would taste herself on him.

Rayne licked his lower lip and smiled up at him, blushing.

Ghost pulled her up. "Come on. We *really* have to go now."

"I love you, Ghost. I never thought I'd say this, but I'm glad I was a hostage in Egypt." Before Ghost could explode, she continued quickly, "Because it brought you back to me."

"Come on, before I tell my friends we can't make the cookout after all."

Rayne giggled as Ghost pulled her out the door.

"Come on, tell me what you did," Rayne cajoled Truck as they rode in Fletch's car.

The big man shrugged. "I called Tex."

"You called Tex," Rayne repeated with no inflection in her voice.

"Princess, drop it," Ghost warned, putting his hand on the back of her neck and squeezing affectionately.

"But Ghost—"

"Do you enjoy your new job?"

"Yeah."

"Then why do you care?"

"Because!" Rayne protested. "It's not normal that some guy named Tex—who I've never met, by the way—is able to not only get me out of my job with a glowing recommendation, but get me hired, without an interview, for a different airline out of Austin instead of DFW!"

"I'll ask again," Ghost said with extreme patience. "Would you rather be flying the DFW international routes again? Taking a chance you'd have to fly into Cairo, or Turkey, or some other Middle Eastern country?"

"No."

"Then drop it, Princess. Seriously."

Rayne huffed out a breath. "Oh all right. But only because you trust and like this mysterious Tex guy."

Ghost smiled at her.

Rayne looked to Fletch. The four of them were finally on their way to Fletch's place for a barbeque. Since he'd been out making a beer run, he'd offered to pick them up...and Truck too, since he'd been over visiting Ghost. They hadn't planned on the extra fifteen minutes it took Rayne and Ghost to "get ready" but neither said anything about it, pleased as hell things were working out between their team leader and his woman.

"I still think you should've let me bring something," Rayne griped.

Fletch shrugged. "Got everything I need. Nothing left for you to bring over."

"But something...brownies? Chips? Something?"

Fletch laughed. "Nope. Got it all."

They pulled into the driveway of Fletch's place and Rayne looked toward the apartment over the garage. "Is your tenant going to join us?"

"No."

The word was bitten out.

"Why not? I thought you said she was nice?"

"She *is*. But she's busy," Fletch said flatly.

"Oh. Did you ask politely?" Rayne pushed. "Sometimes you can be a bit abrupt. You said she had a little girl. Maybe they both could've come over."

"Of course I did. I'm not a Neanderthal. And she has a boyfriend, so get that matchmaking gleam out of your eye right now, Rayne," Fletch warned, putting his car in park.

"Oh, that's a bummer. There's always Mary then."

Fletch laughed, especially when Truck stiffened next to him. "No way am I mixing it up with that hellion. Your friend is safe from me."

"Well, poo. I still think *one* of you needs to hook up with her." Rayne had been thrilled when Mary had finally done as she said she would, quit her job and moved down to the Fort Hood area. She'd been offered a job at the same branch as her old bank and hadn't even missed too much work with the move.

Rayne was going to move in with Mary after she'd found a place nearby, but Ghost had convinced her, in the best way possible—namely, making her orgasm over and over again until she agreed—to move in with him. And while they had their moments, she'd never regretted it.

They all tromped into the house, ready for some good food and a nice visit with friends.

But they didn't notice Fletch turn as he was closing his front door and look at the apartment over his garage longingly, before shutting the door with a sigh and joining the rest of his teammates.

Look for the next book in the *Delta Force Heroes* Series, *Rescuing Emily.*

To sign up for Susan's Newsletter go to:
http://bit.ly/SusanStokerNewsletter

Or text: STOKER to 24587 for text alerts on your mobile device

Discover other titles by Susan Stoker

<u>Delta Force Heroes</u>

Rescuing Rayne

Assisting Aimee – Loosely related to Delta Force

Rescuing Emily

Rescuing Harley

Marrying Emily

Rescuing Kassie

Rescuing Bryn (Nov 2017)

Rescuing Casey (TBA)

Rescuing Wendy (TBA)

Rescuing Mary (TBA)

<u>Badge of Honor: Texas Heroes</u>

Justice for Mackenzie

Justice for Mickie

Justice for Corrie

Justice for Laine

Shelter for Elizabeth

Justice for Boone

Shelter for Adeline

Shelter for Sophie (Aug 2017)

Justice for Erin (Nov 2017)

Justice for Milena (TBA)

Shelter for Blythe (TBA)

Justice for Hope (TBA)

Shelter for Quinn (TBA)

Shelter for Koren (TBA)
Shelter for Penelope (TBA)

SEAL of Protection

Protecting Caroline
Protecting Alabama
Protecting Fiona
Marrying Caroline
Protecting Summer
Protecting Cheyenne
Protecting Jessyka
Protecting Julie
Protecting Melody
Protecting the Future
Protecting Alabama's Kids
Protecting Kiera (June 2017)
Protecting Dakota (Sept 2017)

Ace Security

Claiming Grace (Mar 2017)
Claiming Alexis (July 2017)
Claiming Bailey (Dec 2017)

Beyond Reality

Outback Hearts
Flaming Hearts
Frozen Hearts

Connect with Susan Online

Susan's Facebook Profile and Page:
www.facebook.com/authorsstoker
www.facebook.com/authorsusanstoker

Follow Susan on Twitter:
www.twitter.com/Susan_Stoker

Find Susan's Books on Goodreads:
www.goodreads.com/SusanStoker

Email: Susan@StokerAces.com

Website: www.StokerAces.com

To sign up for Susan's Newsletter go to:
http://bit.ly/SusanStokerNewsletter

Or text: STOKER to 24587 for text alerts on your mobile device

About the Author

New York Times, *USA Today*, and *Wall Street Journal* Bestselling Author Susan Stoker has a heart as big as the state of Texas, where she lives, but this all-American girl has also spent the last fourteen years living in Missouri, California, Colorado, and Indiana. She's married to a retired Army man who now gets to follow *her* around the country.

She debuted her first series in 2014 and quickly followed that up with the SEAL of Protection Series, which solidified her love of writing and creating stories readers can get lost in.

If you enjoyed this book, or any book, please consider leaving a review. It's appreciated by authors more than you'll know.

CPSIA information can be obtained
at www.ICGtesting.com
Printed in the USA
LVHW051358070419
613260LV00017B/308/P

9 781682 306697